See You

a love story

by

Dawn Lee McKenna

A Sweet Tea Press Publication

First published in the United States by Sweet Tea Press
©2014 Dawn Lee McKenna. All rights reserved.

Cover Design by write.DREAM.repeat
Front cover image: keepingtime_ca
Back cover image: Jo Naylor

See You is a work of fiction. All incidents and dialogue, and all characters are products of the author's imagination. Any similarities to any person, living or dead, is merely coincidental.

Prologue

1994

SHE WAS THE BEST last thing to see.

Every year when he got ready to leave again, he watched her from this same grassy hillside. He always told her he was going off by himself for a few minutes and he knew she thought, or at least hoped, that he was going off to pray.

Sometimes he did, but mostly he just watched her while she wasn't watching him. He soaked in the sight of her as she drank her coffee on the front porch or, like today, worked in her front garden.

Jack Canfield had been coming to and leaving Locust Grove, Alabama for almost twenty years. He'd grown up here, but he'd left the first chance he'd gotten, off to Ole Miss and then the Marine Corps.

He came home every year on leave and every now and then he made it back for Christmas, but there was nothing here for him but these nine acres here on this dirt road and the woman that lived there.

He was thirty-seven years old and still hadn't found some place he could be that wasn't here. But he couldn't be here, either.

Every year, he got off the bus out on Highway 9 and walked the two miles to her place here just outside of town. He never told her when he was coming, in case his leave was cancelled or his orders changed.

But come he did, for a few days every year, and then he would leave, taking the memories of her with him so he could ration them out to himself when he was gone.

From his spot on the knoll, he had a perfect view down into the only place he'd ever thought was home. A gravel drive led from the dirt road and circled around to the back of the house, beyond his vision. Next to the drive and set back a ways was the old white farmhouse.

It wasn't the farmhouse that rich people bought when they decided to take a place in the country, though they wouldn't have come here, anyway. It was the farmhouse of people who built something small but sturdy and then added to it through the years, when more babies made it necessary and a piece of money made it possible.

There was a front porch that ran the width of the house and one just like it on the back. At one end of the porch, a white wooden swing and her pots of flowers. At the other, a few scattered chairs and a white wooden table that had his initials carved into the top. For most of his life, that porch was where a lot of his best living got done.

Sweet tea in the afternoons, when the sun was hot but the two big magnolias gave shade. Cribbage at night, or maybe some storytelling, laughing so hard the cicadas stopped their racket to see what was so funny.

Now his battered sea bag sat by the front door, waiting for him to take it up and be gone again.

When he was gone, when he was back to whichever far away the Corps had sent him, he would sometimes sit and imagine he was on that porch with her, listening to a late afternoon rainstorm pounding on the faded green tin roof. Next to her laughter, it was the finest sound he knew.

He watched her now, digging in the flowerbed that ran along the front porch. Hollyhocks so blue the sky got embarrassed about it. Larkspur as purple as her homemade jam. The pink and red kalancho that she was digging now, dividing and replanting them along the rock edging he'd put down for her last year.

She could grow anything, from tomatoes to pumpkins to her giant gardenias by the picket fence; gardenias you could smell before you even turned onto the road. Everything she touched grew well, even the things that were half-dead when she found them.

He watched her digging and even though her back was to him, he knew she wore her faded flowered gloves, the ones that had the holes in both thumbs. He knew a glisten of sweat was on her brow and that it irritated her. Knew she had a handkerchief tucked down in between her breasts and that she'd pull it out to wipe the sweat away before it salted her eyes.

He also knew that she knew he was almost gone, and that she was busy making something the way she wanted it to be, because other things just weren't.

He watched her looking like she wasn't waiting, as he sat there looking like he wasn't leaving. He watched her until the familiar resignation pressed into his chest and he knew it was time. He stood and pinched his cigarette out, tucked it into his pocket. Then he blew out a breath he hadn't noticed he was holding and went to say goodbye to the only woman he had ever loved.

❦

She looked over her shoulder when she heard the picket gate scraping across the fieldstone walkway. Her silver hair, shiny as a wedding ring, was damp along her forehead and her face was flushed from the heat. She got to her feet before he could get there to help her and she pulled off her blackened gloves as she met him halfway down the walk.

She was four feet, eleven inches if there wasn't any wind and she had to look straight up just to meet his eye. She was seventy-five years old and generously proportioned beneath her variety of flowered muumuus, but he thought she was beautiful.

Her skin was permanently tan from working out of doors but every line on her face seemed like a laugh line and she had the warmest brown eyes he'd ever seen.

"Morning, Miss Margret," he said.

"Morning, Jack," she answered. She looked at him only half hopefully. "You have time for one more coffee?"

"No, ma'am. I'm running late." And he was, but he'd stolen his own time with her to spend it watching her, instead of feeling the awkwardness of goodbye between them.

She swallowed and her eyes got wet before she could catch it. He was sorry.

"Well," she said, collecting herself. "I appreciate everything you've done the last couple of days. You know that."

He did. He couldn't say "I love you" without promising to stay, so he came and he fixed things around the farmhouse, spent his few days mending fences and porch steps, painting rails and planting trees. She knew what he meant.

She couldn't say "I love you" without asking him to stay, so she fed him instead. She brought zucchini bread out to the barn, warm and spicy and moist. Sat him down on the porch with plates of tuna sandwiches and her potato salad with the bits of sweet pickle in it. She fed him every time he stopped moving and he knew what she meant by that, too.

"Emma!" she called back toward the house. "Emma Lee!"

The screen door squeaked open and thirteen year-old Emma stepped through it, wearing faded cut-offs and a big white tee shirt. She was still a tiny little thing, but when he'd first seen her the other day it had rocked him.

In his mind, she was always nine or ten. Seeing her growing up reminded him that time passed here while he was gone. Emma Lee was growing up and Margret Maxwell got older, too. She would continue to do so until one day she stopped, and the idea of it was intolerable.

He squinted across the porch at Emma Maxwell, the only child of Margret's only child. His best friend Daniel, now dead. Both of them dead, Daniel and Michelle, leaving four-year old Emma and her Grandma to go on together.

He'd joined the Corps four years before the accident that took them both, right out there on the dirt road. He'd thought about leaving when his time was up, but while he knew Margret waited for his visits home, he also knew she couldn't look at him without seeing her only boy. So he left, always.

"Emma, bring me that banana bread, please."

"Yes, ma'am." Emma went back into the house and Margret looked back up at Jack.

"Where are you off to now?" she asked.

"Back to Kuwait," he told her.

"Well, I don't like it," she said and set her lips that way she did when she disapproved.

"Yes, ma'am. I reckon they don't care for it overmuch, either." Trying to get her to smile. She almost did.

He walked up onto the porch and grabbed his sea bag. When he headed back down the steps, Miss Margret was busy not looking.

Emma came back out the screen door and down the steps, a loaf of Miss Margret's banana bread wrapped in foil. Emma's brown hair had all kinds of gold in it, like her Grandma's used to have. He wondered if she'd go silver, too, one day. Emma handed the bread to Margret and stepped back.

"See you, Little Bit," he told Emma.

"See you, Jack." She gave him a shy-girl wave and they watched her go back into the house.

Margret pressed the banana bread into his hands. It was still warm and he could smell the allspice and the nutmeg.

"Thank you," he told her.

"Well." She fussed with the embroidered handkerchief tucked between her breasts but didn't pull it out. He knew he'd better go. She hated it if he saw her cry.

"Bye, Miss Margret."

She slapped him on the cheek, almost softly.

"What did you just say to me?" she asked, only half joking.

"Sorry, ma'am. See you, Miss Margret." He smiled, kissed the top of her head. Her hair smelled of hot sun and lavender shampoo and he memorized it.

"See you, Jack." Her voice broke and again he was sorry.

She squeezed his hand and he started walking away before it just got too damn hard.

Margret watched him walk out through the picket gate, and she pulled the handkerchief from inside her bra. She loved him so much that sometimes she forgot she hadn't given birth to him. He and Daniel had been best friends since first grade, inseparable and yet so different.

Daniel mischievous and fair-haired, always laughing. Jack tall and broad-shouldered, the football star, with his lush black hair and those sharp blue eyes that always seemed to look right into a person's bones.

The two boys had done everything together, most of it right here. When Jack was twelve, his people had moved off to Natchitoches, seeking someplace new to be of no account, and Jack had stayed here with her and Daniel.

She desperately wanted him to stay right here with her and Emma Lee. Every time they did this, she wanted to grab onto him and beg him not to go. She didn't, because she knew that he would stay for her. But she also knew he couldn't look at her without seeing Daniel and that 'caused him pain.

So she never asked, she just watched him go. It wasn't her job to make it harder for him to leave; it was her job to make it possible.

Margret watched him round the bend where the pecan trees stood and then he was gone. She kept watching anyway. She'd let herself cry for just a minute and then get back to her flowers.

Emma ran through the backside of Grandma's land, past the little orchard and down the hill that led to the old pasture. She was a tiny thing, five feet tall and ninety pounds soaking wet, but she could run. Years of being the smallest kid in class had taught her to run fast.

Until last year, she'd been nothing but knees and elbows, but then Grandma's big boobs had come flying out of nowhere and landed directly on her chest. They made running a little uncomfortable, but she was still fast and she was awfully motivated.

She'd always done this; run from Grandma's through the Peterson's land and cut across to the river that ran parallel to Highway 9. Every time Jack Canfield said goodbye and walked out that gate, she'd run this path to the river. She'd been doing it since she was about six years old and if Grandma ever noticed, she hadn't said.

Once she reached the river, Emma ran across the footbridge, her sneakers thumping along the aged wooden planks, and hit the other side without breaking stride. She could see Highway 9 from here, a good couple of hundred yards away, but Jack wasn't on it yet.

She got to her special tree, a huge old oak forty feet high and with at least a dozen fine places to sit. She climbed up it without even thinking about it, muscle memory and hurry were all she needed.

She had just settled into her favorite crook, a comfortable "V" about halfway up the tree, when Jack appeared on the road. She made herself quite still and watched him come. The sun was hitting his black hair just right, making it glint like onyx.

She couldn't see the details of his face, but she knew that he'd be squinting against the sun and she wished that she could see it. She liked it when he squinted. He had a craggy face, even at his fairly young age. He was striking more than handsome, but she thought him the most beautiful man she'd ever seen.

Every time he left, she came here to watch him go. Not just to get one more look to last her another year, but because it allowed her to watch him unnoticed. He rarely noticed her anyway, but if she'd ever stared at him this long at home, Grandma would have caught it for sure. And she would have known that Emma had feelings for this man that she really had no business having. This man that, if someone had demanded a label, would probably be described as an uncle more than anything else. But she didn't think of him that way at all.

When she was a little girl, she'd wanted him to stay and be her daddy. He was so manly, with that gravelly voice and his crinkly eyes. He'd always seemed so strong, the kind of strong that would protect her, though she had no idea what from.

She liked his roughness, his jagged edges and his quietness. He had an unforced strength that made him seem like he would be the perfect daddy for her.

Somewhere around eleven, though, she started looking at Jack in a whole new light. When he'd come home that time, his role in her daydreams changed. In her daydreams, she had changed, too. She was older, taller and much more sophisticated. Not much older, but grown into her boobs and of legal age for sure.

In her daydreams, this new version of Jack would come home and fall almost instantly and irretrievably in love with her and tell her how surprised he was that his soul-mate had been right here all along.

She wrote these daydreams down sometimes, in her notebooks full of stories. But these stories were her own; they didn't get turned in at school or shared with Grandma in the evenings. These stories were for her and her alone.

Emma thought about the Jack of her daydreams until the Jack of the real world passed her on the road, his sea bag over his shoulder. He wasn't going to see her, but she wondered what he'd do if he did. Probably tell her to get her bony ass outa the tree and go find something to do.

She would have to explain and she couldn't think of a single good lie, so she made herself very still and watched him until she couldn't see him anymore.

Then she climbed down out of the tree and went home to kill another year.

Chapter 1

Twenty years later - 2014

JACK OPENED THE DOOR to the diner and walked straight back into 1970s Alabama. It had been eight years since he'd been home and nothing had changed. The same dozen booths with the same red vinyl seats that had maybe a little more red duct tape on them. The same yellowed clippings on the walls. The same yellowed counter with a handful of stools.

The only thing that seemed different was that he didn't know any of the half-dozen people that were scattered around the room. He figured that figured. The people he'd known had been leaving or dying for years.

He walked over to the empty counter and took a seat at the end. He smelled coffee and bacon and small town. All he wanted was the coffee. His head was pounding and the ketchup bottle didn't look as still as he thought it ought to. He heard pots banging beyond the swinging door, behind the counter and halfway to the big front windows. He'd appreciate it if that stopped.

Just then the door swung open and a tall, skinny black girl came out carrying a plastic dishpan full of silverware. She saw him and smiled, a pretty smile, her teeth big and bright against her black-black skin.

"Hey, sir, how you doing?"

"Fine, thanks," he lied.

"You want coffee or sweet tea?"

"Coffee, please."

She put down the tub and brought the pot and the thick white mug, poured him a cup of coffee.

"Can I get you something to eat, sir?"

"No, thank you." He tried to smile but he was pretty sure he'd grimaced at her instead. "This'll be just fine, thank you, sweetheart."

"Okay, then," she said, still smiling as she gave him a spoon. "You change your mind, just let me know."

"I will thanks."

He stirred real milk into his coffee while

he watched her take the dishpan and a package of napkins over to a booth by the window. As he drank his coffee, he watched her roll silverware up in the napkins and he wondered who her people were.

She looked like she might be a Wayne, but she also looked like she had some Brantley in her, if they still had Brantleys. Bo Brantley had been one heck of a football player back in high school. Jack had appreciated Bo saving his butt a time or two.

Jack was on his second cup of coffee when the swinging door swung again and Emma Lee Maxwell walked through it. She'd been looking at a sheaf of papers in her hand and immediately turned to walk toward the black girl, so he'd only glimpsed a piece of her face, but he knew her and it punched him in the chest. She was supposed to be married and gone off to Birmingham.

She was still tiny, but her hips were a bit wider in her faded Levis. Her hair was pulled back in a long, messy ponytail, longer than he remembered seeing it. The glimpse at her face had let him see that she had just a few fine lines starting up around her eyes and that she looked tired.

How old was she now? Thirty-something. He calculated. She was thirty-three or thirty-four. It didn't seem like she should be. He'd last seen her nine years ago, at Margret's funeral. He'd come back the following year, as he always had, thinking he should keep checking on her, keep an eye on the house, but she'd been gone. Gone and married to Birmingham and then he'd seen no reason to come back until now.

He watched her walk over to the black girl at the booth by the window.

"Lucinda, honey, I got your paperwork all filled out for you," she said to her. Her voice was deeper than he remembered it, stronger.

"Thank you Miss Emma," Lucinda answered. Another big smile.

"Just be sure you get your daddy to sign it and that you get it sent in," Emma said. "Otherwise they're not gonna pay the doctor bill. Okay?"

"Okay, Miss Emma. I will.'

"You can go ahead and go home once you get that silverware rolled, okay? Mary'll be here soon."

"Yes, ma'am."

Jack watched Emma stare out the window and thought that she looked tired or sad or both. He watched her for a minute and then decided to get it over with.

"Hey, Emma Lee," he said quietly.

Emma's first thought was that she must be having a stroke, because Jack Canfield didn't come home anymore.

She turned her head anyway and saw him where he shouldn't be, just ten feet away. The late morning sun, brutal already, was shining right into his face from the window. But she saw him and knew him anyway and suddenly couldn't remember whether to breathe in or out.

Out apparently, because out it went with a rush and she swallowed hard before she tried to sound unsurprised.

"Hey, Jack."

They stared at each other a minute and she dragged her hand along the counter like it would help her find her way over there. Her feet weighed at least twice what they'd weighed a minute ago, but they got her to within a couple of feet of him.

She saw now that the lines on his face were deeper and there were more of them, especially around the eyes, but his eyes were still the same jarring shade of blue. There was almost as much gray in his hair now as there was black. He set his spoon down on his napkin and almost smiled.

"How are you, Emma?"

"I'm okay," she answered and even to her she didn't sound like she thought it was true. "When did you get back?"

"Late last night," he answered. He looked at her a minute and she wondered if he really looked sad behind that smile or if he was just tired. It struck her that maybe it was just age.

He coughed, cleared his throat. He seemed

to collect himself a little, like he'd just caught himself falling asleep in the wrong place.

"I didn't know you were still living in Locust Grove," he said. She shrugged a little, almost an apology. "I heard that you got married, moved away."

"Well, I got engaged," she said and was glad her voice was back to normal. "But I never married him. In fact, I got away with a quickness."

"Who from?"

"Trevor Hollings."

He put down his cup, looked at her like he had a question. "Huh. I wouldn't have thought that."

"Me, neither." One corner of her mouth turned up in something that had hoped to be a smile but lost its sense of self. "Didn't seem like the worst idea at the time."

She reached behind her and grabbed the pot, poured him coffee he didn't want more of but would drink anyway. He saw her hand was shaking a little and he wondered if her breakup was still raw, if it hurt her still. He wondered if Miss Margret would want him to stomp the boy and an old sadness pressed down on him as he wished he could ask her.

"Are you back in your Grandma's house?" he asked Emma.

She noticed that her hand was shaking and thought about cutting it off. She grabbed a rag and started wiping the counter instead. "Yeah, we are."

"We?"

"I have a little girl. Becca. She's almost seven."

He sat back, feeling like he'd been pushed.

"That just doesn't seem right," he said quietly.

"She's the only thing that is right," she said. This time she managed a smile.

She glanced up at him and the sight of him there seemed like something she must have conjured without meaning to. She felt the familiar tugging somewhere in her chest. Nine years. He hadn't been back in nine years and everything had changed. So had nothing.

"So you've retired from the Marine Corps, I guess."

"I have."

"What's that like, not doing what you've always done?"

"Different." She wondered if his eyes really got dark or if it was just the angle of the sun.

"Emma, I came back the year after Miss Margret's funeral. You were gone. Regina told me you'd moved away." Emma looked away from him, then looked down at the counter. "If I'd known you were back, I would have come."

Emma swallowed hard then looked back up at him.

"It's okay, Jack. I know you only came back here for her."

"I came for you, too," he answered quietly.

"I'm not saying you didn't care about me," she said. "But your relationship was with Grandma. We barely knew each other." *Which didn't stop me from pinning my whole world on you,* she thought.

"I always promised her that I would look after you, too," he said. "But nobody knew how to contact you."

"I know. It's okay," she said and offered him half a smile. "I'm all grown up now."

He looked at her thoughtfully, almost sadly. "Yes, that's true."

They exchanged a few superficial questions and answers. Who had died. How people were. When the Hardee's had gone in and when the feed store had gone out. Easy questions with easy answers that gave both of them time to regroup. After ten minutes or so, she'd almost gotten used to him being there and he seemed to have remembered where he was.

He set down his empty cup and she started to reach behind her again but he held up a hand.

"I'm good. I need to get going," he told her.

She felt something kind of like panic.

"How long are you here?"

"Few days."

She swallowed, grateful.

"You working tomorrow?" he asked her. She shook her head.

"I'll come by the house tomorrow, see how things are."

He was already standing by the time she figured out what to say.

"You don't have to do that," she said.

He laid some money down on the counter.

"I know." He smiled at her. "But I'm sure there's some stuff needs doing. And I want to meet your little girl."

He was turning away before she got it out.

"Jack, you really don't have to come by."

"I know," he said. "But I will."

"The house is fine," she said and her hands were shaking again.

"Sugar, that house hasn't been fine since the seventies." He was already at the door.

"I don't want you to come fix things, Jack," she called after him.

"I am unconcerned by that," he said back and the door closed behind him.

She stared at the door and felt like life had just picked her up and shaken her. It left her feeling just a little pissed. From her earliest memory, she'd watched him come home and pay some kind of homage to her grandma, fixing and doing like he was paying off some kind of debt. Over the years, she'd wanted to be many things to Jack, but her Grandma wasn't any of those things.

Jack stepped out into the glaring sun and the thick, almost wet air was just as he remembered. He appreciated that, because he'd had enough startling crap for one day.

Chapter 2

*I*T WAS banging.

With one ear buried in her pillow, she identified the sound as banging. It was banging and it was scraping. She opened one eye to look at the clock and saw that it was banging and scraping at 6 a.m..

The sound was coming from outside her bedroom window, in the vicinity of the back porch. She wondered if last night's storm had stuck around and was playing with the screen door. She untangled herself from the covers and went to the window, pulled back the old white lace curtain and several bad words came instantly to mind.

Jack was fitting the gate back onto the chicken run. One of the hinges had been broken for a good six months and she'd spent a good amount of that time running around after The Girls and stepping on eggs that were laid where they didn't belong. Now Jack was here fixing it at the crack of are you kidding.

Emma rushed to her closet and started flinging hangers back and forth. Not the yellow dress, it made her look like a Peep. The light blue skirt was too dressy. What did she want? Was she going for sexy, for mature, what?

She stopped herself on her way to the dresser and realized that she wasn't 13 or 16 or 20 anymore. She didn't have to waste two hours choosing the right outfit to spend five minutes with a man who would never actually see her. It didn't matter whether she went for sexy or for pretty so she decided to skip it altogether and go for banged and scraped out of bed.

A few minutes later, she carried two mugs of coffee with her left hand and pushed the back screen door open with her right. The sky was pink and there was just a hint of rain still in the air. She put one of the mugs on the porch rail and cupped the other in both hands, took a long swallow.

He was across the yard with his back to her and she watched him. He was wearing old jeans and a white tee shirt and a baseball cap of some kind. Worn boots that might be the same boots he'd always had.

She could tell that he was only a touch softer of body than he was before. He held the gate up with one hand and worked the screwdriver with the other and his muscles were the kind that men earn by working hard, not by working out.

When she was a little girl, she'd thought he was huge. Six-foot-one, with that gravelly, raspy voice and quick, sharp laugh. He'd seemed so large. Later, she used to try to picture what it would be like to dance with him and she'd sometimes watch when Grandma was standing right up next to him so she could see how they'd look. She was an inch taller than Grandma when she stood up straight.

She watched him work as she sipped her coffee and she thought how surreal it was that he was there. She had finally gotten used to him not coming back and now here he was. It excited her and intrigued her. But it also scared her and that pissed her off.

"I brought you some coffee." She didn't have to yell. The air was still and her voice carried without much raising.

He turned around and was about to answer her when he stopped. She was standing there on the back porch, wearing nothing but a man's well-worn chambray shirt. Her warm brown hair was longer than he remembered and it was messy and bent and covered half her face. The tails of the shirt almost reached her knees and the sleeves were rolled up a good half-dozen times.

His first thought was that she looked like a tiny animal in the process of being eaten by a much bigger one. His second thought was that little Emma Lee Maxwell wasn't supposed to have some man's shirt on at six in the morning.

"You got company?" he asked her.

"I'm looking at it," she shot back. It surprised her. She was known for her mouth now, but around Jack she'd always been such a mouse, trying to skitter around the perimeter without being seen.

His eyes squinted just a bit, like something that he expected to slither had just flown. But then his eyes ran up and down her and she looked down herself and got his meaning.

"I got it at Goodwill," she said. "I like to sleep in it."

"Okay," he said and shrugged a little before he started walking toward her.

"I have a little girl, Jack," she said. "Men don't come to this house."

She didn't know why, but she was irritated. Maybe not irritated, but defensive. She thought maybe she should check that because her natural defense was sarcasm and she used it better than anyone she knew.

"Good, 'cause your grandmother'd have a

damn fit," Jack said.

"Well, it wouldn't be the first time," she muttered.

He stopped at the porch rail and reached up to take his coffee. He was about to take a sip when he saw that it was the precise color he liked it to be.

"Just the way I like it," he said. "You remembered that?"

"It was yesterday," she said back. It was none of his business that she'd known how he liked his coffee since she was twelve, and drank it the same way.

He looked at her kind of quizzically, like they'd just met, then took a long swallow of his coffee, watching her over the rim of his mug. She watched him back.

"Jimmy Leland," he said then and she was pretty sure her face had just lost some color.

"What about him?" she asked, though she was positive she didn't want him to say another word.

"You don't remember Jimmy?" he asked, with an almost unkind grin. "I think a few months had already gone by when I got back, and it was one of the first things she told me. 'Jimmy Leland had Emma Lee in the back of his Pontiac out by the driveway.'"

She felt the color coming back to her face.

"It was the front and we weren't doing anything significant," she snapped. If she'd known then that Grandma had told Jack about Jimmy Leland, she would have thrown herself out of the nearest tree.

"Must have been some kind of significance going on," he said, with half a grin. "Miss Margret said the windows were all steamed up out there."

"We were sixteen years old, we could barely steam up the rearview mirror," she said, and she'd had enough of him making fun of her teenaged self, who had compared Jimmy's kisses, rather unfavorably, with what she imagined Jack Canfield could have accomplished.

"Miss Margret said your shirt was on backwards when you got out of that car."

"Well, now I keep my shirts on frontwards," she snapped, "so I don't think you or Grandma or Jimmy Leland have anything to worry about. Now I'm going to go get some more coffee 'cause I don't take a whole lot of crap on my first cup."

He smiled his first genuine smile in months, but she didn't see it, her back to him as she yanked open the screen door.

"I'd love another cup," he called after her.

"You know where it is," and the screen door slapped shut behind her.

"Huh," he said, to pretty much himself.

He walked into the kitchen and it was like walking back in time, walking back to being ten or twelve or twenty. The same Formica kitchen table, with the hideous yellow-flowered chairs. The same Harvest Gold stove and shelves full of cookbooks and canning jars. Even the same rooster wallpaper that he and Daniel had hung when they were fifteen, penance for getting drunk at the sophomore dance.

Jack had actually been stone-cold sober, but when Daniel had fallen through the screen door right onto his mother's tiny feet, Jack had faked it so that Daniel wouldn't have to bear the wrath on his own.

The only thing different about the kitchen was that Emma was putting the dishes away instead of Miss Margret. He walked over to the counter and grabbed the coffee pot.

"So our shy Little Bit grew up to have a real backbone," he said, smiling.

She glanced over at him, closed the cupboard door.

"I'm sorry. My first instinct tends to be snark,'" she said. "For pretty much everything."

He leaned back against the counter. "I don't mind it."

She looked at him again and wanted to say that she'd just introduced herself to him and wondered if the real, grown-up Emma Maxwell would leave more of an impression than the girl ever had.

"Well, that's just as well," she said, turning

back to her dishes. "I have a pretty sharp tongue sometimes and I think you can probably bring that out in me."

"I'll bet when you really get going you could shave your legs with that thing," he said. She couldn't help smiling. "But that's okay. I'm happiest communicating in my native language."

"Well, stick around a while and you'll probably be beside yourself," she told him.

So he did.

Later that afternoon, Emma sat on the front porch, waiting for the bus to bring Becca home from school.

Emma had spent the entire day alternating between finding reasons to talk to Jack and finding ways to avoid it. It annoyed her that she felt so unsure around him, but then she always had. She kept reminding herself that she wasn't a teenager anymore and there was no danger she'd throw herself at him, but what she was really afraid of was saying something stupid, like "Your lunch is ready. I used to be in love with you."

Jack had spent the day just as he'd spent every other day at the farm, at least in her memory. He'd finished the chicken run, replaced the flush assembly on the toilet and tacked down the kitchen linoleum in the places where it was curling up like old newspaper.

He didn't talk much other than saying "thank you" for a glass of tea or cursing at whichever of four cats had just run under his feet. Jack had always professed to hate Grandma's cats and Grandma had taken great pleasure in pointing out a new one every time he came home.

Earlier, he'd been acutely put out by the fact that the fat black cat was the same one that had peed in his boots fifteen years ago. He theorized that Blackie had lived past a comfortable age and should probably be pharmaceutically relieved of the burden of living. Emma had countered that Blackie seemed altogether unburdened but perhaps Jack needed a shot of something.

Now Jack was finishing up putting a new fan belt on Grandma's old Pontiac station wagon in the driveway. He'd seemed amused to learn that she actually drove the thing, that it wasn't just some sentimental piece of yard sculpture.

She had to admit that the old wagon looked kind of forlorn sitting there next to his shiny green Dodge something-something with the Cummins whatever, dual whatnots and some kind of transmission. Her neurotransmitters had fallen asleep somewhere around "Dodge."

Now she was having little trouble staying awake but a hard time not staring at him as he worked. His being there had an aura of unreality about it, as did having actual conversation with him, adult to adult.

She'd spent years praying that he would one day come home and fall in love with her, then some more years praying she'd get over her romantic idolization. Now she was just praying that she could enjoy his presence for a few days and still keep enough distance to maintain her dignity.

"Hey, Emma Lee, come here a second, please."

Emma got up from her favorite rocker and went over to the car. Jack was hidden under the hood, both arms shoulder deep in the bowels of her old car.

"Point that flashlight down here while I tighten this bolt, would you?"

Emma turned on the little flashlight from his toolbox and pointed it down where his hands were.

"You got some money put away to replace this thing soon?" he asked from under the hood.

"I don't want to replace it," she said.

"There's eighty-seven other things wrong besides this belt, Emma. I'm all for driving a paid-off car, but this one's about to start costing you some real money."

"It'll still cost less than a car payment and I can't afford anything much better paying cash," she answered. "Besides, it's got too much sentimental value. It's Grandma's car and I'll drive it 'til it falls apart."

Jack stood up and tossed a socket wrench into the toolbox at her feet.

"You wear her underwear, too?"

Emma flicked the little flashlight off and let it drop into the nether regions of the engine before she turned and walked away. She heard his muttered "Dammitall" as the flashlight plink-plinked its way down, and allowed herself a satis-fied smile before she settled back into her rocker.

A moment later, he slid himself back out from under the car, tossed the flashlight in the toolbox and made his way to the porch.

"I'm gonna go in and wash my hands," he said as he strode past her. "So I don't leave any black marks on your neck."

The screen door slapped shut behind him and she laughed just as the school bus wheezed to a stop at the end of the driveway. Emma waved back at Grace, the bus driver, as Becca ran down the driveway. Her long blond ponytail was a snarly mess and her backpack made her look like a lit-tle purple camel.

"Hey, baby," Emma called to her. "How was your day?"

Becca ran up the steps and plopped onto Emma's lap, her smile making two little dimples pop.

"It was great!" she beamed. "I pulled Bran-don Gray off the monkey bars and he cried."

"Rebecca Margret, that's not great!" Emma said sharply. "Why would you do that?"

"'Cause he said I was just a weak little girl and then he tried to kick me in the face," Becca answered. "So I grabbed his foot and yanked him and he fell off."

"Did you say you were sorry?"

"No. I said if he was such a strong boy he shoulda been able to hang on."

Emma managed not to grin at that, but only by looking away for a second.

"Listen, Joybug. We can't go around yanking on people just because they say something mean. Was he hurt?"

"No, he was just embarrassed," Becca said, shaking her head. "Some of the kids were laughing at him. I had to sit at my desk instead of going to art."

"Well, I'm sorry you didn't get to go to art," Emma told her. "But you did something wrong."

"So did he! He tried to kick me in the face."

"I know and I'm glad you didn't get hurt, but he could have been hurt, too and that's just as bad, right?"

Becca heaved her best sigh before muttering something under her breath.

"What?" Emma asked.

"I guess so," Becca answered. "But I didn't know he was gonna fall."

"Alright, well tomorrow I want you to tell

him you're sorry," Emma said, lifting Becca off of her lap. "But right now I want you to go put your stuff away. We have company."

"Who?"

Just then, Jack came back through the screen door, wiping his hands on a paper towel. Becca looked up at him curiously.

"Becca, this is Jack Canfield. Jack, this is Becca."

"How do you do, Becca?"

"Hi." Becca squinted at him a second. "Are you Great Grandma's Jack?'

Jack smiled at her. "Reckon so. Do you know me?"

"Yes. You're like my Grandpa's brother."

"Kind of, yeah," Jack said, his smile faltering just a bit.

"Does that make you Grandpa Jack or Uncle Jack?"

"Well, why don't we keep it simple and you can just call me Jack, okay?"

"Okay."

Jack seemed to search a moment for something appropriate to say, as some people without children do.

"How was school today?"

"I yanked a boy off the monkey bars 'cause he tried to kick me in the face."

"Good," Jack answered flatly.

Emma sighed as Becca broke into the smile

of the vindicated.

"Becca, go do your homework," she said.

"Okay," Becca said brightly and she ran into the house, tripping over Blackie, who was lumbering out for his daily constitutional.

Jack scowled at the cat as he stopped next to Jack long enough to scratch himself vigorously and fart, then moved on to his sun spot on the steps.

"That cat lives much longer, he's gonna need a colostomy bag."

Jack looked at Emma and she sent up a prayer that she would say nothing that was either mean or stupid. That she would just be nice.

"I'm making beef stew for dinner," she said. "Why don't you eat with us?"

"Miss Margret's beef stew?"

"Is there some other kind?" she asked with a smile.

"Thank you, that'd be just fine." he answered. "What time's it gonna be ready?"

"About five-thirty."

"That sounds good," he said as he headed down the steps. "I'll just go back to the motel and clean up."

The words were out of Emma's mouth before she knew she was forming them.

"Jack, why don't you just bring your stuff back here?" She'd asked God to keep her from saying anything mean or stupid and He'd taken it as multiple choice.

Jack stopped and turned around, squinting back at her.

"I mean, you've always stayed here. Your room's still your room," Emma said reluctantly. "It doesn't seem right for you to stay at Peet's."

Jack looked away for a moment, up at the magnolia that shaded the far side of the porch. Then he looked back at her.

"That'd be nice, thank you," Jack said quietly. "If you're sure it wouldn't put you out."

"I'm sure." She wasn't.

"Alright then." He seemed about to ask a question, then closed his mouth before he spoke again. "I'll be back in a while."

Emma held onto the porch rail as she watched him turn his truck around and pull out onto the dirt road, then she let out her breath.

"You're a laugh a minute, Lord. Seriously."

Jack carried a single duffle bag as he followed Emma upstairs a little while later.

"I never saw any reason to change your room, so it's probably pretty much like you left it," Emma said over her shoulder. "Becca has my old room and I moved into Grandma's."

She turned and smiled at him as they stopped in front of the door to his and Daniel's old room at the end of the hall.

"I guess you probably think that's sentimental, too."

Jack bounced the duffle bag in his hand
and looked down at her. "I didn't mean anything
when I said that about her underwear."

Emma smiled again. "I know that, Jack. I
wasn't offended. I can take it almost as well as I
dish it out."

Emma opened the door and it creaked in
the exact same way it always had. He and/or
Daniel had been caught sneaking in more than
once because of that creak, which no quantity of
WD-40 had silenced.

"I'll let you get settled in," Emma said, heading back for the stairs. "Dinner'll be ready in
about ten minutes."

"Are you sure you don't mind my staying
here a few days?"

Emma waved his question off and started
down the stairs. She really didn't mind, and actually she was glad. While he'd been at the motel, she'd realized that Jack staying at the house
would be a good thing.

She'd gotten over him a long time ago and
the more time she spent getting to know him,
adult to adult, the further she would get from
that lovesick teenaged girl. And that was good,
because aside from Becca, he was all the family
she had left.

Jack set his duffle bag down by the closet door and looked around the room he'd shared with Daniel from the time he was twelve until he'd gone off to college. Miss Margret had replaced the twin beds with a double a few years later, when Daniel and Michelle had married and moved into a trailer just a little way down the dirt road. The trailer was gone now, too.

The first few times he'd come home after that, his nights in this room had been largely sleepless. After a while, the ghosts had faded, though they were never completely gone. Daniel had been the closest thing he'd ever had to a brother. His best friend, never replaced with another.

He sat down on the side of the bed and shook his head. This trip was turning out to be very different from what he'd planned. He was only going to be here for a day or so, just to come by the old house and see it one more time. See if Emma had sold it, if another family lived here now. To breathe the scent of Miss Margret's gardenias and tell her goodbye.

From below him in the kitchen he heard the sounds of Emma and her little girl talking while they set the table.

He let out a sigh and laid back on the bed. He'd spent thirty years being everywhere but here and now he'd ended up right where he'd started, still trying to work off a debt to the women who lived here.

Emma spooned another scoop of beef stew onto Jack's plate and added another roll.

"Thank you," Jack said. "This is really very good.'

"Thank you," Emma said. "I learned from the best."

"You look a lot different than you do in all those pictures in the living room," said Becca, pretending there wasn't a small pile of peas left on her plate.

"I bet I do," Jack answered. "Most of those were taken a long time ago."

"You're still handsome though," Becca said. Jack just smiled and chewed.

"Peas, Becca," Emma said.

"How many?"

"At least five."

Becca proceeded to spear one pea with one tine of her fork, but the fork stopped halfway to her mouth.

"My Grandpa was handsome, too," she said. "I like his wedding pictures the best. Why aren't you in the wedding pictures?"

"Well, I wasn't at the wedding," Jack answered. "I was really far away when your grandparents got married. I didn't meet your grandmother until just shortly after your Mom was born."

The words felt foreign, like a piece of lint on his tongue. He'd never imagined Daniel and Michelle beyond their twenties and yet now he was referring to them as grandparents.

"Mommy was a cute baby," Becca said plainly.

"She was. As babies go."

"Consume the pea, Becca," Emma said.

Becca did. Just the one.

"I was cute, too," Becca said.

Jack put his napkin onto his plate and looked her in the eye.

"I have very little trouble believing that."

"Does that mean I'm prob'ly right?"

"Yes."

Becca noticed her mother's eyebrows and speared another pea.

"What kind of a soldier were you?" she asked.

"I was a Marine," Jack answered.

"What kind of a Marine?"

Jack seemed to think about it a second. "The lucky kind."

"'Cause you didn't die in a war?"

"That's right," Jack answered.

"I don't want to be in a war," Becca said, pushing one more pea past her lips.

"Good," Jack said. "Most wars aren't as big and dramatic as they look on TV, but they're a lot scarier."

Emma stood up and grabbed the pot of stew from the table.

"Becca, it's a school night," she said. "Time for you to get in the shower."

"You go ahead and get her squared away," Jack said, picking up his plate. "I'll take care of this."

"That's okay, I can get it," Emma said.

Jack gave her half a smile as he headed to the counter.

"You're forgetting we were raised by the same woman," he said. "She who cooks does not clean."

Emma smiled at the words she'd heard many times.

"Okay, suit yourself," she said. "Come on Joybug, take your plate to the sink and come upstairs."

Emma tucked the sheet around Becca's shoulders and handed her Ralph, her leprous bunny.

"I like him," Becca said sleepily. "He's nice."

"Yes. Yes, he is," Emma said quietly.

"Does he like fishing?" Becca asked. "Maybe he can take me fishing before he goes home."

"Maybe," Emma said.

She felt a twinge of déjà vu and wondered if

she and Grandma had ever had this same conversation. She looked around at her old room, which wasn't much different now from when she'd been a child. It still had the same yellow striped wallpaper with little purple pansies. Most of the furniture had been hers, including the little white desk where she'd spent most of her free time.

On the bottom right corner of the desk was a little picture of a cat, drawn with an excess of blue ballpoint ink. When she was fifteen, she'd doodled her and Jack's initials on the desk before she'd realized that Grandma would see them, then drawn the cat to cover them up.

For just a moment, she felt stuck between one reality and another. She'd been a six-year old child in this room and now her little girl was falling asleep in her old bed. Underneath that cat were the initials of a partly made-up man, half action hero and half Prince Charming, who she had believed in without question.

Now the real man sat downstairs, and moment by moment was replacing that old image with something else entirely. In a way it made her sad, but she couldn't say she was sorry.

"Good night, Joybug," Emma said, and leaned over to kiss her daughter's forehead, but Becca was already asleep.

Chapter 3

EMMA SAT BACK in her chair, her bare feet up on the back porch rail. She was feeling oddly content and figured it was partly the late summer breeze, partly the easy familiarity of dinner and partly the glass of blackberry wine that she was slowly sipping.

The screen door creaked open and Jack came out onto the porch, settled himself in the other chair and propped his boots up on the rail.

"That was really fine, Emma, thank you."

"I'm glad you liked it," Emma answered.

"Kind of surreal, really, sitting there with you and your little girl," he said after a minute. "Like watching a remake of an old movie with different actors."

"Yes." Emma took another swallow of her wine.

"What's that you're drinking?" Jack asked her.

"Blackberry wine," Emma answered. "The only kind I actually like."

"Brother Fillmore's blackberry wine?" Jack asked with a smile.

"Yeah."

"You mind if I have a sip of that?"

"Sure," Emma answered and handed him the glass.

"Oh, that's a beautiful thing," he said after he took a sip.

"Do you want a glass?"

"Maybe later," he said.

They sat in silence for a moment, or human silence at least. The cicadas were in their usual uproar and they could just hear the chickens exchanging a little last-minute gossip before they went to bed.

"You've got a fine little girl, Emma," Jack said finally. "Smart as a whip."

"Thank you," Emma said.

"It occurred to me tonight that we've had more conversation today than we've probably had in your whole life prior," Jack said. "I'm sorry if I never paid you much mind when you were growing up, Emma Lee."

Emma pictured Jack engaging her in an actual conversation when she was young and saw her twelve-year-old self exploding like a dandelion from the stress of it.

"It's okay, Jack," she said. "I didn't feel ignored. You were always here for a just a few days and I knew you were here for her."

"We did talk an awful lot about you, though," Jack said. "You were her pride and joy when you weren't making her crazy.'

Emma smiled.

"Well, the crazy-making was mutual, but I loved her, too."

They were quiet for another minute or two. Jack took another sip of her wine.

"Why are you here, Emma?"

Emma looked him.

"What do you mean?"

"I always figured you'd be a famous author by now," he said. "You still writing?"

The question took her by surprise.

"Not so much, not lately," she said and took her wine back.

"Every time I came home, your grandma'd show me one of your new stories. They were good."

Emma was having a hard time assimilating the fact that he'd ever read one.

"I think my favorite one, you were about sixteen or seventeen maybe, that story about the girl that lived on the beach up north." He looked at her. "The girl who was taking painting lessons from her father, only she didn't know that was who he was. It was very good."

"Well, maybe for a teenager," Emma said, feeling slightly uncomfortable.

"That was one of the best things you ever wrote." Jack answered. "Maybe it was one of the best things I ever read."

Emma laughed nervously. "Maybe you haven't read enough."

"Well, that just proves the point about making assumptions," Jack said. "You forget that I got my degree in literature?"

Emma's jaw wanted to drop but she refused to let it.

"Actually, I don't think I ever knew that," she said finally. "I wouldn't have forgotten it. I majored in creative writing."

"I know."

"Although, I didn't play football, so I had to go to Troy," she said, grinning and hoping to change the subject.

"See, there you go again," he said. "I played for Ole Miss, but I wasn't on a football scholarship. I went on an academic scholarship. Full ride."

"Huh," was the best she could come up with.

"Yeah, 'huh'" he said back. "Put that in your pipe and smoke it."

He grabbed her glass and swallowed the rest of the wine.

Two days later, Emma was running serious-ly late for work. She raced through her shower and tried to climb into her jeans while she was still wet. They took issue with that, which only served to degrade an already ill mood.

She didn't mind her job; in fact she some-times liked it. It required very little of her mental energy and the hours were good as far as being home for Becca. It was a comfortable part of her intentionally small life, a small life she'd grown up in, left and then knitted back around her like an old baby blanket.

But today she resented having to spend eight hours pouring coffee, cashing out custom-ers and ordering supplies. Jack hadn't said when he was leaving, but he'd said he was only here for a few days. If this was his last day, she was going to hate having been gone.

They'd spent most of the day yesterday pick-ing some of the last of the peaches. She'd canned or frozen quite a bit and of them and they were madly eating the rest out of hand. Later, when all that was left was bruised or overripe, she'd take them in baskets to Brother Fillmore down the road. He got the bruised fruit for his hogs, just as he would a ton of apples later on, for making the most popular cider in three counties. In exchange, she and Becca got a hog every fall.

In the evening, after Becca had gone to bed, they'd played a mercenary game of cribbage out on the porch and debated the merits of various Southern writers. She'd kicked his butt at cards, but had let him think he'd prevailed on the matter of Thomas Wolfe. Things had gotten a little heated when discussing Faulkner and they'd both needed a break from conflict.

Last night, she'd lain awake for just a while and thought that, as much as she'd adored Jack in her youth, she'd never realized he'd be such good company.

Now she was obligated to spend the day cleaning grease traps and listening to locals coming up with new solutions to problems they'd been solving for years. She loved some of her regulars, but she'd rather stay home and keep discovering Jack.

He was drinking a cup of coffee on the front porch when she shoved the screen door open and charged out, tripping over the orange tiger who was charging in.

"Move it, Killer!" she snapped at him and exchanged a wave with Jack as she rushed down the steps. Halfway to her car, she stopped and turned around.

"Are you leaving today?" she asked him.

He thought about it a second.

"I can, Emma."

Emma shook her head. "No, I'm sorry, that's not what I meant," she said, and took a deep breath. "Are you planning on leaving today?"

Jack thought a bit longer.

"I hadn't really planned to leave today, no," he finally said.

"Okay. Well. Good, then," and she dashed for her car.

Grandma's old Pontiac usually took some romancing to get started, but after the fourth try, the old heap made a sound like it was drowning and then just quit. When Emma tried to turn it over again, it just clicked.

Emma looked up to find Jack standing at her window with his coffee, looking amused.

"Can you push me off or something?"

"Push you off what, the Grundy Bridge?" he asked. "This thing's not going anywhere. Come on, I'll give you a ride to work."

Emma stuck her head out the window as he started for his truck.

"I think it'll be okay if you can just get it going," she called.

"As usual, you're wrong," he hollered back as he got into his truck.

He started it up and Emma sat there staring at him while he stared back at her in his rear view mirror. Finally, she got out and climbed into the passenger seat.

"What do you have against my car?" she asked him as he pulled onto the road.

"I like things to do what they're supposed to do," he said. "Cars should run, cats should stay out of the damn way and toilets should flush. When they do, I'm rather friendly towards them."

Emma rolled her eyes and looked out the window for a few minutes as they got onto the blacktop and headed the four miles into town.

"You know, if you'd do something with your writing, you could afford a decent car," he said after a time.

"I plan to, Jack," she answered. "I just need to find the time."

"Make the time," he answered.

"Out of what?" she shot back. "I'm raising a child, working full time, taking care of the farm. I'm not sitting at home watching TV."

"I understand that," he said evenly. "I just don't like to see you struggle. You shouldn't have to and you sure as heck shouldn't have to when you have a true gift that could make your lives better if you'd use it."

"Jack, I understand what you're saying, but it's not all that easy. I'll get back to it, but maybe just not right now."

"When was the last time you wrote something" he asked her, his eyes leaving the road for just a moment.

Emma sighed.

"I don't know."

"Look, Emma, I'm not trying to give you a hard time," he said after a moment. "I just know that you're wasting your talent and you're wasting your time wiping counters at Cookie's."

"Not if I'm buying bread and milk with that time."

"Point taken," he answered.

"Look, Jack. I know my life isn't necessarily what Grandma wanted for me," Emma said. "And I've never aspired to manage a diner in town. But I'm content. The diner doesn't pay much, but the house is paid for and we're poor but we're rarely broke. Stop feeling sorry for us."

Jack thought about that for a moment.

"Okay, I'm going to say something and I would appreciate it if you'd hear me out before you start gagging on all that righteous indignation you got going."

Emma opened her mouth to remark on that, but shut it again when he raised his hand.

"I think you should let me buy you a decent running car—" he started.

"What? No!"

"Tie a knot in that tongue for one second, Emma," he said. "I have savings, I have no real expenses, it's not going to hurt me to help you a little."

Emma sighed out the window as they pulled

into the diner's tiny parking lot.

"Jack, I appreciate it, really," Emma said as Jack pulled to a stop in front of the door. "But I don't want you to buy me a car."

She got out of the truck with an almost total lack of grace or dignity, as her legs couldn't reach the ground.

"Emma, there's nothing wrong with accepting a little help," Jack said as she shut the door.

He looked over at her and could only see her face from the nose up, but her mouth was moving, as usual.

"Listen, Jack. I know you felt obligated to Grandma for taking you in and for some reason you felt like you needed to pay her back for loving you," Emma's forehead said. "But I'm not Grandma and you don't owe me anything."

Jack was going to answer her, but she'd spun on her heel and stalked off. He watched her go into the diner behind an elderly man wearing blue coveralls that he probably didn't need anymore.

He respected her independence and he admired how hard she worked to make a life for herself and her child, but that didn't interfere much with his somewhat therapeutic vision of grabbing her by her neck and yanking her right out of those ugly black shoes.

Jack spent the day mudding a hole in the wall of the mud room, trying to get Emma's car running and either letting cats in or letting cats out, often the same cat at the same time. But throughout the day, his mind was on Emma; on what she'd said about obligation, debt, and Miss Margret.

He had issue with her choice of words. He would have used terms like honor, gratitude and love, but he understood her not wanting to feel like a note that needed to be paid.

By the time he'd cleaned up and sat out on the porch with a glass of tea, he'd decided that he needed to talk to her and that maybe he needed to say more than he'd expected to say.

Chapter 4

WHEN JACK PICKED Emma up at two, she had either put their discussion that morning out of her mind or wanted to pretend she had. She thanked him for coming to get her and asked about his day. He told her the hole was fixed, the car was not and his day was fine, outside of all the cats who lacked follow-through and conviction.

They spent the rest of the short ride mostly in silence, aside from him asking if so-and-so still lived in such and such house and what had happened to the Grandys, who used to own the farm near the turn to Miss Margret's road.

As Jack got and Emma tumbled out of the

truck, Jack decided to get on with it.

"Emma, I need to talk to you about a couple of things," he said as they walked into the house. "I'd like to do it before Becca gets home. It's important."

Emma looked at him curiously for a moment as he held open the front door.

"Okay. Well, Becca's not going to be home 'til after dinner," Emma said. "She's eating at Grace's tonight so she can see Kyla's new puppy."

They walked into the hallway and Emma hung her purse up on the hook by the stairs.

"Well, I'd like to talk to you now, if that's okay," Jack said.

He seemed nervous and that made Emma nervous.

"Okay," she said. "Let me just go up and change."

As Emma pulled off her work clothes that reeked of bacon and hash browns, she wondered what was on Jack's mind. She had a feeling it was something she wouldn't want to hear. She already knew he was leaving, so what was it? Was he leaving today after all?

She threw on an old flowered dress that she called her French farm wife dress, pulled her hair out of its ponytail and went on downstairs.

Jack was making coffee when she got to the kitchen.

"Do you want a cup?"

"Sure. Thank you."

He went to the refrigerator to get the milk.

"Why don't you go out on the porch where it's cooler? Go on and I'll bring this out."

"Okay," she said and felt off-balance and stupid.

She went out on the back porch, where there was at least some small breeze, and started to sit in her chair, then decided to sit on the steps. He was leaving. Probably today. But why wouldn't he just say that? He wouldn't have any reason to not just say it.

Jack came out and handed her a cup. He seemed about to sit down next to her, but then he went down the steps and stood in front of her instead. When she looked at him, he looked down into his cup and took a drink.

Suddenly she knew that he was trying to be careful and he was trying to be kind, which meant that somehow or another, she was about to feel humiliated in some way.

He was leaving. He sensed that she liked him maybe a little too much in too wrong a way and he was going. He sensed this and was going home to a wife and kids. He was going home to his wife of twenty years and his teenaged kids.

She thought all of this in just a few seconds and had already mentally thrown up six times before he finally spoke.

"Uh. This is not going to be an easy conversation for me. I actually have two things I need to say to you and I've spent half the day trying to figure out which one to say first." He turned the cup around in his hands a few times. "Unfortunately, as conversation starters go, they suck pretty much equally."

Emma opened her mouth to speak, though she had no idea what she wanted to say. But Jack held up a hand.

"Wait. Let me just say what I need to say. Don't talk just yet," he said.

Emma closed her mouth and waited while he took another sip of coffee, then looked at her.

"I'm about to die, Emma Lee."

Just like that he said it, and it was as though sound wasn't traveling at the same speed that it normally did, because she didn't even understand this arrangement of vowels and consonants until a few seconds later.

"I lied to you a little about where I've been the last nine years," he said. "I did retire four years ago and I did go live on the Outer Banks for a while. But I've spent most of the last two years in and out of Bethesda Naval Hospital."

Emma was having trouble breathing. It wasn't that she couldn't get enough air; it just suddenly seemed to have too much oxygen in it.

"It's called malignant astrocytoma. A brain tumor."

Emma wanted to start over. She wanted

him to go in the house, come back outside and tell her about his wife and kids. She swallowed hard and found her voice.

"What about – wait," she said. "What have they done? What can they do?"

"They've already done it," he said. "They did surgery and chemo and immunotherapy and radiation. It's been done."

Emma felt the tears start to flood her eyes and she blinked them away, looked away for a minute, at Jack's shirts hanging on the clothesline.

"I don't understand. They didn't get it out?"

"Not it, Emma. Them," he told her. "They got the first one out two years ago. It came back. Then I got a bunch of smaller ones. That's what they do, these types of tumors."

"So have surgery again." she said.

"Emma, I've had three."

"Have you tried seeing someone else?" she asked him. "Did you get a second opinion?"

"Yes. Listen to me, Emma," he said. "I'm sorry. I didn't come here to burden you with my problems. I was just here for a day or so to see the house one more time. I didn't know you were here. But you're here and it was right to tell you."

Emma took a deep breath, a slow breath. She wanted everything to slow down.

"How long, Jack?"

"Last month they said at most fourteen

months. But it could be next week, next month. Anytime really."

"But maybe fourteen months?" Emma asked. "More than a year maybe?"

"My chances are unimpressive."

"But you don't look sick. You're fine."

"No. I get hellacious headaches. I throw up. I throw up behind your barn."

Emma started blinking again. Someone she cared about deeply was telling her he was dying. She would do him no favors by bawling. She swallowed again, feeling like something sharp and poisonous was caught in her throat.

"Jack. I'm so sorry," she said. "I'm so – maybe there's something else, they're always doing research and trials, right?"

"No, Emma."

He squatted down then in front of her and he was just so close. She wanted him to reach out, to hold her, but how do you ask someone who's just told you they were dying to comfort you in your brand-new grief?

His face was just a couple of feet away and she wanted to put her hands on it, to make him understand that she was sorry. But then she realized that she didn't remember ever touching Jack or him touching her. It just wasn't something that they'd ever done.

"Emma, I need to talk to you about something else and I want you to hear me out," he said. "I need you to just listen to what I have to say."

The idea that there could be something else made it difficult to say anything, so she just nodded. Jack turned his cup around again, then stood.

"I think you should marry me."

"What."

"Just listen for a minute," he said quietly. "I want to help you. You deserve help, both of you. I've got savings I'm not going to spend. Life insurance."

"Jack, I don't want your money!"

"Listen to me, Emma. I worked hard for that money," he said. "I spent thirty years in the Corps and it ought to count for something for somebody because it didn't do anything for me."

Emma started to speak again, but he held up a finger.

"I'd get something out of it, too, Emma. This is the only place that I've ever called home. I don't want to keel over in some motel at the beach or in a Denny's bathroom somewhere. I sure as hell don't want to go back to Bethesda. I would like to die here, Emma Lee. I'd like to spend the rest of my time here and I would like to be here when it's done."

"Jack, you don't need to marry me to stay here!" Emma cried. "This is just as much your house as it is mine."

"But it's your home."

"It's your home, too!" Emma stood up on shaky legs, wishing they'd had this conversation inside. Wishing they weren't having it at all. "Jack, I don't want your life insurance, but even if you want to give to us, you can give your life insurance to whoever you want. You don't have to marry me."

"I understand that," he answered, and she marveled at how calm he sounded. "But here's the thing. There's not much chance that I'll last a year, but if we're married for a year when I die, you and Becca will qualify for survivor's benefits. That's a big deal and you need to think about it. You need to think about Becca, about her future. About your future. I worked for those benefits, Emma. Somebody should get them."

Emma took a deep breath and let it out again.

"This is too much, Jack," she said. "I can't think."

"I'm sorry, Emma. Really. I am. But I want you to seriously consider what I'm saying."

"I need to think, Jack. I need to process this."

"I know."

Emma looked out past the orchard to the pasture. Everything looked so normal. It looked exactly the same as it had ten minutes ago and she felt insulted by that, as though it didn't matter to the rest of the world that one-third of *her* world had just announced its imminent destruction. She felt like her internal organs were rearranging themselves inside her and she knew that she was about to fall apart. She hugged her arms to her stomach and looked at Jack.

"I need to go for a walk, okay?'

"Okay."

"I'm sorry."

"You shouldn't be," Jack said.

"I need to go off and think and I'll come back with an answer."

"Emma, you don't have to tell me today," Jack said. "I know it's a lot. You need to decide soon, but it doesn't have to be today."

"I'll tell you in an hour."

Emma set her cold coffee down on the porch step and started off across the yard.

Emma got her crying over with on the way to the river.

She'd worked so hard to hold it in while Jack was looking that when she finally let it go it actually hurt. She felt something clenching in her chest with every sob. She didn't know if it was her heart breaking on Jack's behalf or if it was because she was trying not to let herself cry too freely. She had to face him again in an hour and she had no intention of saddling him with some sort of responsibility for her pain.

By the time she crossed the footbridge to the grove of oak trees, she'd stopped her crying and pulled herself into some semblance of together. She needed to really think about everything he'd said, to process it, package it and decide where to put it.

She found herself standing next to her favorite tree, the one from which she had often watched Jack walk to catch his bus back to Beaufort.

She put a hand on the trunk of the tree and tilted back her head, squinting up through the branches and the sun-bleached leaves to her old perch fifteen feet above the ground. She thought about the teenaged angst that had been her companion on those short vigils and wished that she could trade the sorrow she felt now for the sorrow she'd felt then.

She wondered for a moment when she had last come to this special place of hers. She realized with some surprise that the last time she'd been here, she hadn't come to make a decision about Jack but she had made one all the same.

It was the summer before Grandma had had her stroke and left her here alone. It was also the one and only time that she had ever missed Jack's coming home. She was twenty-five, had recently dropped out of graduate school and was waitressing for the summer at an oyster bar in Mobile while she tried to finish her first novel.

It was a month during which she was trying to figure out who she really wanted to be and get herself pointed in that direction. She'd finally gotten around to testing the waters of drinking and socializing with her friends, but it hadn't taken and she'd gone back to her hermit-like ways.

She'd gotten a wild hair a few weeks earlier, after watching *The Misfits,* and dyed her hair Marilyn blonde, an unfortunate mistake that she couldn't wait to color back out and that she wasn't looking forward to unveiling to Grandma.

That Saturday morning, she'd gotten out of the shower to find a missed call and a message from Grandma on her cell phone.

"Emma Lee, when you come home for the fair tomorrow, stop at the Home Depot in Dothan and get me some more of those pink peonies you brought me," Grandma's nasally voice had said. "They're doing really well out by the hen house. Don't forget we need to leave for the fairgrounds by ten if we don't want to carry these pies all the way from the back forty. If you set your alarm early enough, you won't have to speed. I don't want to see any more tickets."

She'd sounded like she was hanging up the phone, then spoken again.

"Oh, I forgot to call you the other day and

tell you Jack was home. He's leaving today but he said to tell you 'hello.' Okay then," and she'd hung up.

Emma was still damp from the shower when she'd jumped into her old Honda, a beaten-up Civic that she'd ended up selling a few years later, when Trevor had lost his fourth job. She had, of course, ignored her grandma's edict and floored it all the way through.

It was a four-hour drive and she needed to make it in three, since Jack's bus left at 11:30. There was one other Greyhound that passed through each day, late in the afternoon, but it ended at Atlanta and Jack despised Atlanta, and preferred the route that let him change buses in Savannah.

Emma had blown right past Dothan without stopping, but road work on 231 had cost her a good half hour anyway. She was just ten minutes from the exit to Highway 9 when she saw Jack's bus pass her going the other way.

She'd slowed down once she pulled off onto the two-lane highway and her eyes started to sting when she passed the gas station-slash-bait store-slash lunch counter where Jack caught his bus.

On impulse, she'd parked her car in the little gravel lot at the river that fishermen used and walked over here to her tree. She hadn't known why she was there; Jack wasn't going to be walking up the road. But she was feeling frustrated and depressed and not eager to go home to Grandma's just yet. She'd plopped down on the grass by the riverbank, and let the flowing water focus her mind.

She was twenty-five years old, had a dead-end job, a half-finished education and a half-finished book. She was a bona fide adult and yet at the mention of Jack's name, she'd come flying home, hoping to catch a few minutes in his presence or at least see him from a distance as he made his way to the bus.

She'd raced to get home to catch a glimpse of a man she'd known her whole life and yet didn't really know. It had embarrassed her and made her feel ashamed of her knee-jerk pursuit of an infatuation she should have let go of years before. Was it really because of Jack or was she just afraid of the responsibility of growing up and actually trying to achieve something?

She'd never had a relationship that was anything more than casual dating and it was because she refused to stop comparing the boys she knew with the man she thought she knew.

She'd sat by the river for over an hour and could have sworn she felt herself maturing by the minute, almost perceptibly catching up to her actual age. She'd felt stupid for holding men up to her idea of Jack; none of them was ever going to measure up to the romantic and sometimes ridiculous ideal that she'd built up over the years. Truth be told, Jack probably couldn't live up to himself, either.

By the time she'd left the river that day, she'd decided to finish growing up and put Jack out of her mind. Six months later, she'd met Trevor.

Now she was back at the river, sitting on the bank with the sun hot on her back. But she knew there really was no decision to be made. She would do what Jack asked because he'd asked it and because he deserved to have what he thought he wanted.

But she also realized that, by saying yes, she was volunteering herself for a hurt she might not be prepared for. After just a few days with Jack, she was finding him so much more compelling and so much more interesting than the Jack that she'd invented on her own.

She knew, without question, that whether he was there for a month or a year, she would not come out the other side of it without loving him. And she knew that this time it would be for real and later on she wouldn't be able to put it away with her footless Barbies and her high school yearbook. It was gonna stick and it was gonna hurt.

But there was no real question about what she was going to do and so worrying about what it would mean was pointless. Jack didn't need or want her mooning and there was no good to come from feeling tomorrow's pain today.

So she did what she'd always done, what she was raised to do; she prayed. She asked God to please make it better, she asked God to please make it stop and finally she just asked God "please" because she really didn't know what she needed to pray for.

For just a moment, she wondered why God was being so unkind. She'd prayed most of her life to be married to Jack and now He was saying "Yes." But it wasn't for love and it wasn't forever and though it shamed her to admit it, she wondered if He was being intentionally cruel.

She started to ask Him why He was doing this to her, but only got halfway through the question before the guilt shut her up. None of this was about her and if she cared for Jack as much as she'd always believed, she would suck it up and remember that it was about him.

Jack was sitting in his chair on the back porch when she came walking back across the yard. He had one boot propped on his knee and he was wearing the Crimson Tide cap that he liked for when he was working out in the sun.

Black clouds were converging just to the south, like the sky had sent emissaries to convey its sympathies. A breeze brushed across Emma and she wrapped her arms around herself as she watched Jack watching her return.

"Hey," he said quietly as she came up the steps.

"Hey," she said and sat down in her chair.

She watched him as he took off his cap and ran a hand through his thick, gray-black hair; hair that she used to wish she could roll around in, it was so beautiful. It still was, though she'd noticed it was thinning a bit at the back of his skull.

Jack placed his cap on the toe of his boot and looked about to say something, so Emma spoke first.

"Jack?" He looked over at her and she saw him seeing that she'd cried. "Are you scared?"

"No, Emma. I'm really not," he said quietly. "But I've had some time to get used to it."

Emma was going to reply, but found herself distracted by a sudden need to try to memorize every crease near his mouth, every wrinkle at the edges of his eyes.

"Emma, I know I put a lot on you all at once and I'm sorry," he said.

"It's okay," she said. "We'll get married, if you're sure that's what you want."

He looked her in the eyes for a long minute, like he was searching them to see if this was really the best idea for her.

"I think it's the right thing to do."

"The right thing to do, or the thing you want

to do?'

"Both. It'll make me happy, Emma, if that's what you're asking me."

"Yes."

He got up and put his cap back on as he looked out towards the back field.

"When do you want to do this?" she asked him. He looked over his shoulder at her.

"Tomorrow," he said.

"Tomorrow?"

"There's not much chance I'll make it the whole year, for you to get those survivor benefits, but the odds against it get bigger every day," he said to the yard. He turned back around to face her and leaned back against the rail. "So I'd like to hurry up and get it done."

"Okay," she said dully. Tomorrow was so soon. All of this was fast and soon.

"Good," he said.

"Well then." Emma said. She couldn't think of anything else to say that she should say, so she got up and headed for the door. "I'm gonna go make dinner."

"Emma?"

She stopped, one hand on the open door.

"I've never been able to tolerate pity," he said. "I'd appreciate it if you didn't subject me to it."

The idea that her Jack should be pitied made Emma's eyes sting and she blinked back fresh tears.

"Okay," she said and went inside.

Chapter 5

JACK AND EMMA spent most of dinner in near silence. It wasn't the uncomfortable silence of strangers, but the silence of two people who knew they were thinking about the same thing; who knew they shared the topic, if not the particulars. After a meal that passed with little more than "Please pass the tea" or "That rain's really coming down", Emma got up from her place and took her plate to the sink.

She filled the old porcelain sink with hot soapy water while Jack cleared the table, then he came to stand beside her.

"If we're going to go ahead and do this tomorrow," she said, wondering why she couldn't say the thing they were actually going to do, "then we need to talk to Becca tonight when she gets home."

Jack took a plate from her and started to wipe it down it with Grandma's Community Coffee dish towel.

"What are we gonna tell her exactly?"

Emma finished washing another plate and handed it to him before she spoke.

"The truth."

"All of it?"

Emma turned and leaned her hip on the counter.

"No. I mean, she's not going to ask why we're getting married, she doesn't really understand why people do," Emma said. "She knows we've always known each other. She's just not going to think about that. But we have to tell her about the ... about you."

Jack put the plate in the cupboard and set the towel down on the counter.

"Are you sure about that, Emma?" he asked. "I know we have to tell her at some point, but she's just a little girl. That's a lot to lay on her at one time."

"I know that, but if we don't tell her, it could end up really hurting her later on. We need to go ahead and tell her now."

"Emma, it's not like taking cod liver oil," he said. "It doesn't all have to be at once."

"It does, Jack," Emma answered quietly. "She may not think about why we're getting married, but she does think that getting married means happily ever after. And I know Becca; she's going to be attached to you within another week."

Jack picked up the towel again and twisted it in his hand.

"Besides, Jack. What if we don't tell her and you—something happens sooner than we think?"

"You're right," Jack said.

"There's one thing, though," Emma said. "I'll tell her about tomorrow, but I think you should tell her about you. You seem so calm about it and I don't think can do that. It would help her I think."

"I can do that, Emma," he said. "Of course."

"Thank you," she said and she started washing the salad bowl.

"I've been thinking," Jack said after a minute. "I think we should have a barbecue Saturday. I think we need to tell people, you know, just our friends on the road, Regina and Dew, especially. Invite them all over here for a barbecue to celebrate."

"What? Why?"

"Were you planning on keeping it a secret?" Jack asked her.

"Well, no, but I just didn't get to thinking about that part yet," Emma said. "But why? I mean, it's not like it's a real wedding or anything. We're not actually celebrating, to put it plainly."

"Here's the thing, Emma Lee," Jack said. "They're all going to know eventually anyway, or they'll just think we're shacked up here or some other kind of oddness. There's no harm in just telling them straight out and I don't want you worried about what people are thinking."

"I don't really care what people think."

"Sure you do. And what about Becca? She's going to talk about it anyway."

Emma put the salad bowl on the counter and sighed.

"I did not wake up expecting this day," she said.

Jack smiled at her as he started drying the bowl.

"Look at it this way, Emma Lee," he said. "We tell everybody we got married and then I drop dead shortly thereafter and it's just the sweet-est tragedy. The Junior League Ladies'll be tick-led pink and you and Becca will be swimming in casseroles and Jell-O salads for a year."

Emma looked at him and couldn't help smil-ing just a little bit.

"You're such a jerk," she said.

Jack started to say something back, but just then the front door slammed shut and Becca came running down the hall.

❧

As Emma had predicted, Becca took news of the immediately pending marriage in stride. They'd sat in the kitchen, Emma scratching at the little boomerang designs on the Formica table while Jack and Becca had blueberry cobbler.

Once she found out that there would be no wedding dress or wedding cake, Becca had no further questions. But once they'd gotten that out of the way, Emma's stomach began to tighten.

Her instinct was to shelter Becca, to wrap her in a protective coating of Disney movies and dollhouses filled with happy families. Becca had a farm girl's pragmatism about life and death, but she hadn't as yet experienced the death of someone she knew. Her opinions about people dying were based on short question and answer sessions with Emma and talks about Heaven in Sunday school.

As Jack pushed aside his dessert bowl, Emma took a deep breath and willed her baby not to be stricken.

"Becca, I have to tell you about something else, too," Jack said quietly.

Becca licked the last of the blueberry sauce from her spoon and looked at Jack expectantly.

"I have a thing wrong with my head. It's a bad thing and the doctors can't fix it, so one day soon, maybe a few months or a year, I won't be here anymore."

Becca looked at him for a moment, her blue

eyes wide.

"What I mean is that I'm going to die pretty soon," Jack said.

Becca looked at Emma and then looked back at Jack. Her expression went from surprise to sadness to the kind of compassion you see on the face of a nurse or a pastor, like she was the one delivering the news.

"That's really sad," she said finally.

"Well, we all die eventually and I've had a fairly decent life," said Jack.

"Are you scared?" Becca asked him.

"No," Jack answered.

Becca looked at him for a moment.

"You don't look sick. Just a little old maybe."

Jack smiled at her. "Just a little."

"Will it hurt?"

Jack thought about the answer for a second.

"No."

"Are you just going to go to sleep?" Becca asked him. "My rabbit just went to sleep one day and didn't wake up."

"I don't really know exactly," Jack said.

Becca looked down at her bowl for a second, the fingers on one hand picking at the nails of the other. When she looked up and spoke again, her voice wasn't much louder than a whisper.

"Please don't do it in my room," she said.

"Okay," Jack answered.

A little while later, after she had bathed Becca, joined her in praying for Jack and tucked her into bed, Emma grabbed a glass of tea and found Jack sitting on the front porch with a glass of tea of his own.

Emma sat down in Grandma's old white rocker and they sat for a few moments, with nothing but the crickets and cicadas breaking the silence. That and the remnants of the rain dripping from the green tin roof onto the flowerbeds.

"Can I ask you a question?" Emma finally asked.

"Sure."

"Are there things you want to do? I mean, is there anything you want to accomplish or anything?"

Jack looked at her and smiled.

"You mean do I have a bucket list?"

"Well, yeah. For lack of a more palatable phrase," she said.

"No, I don't," he answered. "My plan was to just travel around a little, see some things I only moderately cared about seeing and just wait for it to happen."

He sat back in his chair and crossed one bare foot over the other.

"But now that I'm going to be here, I just want to go through the motions of living," he said. "I want to kick back on a Saturday and watch the Tide pretend to work hard at beating the Gators. I want to go fishing over on the river. I just want to live my life."

He looked over at her.

"What I want to do is what we've been doing," Jack said.

"Okay," Emma said and she looked out at the picket fence that ran along the driveway, where Grandma's gardenias were blooming like crazy. "You know, it's Grandma's birthday next month. I tell Becca stories about her and we bake a German Chocolate cake. It was her favorite."

"I remember," Jack said and he smiled.

He watched Blackie lumber up the front steps and flop like half-melted butter onto the braided rug in front of the door. Then he looked back at Emma.

"You know, Emma, I didn't come back here all the time just because I owed your grandmother. I loved her beyond reason."

"She sure did love you," Emma said.

Jack looked out into the yard for minute, then turned to her and smiled just a little.

"Did Miss Margret ever tell you about the time she beat up my daddy?"

"No!"

"It was the summer after third grade. Daniel and I were eight. We'd been friends since first grade and I was over here all the time, but Miss Margret had never met my daddy, except in passing. We had a crappy little house out on Piedmont Road, where that storage place is now."

Jack sat back in his chair and took a sip of his tea.

"One Sunday evening, Daddy and I were in the yard, ostensibly practicing baseball," he said. "The day before, I'd gotten struck out in the last inning because I stepped back from a fastball that was high and inside."

Emma took a sip of her tea and thought about the pictures she'd seen of Jack and her father when they were about that age. Jack had been slim but not slight and his hair was jet black and slightly mussed.

"Anyway, we were out in the yard and Daddy was throwing one ball after another, right at my chest, while I just stood there, and he kept saying 'Don't you move, boy, don't you flinch,'" Jack went on.

Emma felt a heaviness in her own chest at the thought of this man as a helpless boy. But Jack sounded so matter of fact and downright conversational about the whole thing, as he stared out into the dark.

"We'd been out there for a while and all of a sudden Miss Margret and Daniel pulled up in her old Impala," Jack said. "They'd just come from church and she wanted to ask if I could come to Vacation Bible School the next week."

Jack took another sip of his tea before he went on.

"She came flying into the yard like a little Banty hen, yelling and asking my daddy what he thought he was doing," he said quietly. "I didn't catch what he said, but next thing I knew, she'd picked up one of my bats and commenced to beat my daddy down to the ground. Then she threw the church flyer down on him, said 'We'll be picking Jack up at four' and got back in her car and left."

He looked over at Emma and smiled. "I loved her with a vengeance from that day forward."

"Holy crap," Emma said.

"That Miss Margret. She was every bit a southern lady, but there wasn't an inch of dainty to her."

Emma smiled and looked back out at the gardenias. The white blossoms were barely visible in the dark, but the fragrance was intense and close.

"I still talk to her every day," Emma said.

"Me, too," Jack answered.

The next morning, Emma washed the coffee pot in the sink and tried not to focus too much on the fact that this was going to be one of the weirder days in her life. She was going to marry Jack Canfield in just a little while. All those years of practicing her signature were about to pay off, but not for any of the reasons that she had imagined as a girl.

She'd decided to wear her French farm wife dress because she thought she should, but she'd drawn the line on extra makeup or messing too much with her hair. The last thing she wanted was to look like some blushing bride who expected everything, or even anything, to be different after today.

She thought about the wedding phase she'd gone through when she was about fourteen or fifteen. She'd spent too much of her allowance on bridal magazines, dog-eared all of her favorite wedding dresses, scratched and sniffed the scented perfume cards, boned up on shower etiquette and tried to picture Jack in each of the tuxedoes.

She'd finally decided he'd look best and be most comfortable in a standard black tuxedo; no cummerbund, and that they'd both enjoy the mandarin orange wedding cake with the purple marzipan flowers around the edge.

As she scooped coffee grounds into the filter for later, she could still remember her vision of their first dance as a couple, with white Christmas lights strung in every possible location and the deejay playing "Kiss Me" by Sixpence None the Richer.

She had to smile at how those details had stuck with her, but then she'd thought about the whole thing every day for about a year and in such minute detail that she could get herself outright twitterpated over it all.

Now it all seemed so silly and that embarrassed her. Jack probably hated that song. And tuxedoes, and marzipan, mandarin orange or otherwise. But it was a sweet memory of a sweet time.

Just then Jack walked into the kitchen. He was wearing pressed jeans and a bright white polo shirt and his hair was still a little damp at the ends. He picked up his cup from the table, swallowed the last of his coffee and put the cup in the sink. She got the barest whiff of Nautilus when he passed by her.

"Well, Emma, let's go get legally wed," he said.

"Okee-doke," she said and followed him to the door.

Chapter 6

THE DRIVE TO the Henry County
Courthouse in Abbeville took them just
a little more than half an hour and they
talked about all kinds of things that were neither weddings nor tumors. When they got to the
county clerk's office, they took some forms, took
a number, and took their orange plastic seats in
the crowded waiting area.

They'd filled out their forms, lost two dollars
in the soda machine and read every sign on the
wall by the time their number was called an hour
later. A round little blonde in her forties with a
lavender bow in her hair sat behind the window
and took their paperwork.

"Good morning," she said in a doll voice. "How y'all doin'?"

"Just fine, thank you," Jack said. Emma was starting to feel nervous again and just smiled.

"Okay, I see y'all are getting a marriage license," the woman said. Her name was Marsha Poole according to the little plastic sign. "Are you getting married elsewhere or are you wanting to be married today by a clerk of the court?"

"We'd like to do it today," Jack said.

"Alrighty," Marsha Poole said and started stapling little tags to their papers. "If y'all have ever been married to anyone else, I'll need your divorce decrees."

"No ma'am, neither of us has ever been married," Jack said.

Marsha Poole gave him a dimply smile.

"Good gracious, I find that hard to believe," she said, blinking all over Jack. Then she grinned at Emma. "Don't worry, hon, I'm just teasing.

Emma smiled that it was alright, but it wasn't alright much. She had a quick vision of snatching the stapler and stapling the woman's nostrils shut. The twinge of jealous irritation surprised her just a little, but she didn't feel particularly repentant about it.

"Well then," said Marsha Poole. "I just need to copy y'all's driver's licenses or state-issued photo IDs and your Social Security cards."

Jack and Emma got out their driver's licenses and Social Security cards and when they put them on the counter, Emma glanced at Jack's.

"Huh," she said. "I always just assumed your given name was John." Marsha Poole glanced up at Emma with her eyebrows raised.

"Nope, it's Jackson," Jack said. "Named after Stonewall, of course. The only upstanding thing my daddy ever did."

A few minutes later, Marsha Poole gave them their marriage license and gave them back their IDs and directed them up one floor and around the corner, where she said the clerk of the court was performing ceremonies from eleven to one, first come, first served.

The waiting room was half-full and most of the couples in it were about eighteen. Half the girls wore prom dresses and the other half wore flip-flops and shorts. After they got their little paper number out of the machine, Jack and Emma found two seats off in a corner.

They'd been sitting there for a few minutes when Jack swore under his breath.

"What's the matter?" Emma asked him.

"We forgot to stop and get some rings," he answered.

"Oh, yeah," Emma said and picked her purse up from between her feet.

She pulled out a little rose-colored velvet bag and tipped two white-gold wedding bands and a simple garnet engagement ring into her palm. Jack reached over and slowly picked up the engagement ring.

Miss Margret's husband Clyde had given it to Miss Margret when she was sixteen. He'd married her the day after her seventeenth birthday and Jack had never seen her take it off.

"Wow. I haven't seen this in a long time," he said quietly.

"Yeah," Emma said.

Jack started to put the ring back in her hand, then held it out to her.

"See if it fits," he said. It did. "You do have tiny hands like she did."

"You don't have to wear Grandpa's wedding band," Emma said. "I just keep them together."

"I'll wear it."

Emma put the rings away and tucked her purse back between her feet.

"Emma, I know this isn't exactly what it's supposed to be, but I hope you understand that as far as I'm concerned, married is married."

"What do you mean?"

"I mean I'm not going to be out at the bars picking up women or flirting with bleached blonde clerks. I wouldn't disrespect or humiliate you that way."

Emma wasn't sure what to say about that, so she looked out the window over Jack's shoulder.

"Crap, Emma!" Jack said then.

"What?"

"I never even thought to ask you if you were dating somebody," he said.

"I'm not. There's nobody," she said.

"Good. This'd probably be a hell of a thing to explain," he said.

Emma just smiled and looked back down at her hands. Grandma's ring looked so familiar, but so foreign on her hand. Everything, all of this, was just so strange. She suddenly thought of something and her stomach churned just a bit.

"Jack? Maybe we shouldn't do this today."

"Why not? Are you having second thoughts?"

"No, but ...." She swallowed hard. "Don't you want to have sex, I mean, at least one last time?"

"I hadn't really thought about it," he said, surprised. "Maybe after we get some decent coffee."

Emma felt the blood rush to her face and all the hairs around her temples standing up. Jack looked at her and grinned.

"I'm sorry," he said. "I'm just trying to lighten things up a little."

"You're an idiot," Emma said.

"That's sometimes true," he said. "To tell you the truth, Emma, I'm a little surprised that it hasn't occurred to me. I guess the last time *was* the last time. If I had known that, I probably would have put more thought into it."

Emma wanted to say something worthwhile, but her head was suddenly filled with sex, Jack and really good coffee all at once and she didn't know whether to look around, check her cell phone or go pee.

Fortunately, a nervous young couple sat down a few seats away and the boy struck up a conversation with Jack. She didn't have to say anything worthwhile and their number was called just a short time later.

The ceremony was performed by a short man somewhere in his thirties, with a round face, old acne scars and blue wire glasses. He spoke in a polite, but bored tone that Emma had to work hard to pay attention to. In the entire room, the only concession to the occasion was a white pillar candle, still wrapped in plastic and stuffed into a plastic ring of dusty yellow carnations.

Jack and Emma listened to the man ask all the usual questions and they answered in all of the usual places. They put on Grandma and Grandpa's rings. Then the man said, dull as primer paint, "By the authority vested in me by Henry County and the State of Alabama, I pronounce you Mr. and Mrs. Jack Canfield. You may kiss the bride."

Emma wondered if he was going to say, "That'll do, pig," and she came out with a nervous giggle just as Jack leaned over.

"It's not that funny," Jack said, smiling, and gave her a peck on the mouth.

He grabbed her hand and she stumbled after him to the door.

"That's not what I—" but then she realized that after twenty-some years of waiting for it to happen, Jack had just kissed her and she'd pretty much missed it, and so she forgot to explain.

Later that afternoon, Jack walked up one side of the dirt road and down the other, stopping at the eight or so houses on the two-mile road where people they knew still lived. His first stop was the Porters' place. He'd gone all the way through school with Regina Porter and three of her brothers and there had always been a variety of cousins, nieces and nephews living in the house.

Regina was out in the yard sprinkling children with a hose and she saw Jack coming up the road. She dropped the hose and teetered over to the fence as fast as her high heels would let her.

She was wearing purple pants that only went just past her knees, and a purple top with all kinds of flowers on it covered her big belly and impressive backside. She'd always been a large girl, but she was pretty and she was fun and she was kind and everybody loved her.

When she got closer, Jack saw that her dark skin was almost as smooth and unlined as the last time he'd seen her, the year after Miss Margret's funeral.

Jack gave her a hug and got himself squeezed all out of shape while she exclaimed over him. A bunch of little kids he didn't know came running over and she introduced all kinds of grandchildren whose names he instantly forgot. Then she shooed the kids away and yelled toward the front door.

"Dew! Get out here!" she yelled and her gigantic husband Dewayne lumbered out onto the porch and squinted at Jack before he broke out in a smile.

"Well, I'll be!" he hollered out, and he started down the steps. "Jumpin' Jack Flash. My man."

He came over and they shook hands and hugged both. Dew had been Jack's best friend on the high school football team, a running back with the speed of a skinny boy and arms like telephone poles.

The three of them chatted a few minutes, talking about where he'd been, how long it had been and what they'd been doing, then he got around to mentioning why he was there.

"So, Emma and I got married this morning and we want a have a little barbecue tomorrow," he said.

Regina stared at him for a second, looking confused.

"Emma who?" she asked and Dew grinned

and said "Emma Maxwell?" at the same time.

"Yeah, Emma," Jack said. "This morning."

"What do you mean, this morning?" Regina yelled. "Why didn't you invite us to the wedding?"

"We just went down to the courthouse," Jack said. "We'd rather just have friends and neighbors over, have some good food, have fun."

"Oh, law!" Regina said, laughing. "Ain't nobody in town gonna believe Jack Canfield finally got around to getting married!

Just then one of the little boys started to cry across the yard and they looked over to see him on the ground, with the other kids circled around. The little boy was holding his knee. Dew started to jog over there, waving back at Jack and telling him he'd see him Saturday.

"What you want me to bring?" Regina asked Jack. "I'll make some collards; I got some real nice collards ready to pick."

"That sounds good, Regina."

"I got to call Byron and James," she said. "They're gonna choke."

"Tell 'em to come on over if they can." Jack said.

"What you think Emma wants me to bring?" she asked. "I'll bring some of them candied carrots you like. What's Emma making?"

"I don't know. Miss Margret's potato salad, of course. I think she said barbecued chicken."

"Does Emma need me to bring some beverages?" Regina asked. "I'll bring some root beer, I just got three cases of it over to the Sam's Club in Montgomery."

"That'll be fine, Regina," Jack said. "Sounds good. I need to head up the road, but I'll see you tomorrow."

They hugged again, Regina's big bronze earrings scraping Jack's neck, and Regina toddled back off toward the house.

"Jack Canfield got married," she yelled over her shoulder, laughing. "I got to call Byron. And Emma! Lord have mercy, that girl can keep a secret."

Jack laughed and got back onto the road and went to invite their other friends and neighbors. All of them were surprised to see him, all of them were surprised he was married, but nobody seemed all that put out that he'd married Emma. A few made remarks about the difference in their ages, but they were playful remarks with no harm intended.

His last stop on the way back to the house was Brother Fillmore's place. Jack couldn't remember what Brother Fillmore's rightful first name was; he'd been a deacon at First Baptist for so long that he'd always just been "Brother." Brother Fillmore had intimidated the life out of him and Daniel when they were kids, but although he was as fundamentalist as they came, he also had a dry wit and an open hand for anyone that needed help.

Jack found Brother Fillmore out back, shooing two half-grown hogs back into their pen. He was the only man Jack had ever seen who could work outside all day and have his overalls as pressed and clean as when he'd put them on.

He was a slim man, just a bit shorter than Jack, but his dignity and bearing always made him seem larger to Jack. He had to be over eighty, though he looked much younger, and he'd lived alone since his wife had passed, back in the nineties.

He didn't seem all that surprised at Jack's news, but Jack didn't recall ever seeing him surprised.

"Well, Emma's needed a good man to give her some direction for some time," Brother Fillmore said. "She's not meant to go it alone."

"Yes sir," Jack said.

"How long have you been home, son?"

"Just a little while," Jack said.

"You've not been living in sin 'til this time, have you?"

"No sir," Jack said. "No sinning at all."

"Well, I'll be pleased to join you in celebrating," Brother Fillmore said. "I'll need to come up with an appropriate gift."

"No gift necessary, sir," Jack said. "Just bring yourself; bring a dish if you like."

Brother Fillmore pointed his cane at the

smaller of the hogs he'd just penned.

"That one just tore up all my Black Krim tomatoes," he said. "I'll bring him."

Chapter 7

THERE WERE ALREADY three ve-
hicles in the front driveway and several families out in the back yard by the
time Emma ran out of things she could do in the
kitchen. Jack had just taken the chicken out to
the fire pit, where they'd laid the racks for a grill
and Emma had sent Becca out several times,
with pickles or paper plates or more tea.

She took the lid off of the big white Tupperware bowl that Grandma'd gotten way back
in the fifties, and stirred the potato salad one
more time as Jack came back through the back
door.

"Emma, what are you doing?"

"I'm just giving the potato salad a stir," she said.

"You've been stirring it since last night," Jack said. "It's done."

Emma looked up at Jack, nervously chewing the corner of her lip.

"I've known everybody out there my whole life and I'm scared somebody's going to try to have a conversation," she said.

"What are you afraid of?" he asked her.

"What if somebody asks me how we ended up getting married when you've been gone for eight years? What if somebody asks me what the heck we're doing?"

"Come on," he said, and he put his hands on her shoulders like he was some elderly country doctor about to give her a shot. "You know how it works around here. No matter how much they might want to know, nobody's gonna ask a direct question. They'll drop a hint that they're wondering and when you don't come through they'll wait 'til you tell somebody else, then they'll hit that person with a full frontal assault."

"I just don't know how to act," she said.

"Listen, these people know us," Jack said. "They're not expecting us to hang all over each other or call each other cute names. We just act like we always act, except maybe a little nicer, and they're not gonna think a thing of it."

"Yeah, okay."

"Everybody's here to have fun and eat. Just be yourself and have a good time," Jack said. "Maybe try not to look like you're on your way to the gynecologist."

Jack smiled at her and she couldn't help smiling back.

"Let's go," he said and they headed outside.

Two hours later, the party was in full swing. Fifty or so adults and children were scattered all over the back yard. Dew and Regina's oldest son Lewis, who made extra money as a deejay, had set himself up a makeshift sound station over by the barn and various teenagers were dancing in the big dirt patch that spread from the barn doors to halfway across the yard.

Lewis had been playing an odd mix of classic rock, country and R&B, but the crowd never seemed to mind all at once.

Card tables, picnic tables and a few old doors on sawhorses were covered with casserole dishes and large plastic bowls of food. Coolers filled with ice, bottled water, root beer, RC Cola and Mountain Dew sat under one of the pecan trees, with several milk jugs of sweet tea beside them.

Everyone had brought folding chairs, old sheets and picnic blankets and those were spread out around the edges of the shade from the peach trees, with a few spots reserved in the full shade for the elderly folks in the crowd.

Dew and Regina Porter had called Regina's two brothers, and between all the aunts, children, nieces, nephews and grandchildren, the Porters made up half the attendance.

Emma had been friends with Regina and Dew's youngest son and daughter, who had since moved off to Montgomery and Birmingham respectively. She'd always envied them their large, loud, but fiercely close conglomerate of relatives. Her grandfather had grown up in an orphanage for reasons no one knew, and Grandma had only had one sister, who'd passed away at the age of seventeen.

Emma sat in a lawn chair by the coolers, enjoying the warmth of the sun on her skin and the sounds of people she loved laughing and talking and playing. Becca was surrounded by a group of younger kids in the two-acre rectangle of grass that stretched down to the berry patch. She was dictating the rules to a game of kickball, by virtue of the fact that this was her yard.

Jack seemed to be in his element, sitting on the porch steps with several other men. He was the only one who wasn't wearing some type of baseball cap. Crimson Tide and John Deere were the predictable standards. Jack was wearing jeans and a blue denim shirt tucked in with a white tee shirt underneath. It occurred to her that, while he did look older, he really hadn't managed to get any less attractive as he aged. If anything, he was even more appealing.

Miss Annie Booth, who had been a lifelong friend of Grandma's, gingerly made her way over to Emma with piece of lemon pie on a little paper plate.

It was warm and sunny, but the lack of humidity on this beautiful September day apparently made it cool enough for Miss Annie to need a thin pink sweater over her flowered housedress. She was on the approach to her ninetieth birthday and didn't have a single fat cell to keep her warm.

Emma held the arm of her chair steady as Miss Annie got herself settled in.

"My, my, I just had to have me another piece of this pie," Miss Annie said. "That Cassie, she sure makes a light crust." She smiled over at Emma, a tiny bit of lemon curd stuck to her bright pink lips. "Not as good as your Grandma's, of course."

Emma smiled at Miss Annie. "I never could get the hang of Grandma's pie crust," she said.

They both watched as a group of teenagers grabbed cold drinks from the coolers and then ran back off toward the dirt "dance floor" by the barn.

"Margret sure must be having a giggle right

now," Miss Annie said. "My land."

Emma swallowed before asking, "What do you mean?" though she asked to be polite and really wasn't sure she wanted to hear the answer.

"Why, you and Jack, dear. You and Jack," Miss Annie said, patting Emma's hand with her paper napkin. "Margret had such a fun sense of humor and this is some real knee-slapping irony right here."

Emma got more uncomfortable really quick and barely managed to smile back at Miss Annie.

"How do you mean, Miss Annie?"

"You remember when you were dating Lou Ellen Briggs' boy … what was his name?"

"Ryan," Emma answered. The Briggs had moved away years ago and she'd almost forgotten about Ryan.

"That's right, that's right," said Miss Annie. "I remember one day Margret was telling me he was always fawning over her and trying to make such an impression, but she just couldn't bring herself to like him."

Miss Annie set her plastic fork and plate down on her lap and winked at Emma with a smile.

"I told her she was going to have to loosen up just a little, 'cause one day you were going to bring some young man home," Miss Annie said. "She got all huffy and said that it was a shame Jack was so much older, 'cause as far as she could tell, the only man that'd ever be good enough was the one she raised."

Emma developed a heart murmur on the spot and just sat there, her mouth hanging open a little ways. Thankfully, she was saved from having to come up with something to say by Brother Fillmore, who came to ask after Miss Annie's wellbeing.

Emma patted Miss Annie on the hand and took her plate for her, then got up and decided that now was as good a time as any to go make more tea.

Just as she came back out onto the back porch, the instantly recognizable first notes of "Sweet Home Alabama" came blasting out of the sound system. There were several "whoops" from around the yard and a bunch of people ran for the spot in front of the barn.

Emma stopped at the porch rail next to Regina, the jug of tea in her hand forgotten, as she saw Jack right in the middle of the crowd. She'd never seen Jack dance, had never even imagined such a thing, outside of her slow-dance fantasies as a teenager. But dancing he was, and doing a fine job of it.

"What is happening right in front of my eyeballs?' Emma asked quietly.

"What?" asked Regina, who was holding a sweating bottle of water up to her neck.

"Jack's dancing," Emma answered, like she

was announcing that frogs were falling from the sky.

Regina's considerably arched eyebrows arched even higher as she looked at Emma. "Honey, you married to this man and you don't even know he can dance?"

Emma just shook her head as she watched Jack twirl one of Regina's sisters.

"Girl, that's my date for the senior homecoming right there," Regina said. "Dew went and broke his foot and Jack took me instead. We danced all night long. Shoot, ever since Jack and Daniel were like thirteen years old, they'd come over to our house on Saturdays and we'd all be dancing to *Soul Train*."

Emma just looked at her as Regina laughed.

"Mm hmm, I still remember me and Jack doing the bump to *Jungle Boogie*," she laughed. "Now your Daddy, bless his heart, he couldn't help how white he was."

Emma laughed. "Unfortunately, I must have gotten my rhythm from him."

She looked back out at the crowd in the yard and then smiled a bit sadly at Regina.

"Grandma didn't really talk a whole lot about Jack when he was young. We just talked about where he was stationed, what he'd said in a letter, stuff like that."

Emma didn't mention that she never asked Grandma much about Jack, either. She'd lived in mortal fear that Grandma would one day figure out that she was infatuated with the man who was supposed to be more of an uncle than anything else.

If she'd asked too many questions, Grandma would have eventually given her that look she always got when she'd figured out something that Emma really didn't want her to know. Grandma's narrow-eyed scrutiny had about the same effect as being Tasered in the bathtub, only with a good deal of embarrassment tacked onto the paralysis.

"Well, I guess that doesn't surprise me much," Regina said. "I don't think you could tell a story about one without tellin' it about the other and I know your Grandma didn't like to talk too much about poor Daniel."

"No," Emma said.

Emma looked back out at the yard and watched Jack. She had always been a sucker for a man who danced, much to her detriment. She found herself doing that thing that Southern women do, fiddling with a string of pearls that she wasn't even wearing. Regina elbowed her gently in the side.

"Ha, look at you!" Regina smiled. "You're gone, girl. It's so cute."

Emma couldn't quite come up with a smile, but she tried.

"You don't think it's weird?" she asked.

"Oh chile, every girl I knew was in love with

Jack," Regina laughed. "All the white girls and half the black."

"Well, I meant … you know, because he's sort of family," Emma said back cautiously.

Regina waved her question off.

"This is Alabama honey and you ain't even blood. Ain't nobody gonna look sideways."

One of Regina's grandsons, a boy of about four, came running up to ask Regina something and Emma looked back out at Jack. She'd seen Jack laugh and she'd seen Jack smile, but she couldn't say that she'd ever before seen Jack look happy.

She had no idea how much of it was because he was surrounded by good people who were lifelong friends and how much of it was because she'd agreed to help him feel like his life's work was actually going to benefit someone when he was gone. But she did know that if her walking to Atlanta barefoot would make him look like he did right then, she would do it without hesitation.

The song ended and Lewis turned the volume down a notch before putting on some pop song Emma didn't know. Just about everyone under thirty was dancing. She watched as Jack made his way to the porch, grabbing his RC from the step before leaning up against the rail.

"Are you having fun?" Emma asked.

"Man, it's good to be home," Jack said, smiling. "Only place in the world where you'll ever see black folks getting down to Lynyrd Skynyrd."

Just then Brother Fillmore walked up in his slightly stiff, dignified way. "Jack. Emma. Thank you for having me," he said, as he stuck his hand out to Jack. Jack shook it.

"Are you leaving already, Brother Fillmore?" he asked.

"I believe so," Brother Fillmore said quietly. "I just came to share your joy and have some barbecue, but if y'all are startin' in on the hedonism, I'll truck on home."

Emma said goodbye and asked Brother Fillmore to make himself a plate before he left, then she grinned at Jack.

"Told you," she said.

Jack waved her off with his RC. "He'll get over it. He always has. Hey, Gina, why aren't you out there dancing?"

"I'm taking a break," she said. "I was out there plenty."

"Come dance with me," Jack said.

"No, fool! You're supposed to have your first dance with your wife," Gina said. "And you were out there dancing with Dew!"

Jack looked at Emma. "That's right. I'm sorry, Emma. Come dance with me."

"I'm really not much of a dancer, Jack."

"Oh, hush," Regina said, then yelled so loudly Emma almost jumped. "Lewis! Turn that crap off and play somethin' slow for the bride and groom."

Whatever Lewis was playing stopped dead and some of the teenagers groaned, while the adults did some polite but encouraging clapping.

"Come on. Emma," Jack said and took her hand.

An old Clint Black song started playing and Emma tried to remember the name of it, but then they were out in the yard and Jack turned, put a hand on her waist and she didn't care what the song was called.

She put her other hand on his shoulder and at first she felt awkward, the way she'd felt a few times when dancing with a stranger at a bar when she was young.

She was relieved that it wasn't like a real wedding reception, with everyone standing around in a circle gawking. Several other couples were dancing around them and Emma started to relax a little.

"Hey, lemme get a picture!"

Emma turned her head and saw Dew and Regina dancing next to them. Regina had her iPhone in her hand.

"Y'all quit moving a second," Regina ordered.

She and Jack stopped and Regina took a picture and smiled.

"Y'all so cute, seriously," she said as she

and Dew danced away.

Jack started swaying again and Emma put her head down on his chest. She closed her eyes and she could feel the sun hot on the top of her head and the vibration in Jack's chest as he said something to someone nearby. She inhaled and smelled sunshine and warm denim and just a hint of cologne. She breathed deeply and tried to memorize it all for later, whenever later turned out to be.

Chapter 8

*I*T WAS WELL PAST nine o'clock by the
time everyone had left with their clean empty casseroles and their foil-covered plates of
food. Dew and Regina and some of the kids had
stayed to help Jack and Emma with the last of
the cleanup. Now Jack waited with Regina on the
front porch while Dew took the cooler and the
carload of kids home and came back to retrieve
her.

They sat on the top porch step, Regina with
her cavernous bright yellow purse on her lap.

"Those grandkids better all be asleep before
I get home or everybody's getting some Benadryl,"
Regina said. "I'm wore out."

"It was a fun day," Jack said. "It was great spending the day with you and Dew."

"Mm," Regina said, and they both stared out at the dark for a minute.

"Why you never even called me, Jack?" Regina finally said without looking at him. "I tried calling you a few weeks after you left, the year after Miss Margret died, and your phone was disconnected. And I never heard one thing from you 'til yesterday."

Jack looked at the side of her face, but she just stared out to the yard.

"I'm sorry, Gina," Jack said. "I got sent out to Camp Pendleton for a while and then when I got back to Beaufort......I don't know. You'd told me Emma'd moved away and I didn't really think it was all that urgent for me to keep coming back, with both of them gone."

He let a big breath whoosh out of him and put a hand on top of hers.

"I just lost touch with everything for a while," he said quietly. "But I still had you and Dew and my other friends here and I should have come home. I should have at least kept in touch."

"I started thinking maybe you were dead," Regina said, finally looking at him. "It wasn't right, you doing that. You and me were closer than you and Dew."

Jack put his arm around her shoulders and pulled her close.

"I know. And I really am sorry."

Regina didn't say anything for a moment, just looked out at the inky dark of the yard.

"Don't go grabbin' on me. You're a jackass," Regina said. "I ain't gonna forgive you just 'cause you're lovin' on me."

"I am inclined to jackassery," Jack said.

"Mm-hm. Obviously, you can get back in touch with Emma at some point, but you can't call your friends," she said. "That's how you are and I don't want you to expect none of my pecan pie this Christmas."

"I'll go on loving you anyway, Gina," he said and kissed her temple.

She finally turned to him and smiled, shaking her head. "You suck as a friend, but I guess I still love you."

"I appreciate that, Gina," Jack said.

"Of course, now you up and married Emma, so you're never gonna have no chance with me," she said, smiling.

"That would sting, Gina, if you weren't so hung up on Dew."

"That man? Please," Regina said, waving him off. "I've been stuck with that fool since we were fourteen. I need to upgrade."

"You're such a lousy liar."

"He's gettin' fat. And old. He's got hairs growing where they're not supposed to grow and he's asleep by ten o'clock."

"Well, yeah, maybe you should get a boy-friend then," Jack said.

"I would," she said, as Dew's headlights turned onto the driveway. "But every day when I hear him coming home from work, I still get a lit-tle excited."

Jack smiled at her and she gave him a kiss on the cheek as Dew climbed out of the car.

"Quit messing with my girl," Dew said calm-ly. "Unless you want to pay for her upkeep."

Jack gently shoved Regina away. "Nah, you can hang onto her."

"I figured," Dew said as he reached the steps and held a hand out to Regina. "You ready to go, baby?"

"Law, yes," Regina answered as she stepped down into the yard. "Tote me on home, I'm tired."

"Night, Flash," Dew said, shaking his hand.

"See you around, Dew," Jack said and stood and watched as Dew opened the car door for his wife.

Dew waved, then got back in the car and turned it around in the circle at the end of the drive. Jack watched them pull out onto the road and he wondered guiltily for just a minute if he ought to tell Gina and Dew what was going on with him. But he wouldn't be able to stand them worrying and waiting and he didn't see much point in making them do it, either.

It occurred to him with some sense of irony

that he'd felt the constant weight of a single secret his entire adult life, but now that he was at
the end of his life, he seemed inclined to start a
collection.

As Emma gently closed Becca's door behind
her, Jack came out of the hall bathroom wearing
pajama pants and a USMC tee shirt, his hair every which way and still damp from his shower.

"Hey," he said.

"Hey."

"I saved you some hot water."

"Thanks," Emma said. "A shower's sounding pretty good right now."

"You have a good time today?"

"I did," Emma said, smiling. "I forget sometimes that I actually like people. I haven't seen
most of those folks since the Fourth of July barbecue."

"Good people," Jack said.

"Yes."

Jack walked to the open door of his bedroom.

"Well, I'm gonna hit the rack," he said.
"Good night."

"Jack?" Emma said as he started to close
his door. "Do you think—I was thinking maybe
you should leave your door open at night."

Jack stopped, leaned on the door jamb. "Why, Emma?" he asked, but his voice said he knew the answer already. Emma thought about her phrasing before she answered.

"What if something happens?" she finally asked.

Jack, too, seemed to consider his reply.

"Something will, eventually," he said. "But I'd like us to not tiptoe around like we're waiting for some evil clown to jump out at us. Okay?"

Emma nodded, but she wanted to say that she was going to make a pallet on the floor beside his bed and listen to him breathe.

That morning, she'd watched from the kitchen window as Jack fed the chickens for her, and she'd had an overwhelming urge to protect him, to stand in front of him and keep everything bad away. But then she'd wondered how she was supposed to get between him and the thing that meant him harm.

"Okay, Jack," she said. "Good night."

"'Night, Emma," he said back and quietly shut his door.

Emma left her own door open as she walked into her room, took a fresh nightgown and panties from her drawer, continued on into her bathroom and shut the door.

When Emma was about fifteen, Grandma had gotten rid of a small spare bedroom in order to put in her own bathroom. It had taken six men and a lot of cursing to get the old claw-foot tub up the stairs, but Grandma had always wanted one.

Unfortunately, Grandma had been so short that she couldn't recline in it without her butt slipping and she'd despised getting her head underwater. So she'd ended up taking showers in her carefully refinished, ten-thousand-pound tub.

The bathroom was part of the reason Emma had changed rooms. Mostly, though, it just made her feel better, as though she were closer to Grandma somehow.

Emma let the water run as she got undressed, then stepped into the tub and let the hot water cascade over her head. It slipped over her shoulders and down her body like a soothing drug and she closed her eyes and lost herself in it.

The beautiful heat of it on her head reminded her of the way the sun had felt when she and Jack had been dancing in the yard. A warmth that had nothing to do with the water spread through her stomach and she got just a whiff of warm cotton and heard the memory of a steady heartbeat.

Then she felt a hitch in her chest and she covered her face with her hands so that no one would hear her crying.

After work a few days later, Emma found Jack in the middle of replacing the shower head in the hall bathroom and decided to go out and tend to the garden, which she'd been neglecting of late.

Grandma and Jack had built these same 4x8 raised beds back when Emma had just started college and Grandma had just started complaining about working on her knees. They'd started with four beds, but by the time Emma had graduated, there were four more. Grandma had nursed this dirt like a child and it was black and loose and smelled of minerals, compost and rain.

Grandma'd been a natural gardener and could grow anything that grew, while Emma had killed a steady stream of houseplants in college; houseplants Grandma had sworn were immortal. But Grandma's dirt was like Grandma, it could nurture anything to fruition. The garden always produced abundantly, even with Emma's hands in it.

The raised beds were about ten yards behind the chicken yard, and while she transplanted some fall collards, Emma listened to the steady stream of chicken conversations that all sounded like they started with "And then she said..." or "Well, I never."

Emma always worked with her bare hands, loving the feel of the loose, black soil. It made her feel more connected with the woman who had made it what it was and then fed them from it. She often talked to Grandma when she worked in the garden and it didn't seem all that peculiar to her that she often heard Grandma talk back.

It wasn't that she heard Grandma's voice audibly; Grandma would never be so base as to haunt the vegetable bed. But as Emma worked and talked things over with Grandma, she could sense Grandma's replies, usually well-worn phrases she'd heard over and over growing up.

Things like "Oh you horse's neck, you" or "Well, talk won't make the rice cook." Every now and then, it was just the sound of Grandma laughing, and that always made Emma smile.

Working in the garden with Grandma's trowel, making Grandma's potato salad in Grandma's potato salad bowl; these things kept Grandma from being farther away than Emma could stand. She wondered what would do that for her when Jack was gone.

Emma had just finished with the collards and was picking some almost overdue green beans when Jack walked up with a couple of glasses of tea.

"Brought you some tea," he said.

"Thank you. I'll grab it in a second," Emma said, as she dumped a handful of beans in her pail.

"Want some help?"

"No, thanks. I'm almost done."

Jack set Emma's glass of tea on one of the railroad ties and hunkered down next to her. Watching Emma, he could see Miss Margret's profile layered just beneath hers, like a double exposure in a photograph. They had the same softly-rounded chin, the same little bump in the bridge of the nose.

He'd watched or helped Miss Margret work the garden more times than he could count. She'd loved growing food as much as she loved feeding people and she'd worked hard at both. She'd worked hard at everything and he'd always admired her ability to get things done. He'd noticed that Emma shared Miss Margret's drive in that regard.

"I respect your work ethic, Emma," he said.

Emma glanced up at him.

"It's nothing special," she said. "I just haven't been paying attention back here lately."

"The diner, the chickens, the garden, the laundry. You're always doing something," Jack told her back. "I'm just saying you work hard and I admire you for it. She'd be proud."

There was no need to say who. With Jack and Emma, there was never any other "she."

"Well. Thanks, I guess," Emma said. She looked up at him a moment, squinting against the sun that hung just behind him, creating a painfully bright halo around his head. "But I'm just doing what I need to do."

She reached over to start picking beans from the next plant and heard Jack drumming his fingernails on his glass for a moment.

"So I have a request and I want you to hear me out," he said.

Emma glanced up at him cautiously, then turned back to her beans. "It already sounds like something I don't want to do," she said with half a smile.

"I think you should quit the diner."

She looked back up at him.

"What? No, Jack," she said and went back to picking. "Why would I do that?"

"Because my pension check goes in the bank and just sits there. I don't have any expenses aside from gas and insurance on the truck, and I had to fight you for the privilege of going to get milk for you the other day."

"I don't care, Jack. Your money's your money. Do what you want with it," she said.

"I'm trying to. I think—"

"Jack, you praise my work ethic in one breath then tell me to quit my job in the next—"

"Because you don't have to work, at least not at some diner. You need to get back to your book," Jack said.

"I'm not living off of you, Jack."

"Emma Lee, everybody's got something that they're meant for. For some people, it's a big important thing and for others it's a small important thing, but everybody's got one thing they were just meant to do. For you, it's writing."

"And what's your thing?" she asked him.

"We're not talking about me," he told her back.

Emma stared at him and he thought about it a minute.

"I don't honestly know. I guess I don't have one."

"But you just said everybody does."

"Well. I guess I missed it," he said. "But you and I both know what yours is and you need to get on it before you let another ten years go by."

Emma opened her mouth to speak, but he held up a hand to stop her.

"Not your turn. You'll have plenty of time to be wrong when I'm done," he said.

Emma shut her mouth and glared at him.

"Whatever I don't spend now is going to end up in your bank account eventually, so you might as well let me choose how to spend it. What I choose is to see you doing what you're supposed to be doing before I'm gone."

"Let me explain something to you, Jack," Emma said, standing up to her full five feet. "You'd be here with or without your life insurance and your benefits and whatever. This is your home. I don't care about your money. I don't need you to support me and I wish you'd stop looking at me like some kind of charity project."

"Is that a fact?" he asked mildly, standing up to look down at her. "Well, please be advised that this has nothing to do with charity. It has to do with family. "

"Grandma didn't raise me to let other people pay my way," Emma said.

"She didn't raise you to be a dumbass, either, but trying to get you to see common sense is like trying to suck a squirrel up through a straw." Jack put his fists on his hips and sighed. "You need to write."

"And I will," Emma said.

"When, Emma? Once Becca's grown up and gone?"

"Whenever the time is right."

"You're looking at the right time, Emma Lee. This is it."

"But only if I'm willing to live off of your money," Emma said.

"Who cares, Emma? It's all going to be your money anyway, either now or later."

Emma opened her mouth to speak, but Jack held up a hand.

"I have a 'furthermore'," he said. "Furthermore, I wouldn't mind having your company during the day because I like being around you, particularly when you're not speaking."

Emma was taken aback by that for a second and wasn't sure what to say.

"You need to build some kind of life besides pouring coffee for old farmers. And you know Miss Margret wanted that for you."

Emma propped her fists onto her hips.

"Well, I had a hard time fulfilling her wishes. She also wanted me to straighten up and fly right, learn to fold a fitted sheet, and be happily married," she shot back.

"Well, we're married, aren't we?" he asked. "Get happy."

Emma watched him stalk back up toward the house.

"You don't have to fix everything, Jack," she called out.

Jack stopped and turned back to her.

"I'm not trying—" he started then waved her off. "Ah hell."

He kept on walking and after the screen door slapped shut, Emma went back to her beans.

It might have been the chickens, but Emma swore she heard Grandma clucking in that way she did when she was mildly irritated. Nothing too distinct, but something about pig-headedness. Emma assumed she was referring to Jack.

"You're the one that raised him," Emma said.

A little while later, Emma headed back to the

house with her tea and her pail of beans. She was starting to feel badly about getting her back up, and she couldn't help wondering if Jack was actually uncomfortable being alone all day.

He didn't seem scared, but she imagined there were a lot of feelings that would accompany the thought of dying suddenly and especially the idea of doing it alone.

Jack was sitting at the kitchen table when she walked in, going through the mail that had been forwarded from his old address. A scraggly brown tiger named Ed was sitting on the table, watching Jack with his usual vacant expression.

Ed had the odd habit of leaving his tongue out just a bit at all times, which made him look something like Bill the Cat from *Bloom County*. She'd thought about naming him "Bill" but Ed just seemed to fit.

Emma ran some water into the pail and started swishing the beans around to rinse them.

"Do you feel like some green beans tonight?" she asked finally.

"I do," Jack answered.

Emma looked over her shoulder at him. He was staring back at Ed.

"I'm making pork chops for dinner," she said.

"That sounds good," he told Ed. Ed offered no opinion.

Emma turned back to the sink and dumped the beans into a colander. Jack stared at Ed for another moment, then slowly reached out and touched the tip of Ed's tongue. It didn't retract and Ed didn't really seem to notice much.

"I think this one here's unbalanced or something," Jack said.

Emma looked back over her shoulder and smiled just a little.

"Don't pick on Ed. He's actually a little brain-damaged. He's also my favorite."

Jack looked at Emma and rolled his eyes a bit. "That makes perfect sense to me. How is he brain-damaged?"

"When he was a kitten he got run over by a motorcycle in TJ Howard's yard," Emma answered. "The tire went right over his head. If it hadn't been in the dirt he'd probably be dead. He's not all that bright, but he's incredibly sweet.'

"You and your grandmother. Both of you on some kind of network for special cats."

"Well," Emma said, turning back to stemming the beans. "We are a lot alike."

"Nothing to be ashamed of," said Jack, tossing a piece of junk mail aside.

"No," Emma said. She went to the fridge and took out the pork chops.

Jack put his thumbs to his temples and pressed. He'd had a headache off and on all day and the pain pill he'd taken earlier had long since worn off.

"It's not my intention to make you feel like a

charity project, Emma."

"I know," Emma answered and started un-wrapping the chops at the counter. "I'm not trying to sound ungrateful, either. I know you're just try-ing to do what you think is right and I'll admit you have some good points."

"Does that mean you're gonna quit the din-er?"

"Are you worried about being here alone?" she asked him plainly.

"Not really, no," he answered.

His voice sounded strained to her and she turned to look at him. His eyes were squeezed shut.

"Jack, are you okay?"

"Yeah," he answered without opening his eyes. "Just the usual."

"Do you need something?" Emma felt a twinge of panic rising in her throat like an air bubble.

"I'll take something in a bit." He opened his eyes. "It's not that bad. You know, you'd think that a man in my situation would win every argument by default."

"I suppose you should," Emma said, trying to work up a smile. "But you won't."

"I'll ask again," he said.

"I'll expect it," she answered.

She turned back to the counter and as she took a pork chop out of the package, she saw that her hands were shaking.

Chapter 9

OVER THE ENSUING few weeks, Jack, Emma and Becca fell into a comfortable routine in their living. Emma worked at the diner and in the fall garden, Jack found plenty of things that needed fixing and Becca found Jack wherever he was. Becca asked Jack so many questions as she shadowed him that he once told her he felt like he was on Johnny Carson, and was disappointed when she failed to get the reference.

But Jack found that he missed the little girl's company when she was at school and he wondered sometimes at the fact that he'd never thought himself especially partial to children.

There were times when Becca made him laugh or made him think and he thought that he might have missed something worthwhile when Emma was a child, the way he'd allowed her to stay on the periphery of his visits home.

This thought was especially convincing the more time he spent with Emma herself. With every conversation or every shared joke, he began to realize that by largely ignoring Emma over the years, he'd managed to cheat himself out of one-third of his family.

Late September brought drier air and Jack and Emma spent more time on either the front or back porch. They played Cribbage, over which Jack seemed to have dominion, and Scrabble, the domination of which was hotly debated.

They churned ice cream with the last of the fall strawberries and told Becca stories above the noise of the crickets and the frogs. They drank blackberry wine or sweet tea, depending on the time of day, and talked about William Faulkner and Carson McCullers, Flannery O'Connor and Walker Percy.

September also brought Miss Margret's birthday, the one on which she would have turned ninety-six, if she'd been of a mind to. The day before, a clear, breezy Saturday, Emma stood at the kitchen counter, spreading the coconut filling atop the bottom layer of Grandma's German Chocolate cake. Grandma had always avowed that it tasted better on the second day, so Emma always made it a day ahead, though Grandma was no longer able to tell the difference.

As she spread the coconut and caramel around the cake, she thought back to Grandma's funeral. The last time she had seen Jack until he'd walked into the diner last month.

The funeral had been a very small affair, mainly the friends and neighbors from the road. And Jack. Trevor had taken a job in Birmingham and hadn't been able to make it due to work, but Emma had been glad. She should have taken that as a sign at the time that perhaps she already knew she'd settled too low.

There'd been a small service at the church, then everyone had gathered at the house for the required covered dishes and reminiscence. Jack had only had a day's leave for the funeral, since Grandma hadn't been blood, so he'd actually flown into Birmingham and driven a rental car down the night before.

Emma hadn't had the heart to stay at the house when she'd come in from Mobile, so she'd spent a few days at Regina's. But the day before the funeral, shortly before Jack had arrived, Emma had finally gotten up the nerve to come home and go into Grandma's bathroom with a broom, a pail and some rags.

She'd been alright while she'd swept up the broken glass from the full-length mirror that had hung on the back of the bathroom door. But when Regina walked in a short time later, she'd found Emma on her knees, sobbing.

Emma's hands and knees were tinted red and the rag in her lap had made light brown and red swirls on Grandma's white linoleum. Emma had jumped when she'd heard Regina's "Oh, honey" from the bathroom doorway.

Emma had swiped at her eyes, leaving a red smear along her nose and cheekbone.

"Chile, let me do this here," Regina had said, her own brown own eyes watering.

"I have to do it," Emma had answered, her eyes on the pail full of rags soaking in pink water.

Regina had come into the bathroom then.

"Let me help you then."

"It's okay. I can do it," Emma had answered quietly.

"I know what you can do," Regina had said back and held a hand out to Emma.

"Help me down there and hand me one of them rags."

Emma had taken Regina's hand and steadied her as she lowered herself to the floor. When Emma had let go, she'd seen that Grandma's blood had now colored the other woman's hand.

Jack and Emma barely spoke between the time he'd arrived and when he'd left after the funeral. She'd watched him, of course, soaking in the sight and sound of him partly out of habit and partly out of a sudden sense of her own alone-ness. Every now and then, she caught him watching her, too.

After everyone else had left, she, Jack, Dew, Regina and Miss Mary had said a few words before they took turns pouring Grandma's ashes around the roots of the gardenias out front. Soon after that, Jack had come to Emma on the front porch steps to say goodbye. They'd exchanged phone numbers and now, as she gently placed the top layer of Grandma's birthday cake onto the bottom layer, Emma realized that there had been a time when Jack had touched her.

He'd kneaded her shoulder for just a moment then, as he'd stood in front of the porch steps, and spoken to her without really meeting her eyes.

"You call me if you need anything," he'd said to her and she had answered that she would.

"I'll see you, Little Bit."

"See you, Jack," she'd said and then watched him walk to his car, waving one more time at the others.

Emma had wanted him to stay. She'd wanted to talk to him, to take strength and warmth from him somehow. She'd wanted to run out to his car and beg him to take her with him, but that would have been silly.

So she'd stood there on the step, hugging Grandma's empty urn to her chest and wondering what she and Jack would talk about the next time he came home. But she'd never seen him again.

She had waited months to see or hear from him she had an idea that she might have gone to Birmingham with Trevor to just to end the waiting, to avoid the emptiness she would have felt if he never came home. Of course, now she knew that he'd shown up just a few months after she'd left.

"You gonna frost that thing or just stare at it?"

Emma looked over at Jack, who was leaning in the kitchen doorway.

"I was just thinking about Grandma," she said. "Actually, I was thinking about her funeral."

Yeah," Jack said and looked down at the floor. "Well."

They were quiet for a moment while she started frosting the cake.

"It actually made me realize that I don't know what I'm supposed to do for you," Emma finally said. "When that time comes."

"I suppose I should have talked to you about that already," Jack told her. He walked into the kitchen and sat down at the table.

"Everything's taken care of. I've got the agreement with the funeral home with my other papers in my nightstand. I changed my will last week and took it down to the bank to get notarized."

"What kind of funeral arrangements did

you make?" Emma asked and hated asking it.

"No funeral," Jack answered. "They're cremating me and sticking me in the cheapest container they had. I think it might be a Thermos. Just spread me out underneath the gardenias with her."

Emma stared at Jack for a moment.

"Okay," she said and went back to frosting the cake.

"You should know, Emma, that I have a living will," Jack said. "It probably won't be necessary, but I've made it clear that there will be no machines."

Emma looked over at him.

"No lifesaving measures," he said.

"Jack, why not?"

"Like I said, it probably won't come up," Jack answered. "They say when it comes, that'll probably be it. Dr. Mayer said it's like a catastrophic stroke or a brain aneurysm."

Emma was glad Jack was looking down at the table, because she wasn't sure what her face looked like.

"But there's a slim chance that I might have a less than fatal episode," Jack went on. "If that happens, I probably still won't regain consciousness. I'll just lie there and wait for the real thing. I don't want that. Unless it's before September 15th."

"What's September 15th?"

"Our anniversary, nitwit," he said. "If it's before then, burn the living will and plug me up to a generator if you have to, but keep me going til the 16th."

Emma wasn't in the mood for him to smile, but he did it anyway.

"You really know how to brighten up a birthday celebration," Jack said.

"Well, there's one reason I don't have a social life to speak of," Emma answered.

Jack stood up and headed for the door to the living room.

"You probably married me so you'd have a good excuse not to," he said.

"I just wanted Grandma to stop griping," she said without thinking. She looked over at Jack, who had stopped in the doorway. "I mean, sometimes I just feel like she does."

"You don't have to explain it to me," Jack said. "She looks me up every now and then. I love the woman, but nobody could out-nag Miss Margret."

Emma watched him go back to the nature documentary he was watching with Becca, then she went back to her cake, several times shaking away the thought of spreading Jack's ashes in the front yard.

The next morning was windy and dry and the light looked like it'd been bleached. Regina had taken Becca down the road to play with her granddaughters who were visiting and Emma was hanging sheets on the line. Jack was chopping firewood by the wood shed on the other side of the barn and the steady *chunk-crack* from his axe blended with the snapping of the sheets, making Emma want to lie down in the grass with her eyes closed.

She could smell the Pink Lady apples on the trees behind her and it reminded her that she was behind in picking the last of them. When Grandma was alive, they'd usually have them finished by Grandma's birthday.

At the end of the last day of picking, the two of them would sit on the porch steps with what they deemed the two prettiest apples, count to three and bite into them together. The sweet would burst into their mouths and then right behind it a tartness that would pucker their cheeks and make them squint at each other and laugh.

Emma finished pinning the last sheet and started to pick up the pink wicker laundry basket, then looked over her shoulder at the apple trees and set the basket back down. She walked over to the nearest tree, picked the nicest apple she could still reach and sniffed its skin. She smiled and was about to take a bite when she realized that she hadn't heard any sounds from the wood shed in several minutes.

She turned and looked that way, but the barn blocked her view. She stared for a minute and was going to call out, but started walking instead. When she came abreast of the barn, she called toward the wood shed.

"Jack?"

There was no answer and she picked up her pace and rounded the woodshed. Jack was on his knees with his back to her, one hand on the back wall of the shed. Emma's throat felt like it was closing up.

"Jack?"

Jack put his other hand behind him, palm up, motioning for her to stop. She ignored it and hurried to stand behind him.

"Jack, are you okay?"

"Of course not," he barely said.

Emma skittered around to the front of him, but he was looking down at the ground.

"Look at me! What's happening, Jack?"

Jack looked up at her after a fashion. His face was pointed at her, but his eyes were squeezed shut.

"I need the anti-inflammatory and a pain pill," he finally said.

"Can you walk?" Emma asked him.

"Yes, but I don't want to," he told her, his voice tight and barely audible.

"I can help you get to the house."

"Please. Just get the pills."

Emma wanted to, but she didn't want to leave him kneeling there in the dirt.

"Please!" he snapped then and she ran.

Emma managed to run into the house without tripping over anybody and took the stairs three at a time. Once she got to Jack's room, she found half a dozen pill bottles on his nightstand. She had to pick up and read almost all of them to find the two he asked for and her panic mounted with every second that she wasted.

She nearly fell back down the stairs. She stopped in the kitchen to get him something to swallow the pills with, then decided that eight seconds was too many to pour a drink. She grabbed the pitcher of tea she'd just made and ran with it back to the wood shed, spilling lukewarm tea down her legs the whole way.

Jack was sitting on the dirt now, his back up against the wood shed, his eyes still shut.

"Jack? Here!' Emma said, holding out the two pills. She noticed that she'd sweated most of the red coating off of the anti-inflammatory.

Jack opened his eyes halfway and took the pills. When she held out the tea pitcher, he glanced up at her, but didn't say anything, just took it. Emma watched him, her heart jumping all over the place, as he popped the pills in his mouth, then took a swig of the tea.

His face twisted up again and he swallowed,

then he bent forward, letting out something between a growl and a sob.

Emma dropped to her knees and put a hand on his shoulder. She felt her panic getting away from her, coming up her throat.

"Jack, what?!" she almost yelled.

"No sugar," he said, his face nearly on the grass.

"What? Are you kidding me?" Emma asked him.

"Like to kill me," he told the ground.

"What do we do now?"

"Nothing," he said. He rolled to the side and then was lying on his back in the grass. "Wait."

"For what?"

"Pass," he managed, his eyes still shut.

"How long does it take?" she asked him.

"Depends." He put his hands on his forehead. "How long do I have to keep talking?"

Emma stared at him a second, then leaned back against the wood shed. She was too relieved that he was being snippy to be hurt by it. Her heart was still pounding and her throat felt raw, like she'd had bile come up it, then go back down.

She swallowed a few times, then took a couple of deep breaths, her eyes never leaving Jack's face.

Chapter 10

A LITTLE WHILE LATER, Jack pulled the warm washrag from his eyes and squinted up at the living room ceiling.

They'd stayed out in the yard for a good twenty minutes, then he'd allowed that he felt okay to head into the house. Emma had put one of his arms around her shoulder and helped him to the back steps. He didn't bother telling her that she was too short to be of any real assistance. They'd gotten inside anyway, and Emma had made him lie down on Miss Margret's thoroughly-flowered couch.

He took a few deep breaths and glanced toward the living room window, testing his eyes on the light pouring through. It wasn't bad. He let out another breath and felt his heart rate slowing down to its usual pace.

He looked back up at the ceiling and stared at the same crack that he'd stared at whenever he was home sick from school. Unless he was throwing up, Miss Margret would install him on the couch and he'd drift in and out on her old movies or her favorite PBS shows. To this day, he couldn't hear Bob Ross's voice without feeling a touch of the flu.

But he remembered now, how the scraping of Ross's knife or the whisk of his fan brush had sounded on the canvas while he laid there half-asleep, covered with Miss Margret's big fluffy tiger blanket, the one they only used when someone was ill or heartbroken.

The sun would be bright on his face and he'd hear the sound of Miss Margret's ice tinkling in her root beer behind him. They were peaceful sounds, calming. He had a fleeting thought to see if Bob Ross was on so he could listen, but it wouldn't be the same without the ice.

Just then Emma came back into the room from the kitchen, another warm washrag in her hand.

"Here," she said, handing him the rag. "How are you feeling?"

Jack looked at her for a minute as he traded cloths with her.

"My sophomore year, when we played FSU, I got hit by a car dressed as a football player, then the whole team and what felt like half the stands dogpiled me. I feel better than that."

"Jack, is it always that bad?" she asked him.

"No. Just every so often," he told her.

Emma propped her hands on her hips. "You need to show me what each one of those medications is so I don't have to scramble around trying to find what you need."

"I suppose that would be a good idea," he told her. "It would probably suck if you gave me a double dose of Viagra."

"What the heck are you taking Viagra for?" she almost yelled.

"It was a joke, Emma Lee," he answered, smiling.

"It wasn't funny," she said to him.

"It wasn't unfunny, either," he said, sitting up.

"I'm sorry if I got pissy with you outside," he told her. "Pain makes me angry."

"Well, we're in for a real rollicking time, then," she answered. "Fear makes me angry and your pain scared the crap out of me."

Jack looked up at her and worked up another smile.

"Well, I see you got your mouth working again, anyway."

"What's that supposed to mean?" she asked.

"It means I've been up to here with you tippy-toeing around being nice, because you're afraid you'll say something snarky and I'll just happen to take that opportunity to drop dead."

"That's not true," Emma said without much conviction.

"You have another explanation?" he asked her back.

Yeah. I love you, stupid, she thought.

He stood up, carefully.

"What are you doing? Lie down!"

"No," he answered, carefully making his way around the coffee table. "Becca and Gina'll be back soon and I'm not gonna be lying there like an invalid."

He walked, almost upright, to the recliner that faced the TV, an offensively orange vinyl recliner that had been Miss Margret's official place.

"I'm gonna park right here."

Emma sighed and helped him push the recliner back.

"Do me a favor and put some football on so I can fall asleep like a man."

Emma grabbed the remote and turned on the TV.

"Which game do you want to watch?"

"It doesn't matter. Bama's not playing, the Ole Miss game is over and I'll be out soon anyway."

Emma found a football game and started to

put the remote down.

"Emma, Utah's not a real football team," Jack said. "Try Channel 10."

Emma sighed and changed the channel. It was the second half of a Virginia Tech—LSU game. Even she knew that was official.

"Thank you," Jack said.

"You're welcome," Emma said back. "Are you gonna be awake in time for tonight?"

"Yes, ma'am. I'll only sleep for an hour or so."

"Okay," Emma answered and headed for the kitchen to start Grandma's beef stew with dumplings.

"Hey, don't forget to make more tea," Jack said as she was leaving.

"Bite me," she said over her shoulder.

"Maybe tomorrow," he said back.

She couldn't help but laugh.

"So Miss Margret's screaming 'Kill it, kill it!' and dragging me across the kitchen, only she won't tell me what I'm supposed to kill," Jack was saying as he and Emma cleared the dinner dishes. Becca sat at her place, grinning up at Jack as he told what must have been the tenth story of the evening.

"What was it?" she asked him.

"Hold on and listen right," he said. "So she opens the mud room door and shoves me in there and hands me this little fire extinguisher from 1968 and a dustpan, screams at me to 'Kill it' one more time and locks me out there."

Emma couldn't help smiling big as she put some dishes into soapy water. She'd heard the story a dozen times, but she loved it anyway.

"So I'm looking around, thinking there's a Palmetto bug out there or something, and she's got her face in that little window in the door, still screaming at me." Jack sat back down at the table and took a sip of his coffee.

"All of a sudden, I hear something behind some boxes in the corner and the biggest, ugliest possum I've ever seen comes waddling out," Jack continued.

"What did you do?" Becca asked.

"I pounded on that door and hollered at that old woman to let me back in the kitchen," Jack answered her.

"Did she let you back in?"

"No, she closed that little curtain thing over the window," he said back. "Screaming at me still."

Emma brought the German chocolate cake to the table and set it in the middle, next to three dessert plates.

"So what did you do?" Becca asked again, her eyes wide, a big grin on her face.

"I was thirteen years old and had a broken fire extinguisher and a dustpan," he answered. "What was I supposed to do?"

"You could shoo him out the side door," Becca offered.

"Shoo him? He looked like a heroin addict," Jack said. "He was big and torn up and cussing and hissing at me. So I jumped over him and ran out the side door, ran all the way around the house and back in the front door. I could hear her still yelling at me in the kitchen while I was running up the stairs. Then I grabbed my pistol, ran back down, shoved that old lady out of my way, and shot the fool."

"You shot him?" Becca asked, obviously dismayed.

"Yes, I shot him. He was crazy."

"Aw. Was Great-Grandma proud of you, though?"

"No, she wasn't proud, she was madder than a wet hen," Jack answered.

"'Cause you shot him?"

"No, because the bullet went right through him and killed her Hoover Upright besides."

"What's that?" Becca asked.

"Vacuum cleaner, Little Bit. Brand new, too," Jack said. "Took me three months of mowing yards to buy her a new one."

Emma smiled as she fished a lighter out of her pocket.

"Who's ready for birthday cake?" she asked them.

"Me!" piped Becca.

Emma took three birthday candles out of a little box and pushed them into the center of the cake.

"One candle for each of us," she told Jack. "I wasn't about to poke ninety-six candles into the thing. The year she would have been ninety, I did one candle for each decade. I'm running out of creative ways to not burn the cake down."

Emma lit the candles and sat down. She smiled at Becca and Jack, then she looked at the candles burning in the middle of Grandma's favorite cake.

"Happy Birthday, Grandma," she said and blew a candle out.

"Happy birthday, Great-Grandma!" Becca almost yelled, and had to stand up to blow out her candle.

Jack winked at Becca and glanced over at Emma. She was staring at the one remaining burning candle.

"Happy Birthday, Miss Margret," he said quietly, and blew it out.

A few days later, Jack walked around the house for the third time that afternoon.

He'd been having one of his vague sensations of dread for over a week and it was eating at him. He'd always had them and had even become known for them back in the Corps. They always started out like a niggling, the kind he'd get if he lost his keys or forgot to do something moderately important.

Sometimes they ended up being about something small; other times, they grew in intensity until a mortar fragment came flying through his tent in Beirut or he got word that someone he knew in another company had died.

He'd checked the gas line into the house, looked in on Brother Fillmore, checked the smoke detector and a number of other things, but the dread was still there and no answer for it found.

His one comfort was that the feeling had stayed mild and vague, so it would probably turn out to be nothing much at all. Maybe he'd go to put his boots on in the morning and find a cat turd in one of them.

He was walking up the front porch steps, his thoughts turned to a nice tuna salad sandwich, when he heard his truck pull into the driveway. He checked his watch and then watched Emma jump out of the truck and walk across the yard.

"What are you doing home so early?" he asked her.

She stopped by the bottom step and looked around the yard kind of nervously before she looked up at him.

"I quit," she said.

Jack hooked his thumbs into his belt and looked at her a moment.

"Is that a fact?" he asked her.

"It is," she said.

"Huh. Well, good," he said. "You gonna do some writing today?"

Emma sighed as she climbed the steps.

"No, I thought I would just piddle, maybe catch up on some stuff around the place."

"Well," Jack said, opening the screen door for her. "You could make me a tuna sandwich if you're of a mind."

"I'm not," she said as she went past.

A little while later, they sat at the kitchen table with their tuna sandwiches and some tomato soup.

"Emma, since you're gonna be home now, I want to show you how to do some things around here," Jack said. "I've been thinking about it for a while."

"What kind of things?" she asked him.

"I don't know. How to fix a leaky faucet, how to take care of the truck, that kind of thing."

Emma got a look like something had walked across her tongue.

"Why?"

"Because that insurance money'll last a lot longer if you don't have to pay somebody to do that stuff," he told her.

"But I'm not good at mechanical stuff. Or cars."

"I'm aware of that. Fall back, spring forward is for the smoke detector, not putting oil in the car."

"Look, I told you I'm not going to take crap for that forever," she said. "I'm good at plenty of other things around here. I can hang drywall, I can sand and mud, I can lay tile. "

"I'm not saying you're an idiot, Emma. But if you know how to do some of these things you call 'man stuff,' you won't need to be dependent on anyone else to do it. Later, I mean."

"I get that," she said. "I just don't like that kind of thing."

"You don't have to enjoy it, you just have to know how to do it."

"I thought I was supposed to be writing," she said, grinning.

"Oh, I'll make sure you do," he said and winked at her. "Count on it."

Emma watched him take a bite of his sandwich and wondered stupidly why men didn't wink much anymore. She thought that, if she were a foreign country and he were an invading army, he would have been able to conquer her with just that one wink.

The next morning, after Emma had gotten Becca off to school, she poured herself a second cup of coffee and sat down at the table, luxuriating in the fact that, for the first time since she was sixteen, she didn't have a job.

She didn't mind working, was proud that she always had, but the idea of not leaving every day made her feel free in a way that she hadn't felt since she was a child. The idea of spending her days just writing flat out gave her chills.

She was stirring the milk into her coffee when Jack popped into the doorway, wearing old jeans and a flannel shirt.

"Bring that out to the front yard," he said.

"Why?"

"Because I'm gonna teach you how to change a tire on the truck."

"What's wrong with the tire?"

"Nothing. You're gonna take it off and put it back on."

Emma's upper lip twitched just a little.

"Couldn't I just eat a nice bowl of spiders instead?"

"No. But if you're a fast learner you'll have time for some spiders later," he said as he walked out.

They spent most of the morning getting the tire off and putting it back on. There was a good deal of cussing, a little bit of crying, a touch of blood and a lot of throwing tools involved. By the time Emma had finished up, Jack had learned that Emma might hate changing a tire, but she'd be able to do it. Emma had learned that she'd rather shave her eyeballs than ever do it again.

Jack was reorganizing his tools when Emma announced that she was going to wash up and go pick apples, something she was not only good at, but liked doing.

He got the tools put away, buffed out a ding from a small rock, then went inside to wash his hands. From the window above the sink, he saw Emma about eight feet up one of the apple trees, a half-full burlap bag slung over her neck and a pile of empty ones on the grass below her.

Jack went out the back and walked over to the apple tree. Emma saw him coming and called down to him as he reached the tree.

"Hey, this strap is about to give. Can you catch this and toss me up another one?"

"Yeah, throw it down."

Emma pulled the bag over her head and let it drop. Jack caught it and set it down. He looked up at her and tossed up an empty sack.

"Thanks," she said, catching it.

Then she smiled down at him.

"These smell amazing, don't they?" she asked him.

He looked up through the tree branches

and he looked at her smiling down at him, the sun right above her head, bleaching out all the color from around her, and he realized what that feeling of dread had been for.

It was her.

He wasn't about to get shot at and he hadn't forgotten an appointment. He hadn't even lost his Social Security card. It was just her.

Somehow, he had fallen in love with Emma Lee Maxwell when he wasn't paying attention.

Emma went back to picking her apples and Jack stared out at the back field. He felt sick to his stomach. He felt mad. He also felt relieved that he was actually capable of falling in love with anyone. For just a second or two, he thought about asking her to climb down so he could tell her.

But then he remembered who he was and who she was. He was the almost-sixty year old man that she'd always thought of as an uncle. She was the little girl who had once run up to him with bleeding, scabby knees and proudly announced that she'd finally learned how to ride a bike. The daughter of his dead best friend and the grandchild of the woman who had raised him.

The hairs on the back of his arms stood up like something had jumped out at him and he felt a new heaviness in his chest, heaped onto the old. He'd come here to try to find some kind of ending to his past and then he'd stayed here to try find some way to atone for it.

He bent over, his hands on his knees, and took a deep breath as he wondered if there was anything at all that he couldn't screw up. Then he turned around and headed back to the house.

He wasn't going to tell her anything. It was bad enough that she felt sorry for him for dying. If she pitied him for loving her, he wouldn't be able to die fast enough.

Chapter 11

JACK COULDN'T REMEMBER ever having to try so hard to be hungry.

Emma's roast chicken was good. He knew it was good only because he knew it was Miss Margret's roast chicken; he couldn't taste a thing. There was a knot in his stomach that tightened every time he put a forkful of food in his mouth.

He spent all of dinner trying to rearrange potatoes and carrots in such a way that it looked like he was eating, and looking at Emma in such a way that it didn't look like he loved her. That primarily required not looking at her much at all.

He heard just enough of the conversation at the table to exclaim the right way and in the right places, but he couldn't have reported back to anyone what had been said. Instead, he tried to figure out how he hadn't seen it coming, how he hadn't known, like reworking a physics problem he'd missed on a test.

Jack looked at Emma as she listened to Becca talk about some Christmas program coming up at school next month and he tried to organize all the different ways he knew and felt about this woman.

She wasn't just some woman he'd met and fallen in love with. She was the woman raised by the person he loved most in this world. She was the woman whose father had been his brother and closest friend. She was the little girl who used to jackhammer around the driveway on a bright red pogo stick.

He didn't know what it was like to fall in love in some more ordinary way, but he had an idea that he'd done it backwards. He'd always imagined that a physical attraction, either building slowly or appearing full-grown and all at once, would eventually turn into love.

He'd waited for this to happen several times in his life, but instead the attraction had subsided and left nothing behind in its place. He'd always been honest and he'd tried not to be unkind, but he knew he'd hurt more than one woman in his lifetime.

As he watched Emma get up and take her plate to the sink, the idea of walking up behind her and wrapping his arms around her was almost as compelling as the idea of breathing. He wondered at the fact that he'd known he loved her before he'd noticed that he wanted her.

He stared at her back and wondered why he hadn't known yesterday that he wanted to put his hands on either side of her little waist, to lift up her hair and kiss her neck, to bury his nose in her hair as she laid her head on his chest.

Emma looked over her shoulder at him and laughed.

"Are you going to say something?" she asked and he felt a sharp prick in his chest, like a butterfly that had just been pinned to a board.

"What?" he asked her.

"I asked you like three times," Becca said, laughing. Jack jerked his head her way.

"I'm sorry, asked me what?" he asked her.

"If we could go fishing tomorrow. It's Saturday," she said. "You keep saying we'll go soon."

"Sure. Yeah, we'll go tomorrow," Jack told her. "Get some catfish."

"Finally," Becca told him back and carried her plate to the sink. "Can I finish my book before I take my shower? I only have one chapter left."

"Okay, go ahead," Emma answered, kissing the top of Becca's head.

Becca pranced out of the kitchen and Emma

looked at Jack as she turned the faucet on and waited for the water to get hot.

"You're awfully distracted and quiet," she said. "Are you feeling out of sorts?"

Jack looked at her face, pretty and soft and so much like her grandmother's.

"Sugar, I don't have a single sort left," he said.

Emma smiled at him.

"Anything I can help you with?" she asked.

He got up and squeezed past her to scrape his carrots and potatoes into the compost bucket.

"Not really, no," he said. "There's nothing wrong. I'm just thinking too hard."

He set his plate next to the sink and picked up the compost bucket.

"I'm gonna take this out," he said and brushed past her again as he headed out the back door.

Emma squirted some dish soap into the water and sank her trembling hands into it as it slowly filled the sink.

Jack usually helped her with the dishes while they talked or debated or just gave each other grief. Doing the dishes had become her favorite point of the day, but tonight she was glad to be doing them alone.

When Jack had come behind her to get to the compost bucket, she'd taken a deep breath of what she thought of as 'Jack scent', warmth and cotton with just a whiff of Nautilus. For a moment, she'd had a vision of her pushing him up against the refrigerator and kissing the tar out of him, but then she'd imagined his look of sheer horror and that had pretty much killed it for her.

Even so, her knees were still shaking just a little.

Emma had heard Jack come back up on the porch, but he'd never come in. She'd wondered what had him so anti-social and deep in thought, but she'd thought it best to leave him be, so she'd done the dishes, wiped down the table, swept the floor and put in a load of laundry. Finally, she gave up, poured some blackberry wine and grabbed a sweater from one of the hooks by the back door.

Jack was sitting in his chair, staring out at the back yard with one hand on his chin. The air was breezy and cool and the leaves on the trees rattled like old paper.

Emma handed Jack his glass of wine and settled herself in her chair with hers. They sipped their wine in silence for a moment before Emma spoke.

"I love fall the most," she said, pulling her sweater closed. "Everybody seems to think spring is a beginning, but to me, everything is new in the fall."

"It's late this year," Jack said. "Might be colder than usual."

"I think I might need to put another light in the chicken coop, then," Emma said.

"I'll check it in the morning," Jack answered.

Just then, Becca came out the screen door, wet-headed and carrying a brush. She was wearing slippers and a pink bathrobe with little green frogs all over it. She handed Emma the brush, then sat down between her mother's knees.

"Did you bring a ponytail holder?" Emma asked her

Becca handed her a green rubber band and Emma began gently brushing her hair. When it was wet, it was almost brown and reached the middle of her back. Jack watched Emma hand the brush back to Becca and begin braiding the little girl's hair. He barely heard them as they chatted about some book that Becca had just finished, one of the *Little House* books.

When Emma was done, she gave Becca a bear hug, kissed her and told her "goodnight." Becca came over to Jack and hugged his neck quick and light, like a bird landing just long enough to grab a bug.

"'Night, Little Bit," he told her.

"'Night, Jack," she said and went back inside.

Jack watched Emma take a few sips of her wine and he took a rather large swallow himself.

"You're a good mother, Emma," he said finally. She looked over at him, almost looked surprised.

"Thank you," she said.

She took another sip of her wine and looked at him. He was looking out at nothing in the dark.

"What was your mother like?" she asked him.

He looked at her and thought about that for a minute, then looked back out at the yard.

"I don't really know. She died when I was six," he said quietly. "She fell off a pontoon boat and drowned in Lake Martin. It wasn't her husband's boat."

"I'm sorry," she said.

Emma studied the side of his face, so impassive and hard to read.

"What was my mother like?" she asked him. Jack seemed to come back from someplace else and looked at her.

"I didn't really know her very well," he said. "I only met her just after you were born and I only came home a couple of times after that. She seemed like a nice girl. She was pretty, very pretty. She was a good mother, too. She liked to read."

"Yeah, I have a lot of her books," Emma said. "She loved Jane Austen. I guess that's where I get my romantic ideals from."

"Yeah, I guess she struck me that way," Jack said. "Daniel was my best friend, but I never really understood what she saw in him."

He looked at Emma quickly, apology on his face.

"I'm not saying he wasn't a good guy. He was. Just a little wild."

Emma looked down into her wine.

"Well, I think a lot of people end up loving somebody they don't seem suited for," she said.

Jack wanted to talk to her about the irony of that, but then he also sure as hell didn't.

"I never would have figured you for Trevor Hollings," he said instead. "I didn't know him really, but he always struck me as not much other than a pretty boy."

Emma smiled and shook her head.

"That was pretty much it," she said. "He was charming, too, but there wasn't much else there."

Jack considered shutting up, but his curiosity didn't seem to care much for his feelings.

"So why'd you love him?" he asked her.

"I didn't," she answered. "I just tried really hard."

"Why'd it end?"

Emma looked away from him and he saw her chew the inside of her cheek, like the answer might embarrass her.

"He hit me," she said. "That and I got tired of not loving him."

Jack had never felt an anger that was that instantaneous and yet that intense. He felt his breath ease out of his lungs and his heart rate seemed to slow. He never understood why people used words like "hot-blooded" when they talked about violent anger. For him, rage had always come with an icy calm.

"He beat you?" he finally asked her, steady and quiet.

"No, he slapped me once," she said. "He came home drunk one night, one of many. I called him a whore and he slapped me."

It took a minute for Jack to be reasonably certain he could speak without yelling, or say anything that didn't start with the letter "F."

"Hollings was a tall guy but I've seen bigger muscles on a Cornish hen. Please tell me you kicked his ass for him."

Emma smiled at him, almost shyly.

"No. He rattled me pretty good," she said. "I just shoved him out the door. Then I grabbed Becca out of her crib, threw a few things together and came home."

"Does he ever see her?" Jack asked.

"Nope. I haven't seen him since," she said and looked away.

Jack stared at her, looking so tiny, all wrapped up in a big gray sweater. He wanted to go over there, put his hands on her face and lift her out of that chair. He wanted to pick her up and enclose her. He distracted himself with the thought of driving to Birmingham or wherever and punching the boy in the throat, and how nice it was for him that he'd probably never see jail for it.

Jack and Becca sat on the riverbank this side of the river, in a nice spot that was clear enough of trees to have some good sun on it.

They'd been there for a couple of hours and had three decent-sized catfish on ice in the cooler. Jack figured they'd give it another hour or so and then head home for lunch.

He and Daniel had fished here many times as kids. Sometimes, when they were younger, Miss Margret would come along. She didn't like to clean fish, but she was good at catching them and loved to eat them, especially catfish.

A squirrel jumped from the grass onto the big oak tree just a little ways down and across the river and he remembered the last time he'd been by here.

It was the year before Miss Margret had passed and it was the first time he'd ever missed his bus. He'd dilly-dallied saying goodbye. The bus had already left by the time he got to Highway 9, but he'd been close enough that he could still smell the exhaust when he got to Frank's Truck Stop.

He'd paced around a little bit and grabbed

an RC from the cooler, but he'd had almost four hours to wait for the bus to Atlanta, so he'd left his bag in the back and walked outside to have a smoke.

He'd wandered back down the side of the road a ways as he smoked and considered going back to Miss Margret's for a little while, but saying goodbye twice would have sucked for both of them. Plus she was headed to the county fair shortly, if she wasn't gone already.

He'd stopped walking and ground his cigarette out with the toe of his boot and then looked over at the river. Directly across from him, a woman was sitting by the riverbank, her knees drawn up to her chest.

She was a couple of hundred feet away and had her back to him, so he couldn't see her face, but he was pretty sure he'd remember if he knew anybody with Jane Mansfield-blond hair.

He couldn't have said why, but he felt an urge to walk across the road and say "hello" to her, to start a conversation to help pass the time. He almost felt like he should, like he was supposed to. It was a feeling something like having someone's hand pressed firmly in between his shoulder blades, like a buddy urging him to talk to a girl or a parent encouraging him to go apologize.

In the end, he figured it was just his own loneliness with its hand on his back. For just a fleeting moment, he had wondered what it would be like if he actually made some kind of connection with that woman, something beyond casual conversation, and actually had an excuse to come home for good one day. He'd smoked a whole second cigarette loosely pondering that idea, as he watched the woman sitting still as stone.

But then he'd brushed those thoughts away with the reality that he was a forty-six year old man who had fallen short of every expectation he'd ever had of himself. He still lived in a barracks, couldn't seem to commit to anything beyond lust or companionship and had a good deal of baggage besides. He had nothing to offer a hometown girl.

So he'd ground out his second cigarette and headed back. But he remembered that as he walked back to the truck stop, he'd had a niggling feeling that he'd missed something he shouldn't have.

He'd forgotten all about that day until now. As he remembered it, he thought that at least he had found a way to stay home, although it had taken him ten years.

"Look, Jack! I got one!"

Jack looked over at Becca, then at her line.

"It's about time, Little Bit," he told her. "Careful now, let him out a little, then reel him in a bit, real slow."

He stuck his rod between some rocks and

got behind her, put his hands over hers.

"That's right, you're getting him," he said. "Reel him in some. There you go."

Becca was so joyful when they lifted the cat out of the water that he couldn't help but smile along with her.

"Look how big he is!" she said.

"That's a fact. He's a good three pounds," Jack told her as he held the cat down in the dirt and pulled the hook free.

Becca followed him over to the cooler.

"That's the first time I ever caught a catfish," she said.

"You did good," he told her and shoved the fish down into the ice.

"Mr. Dew keeps 'em on a stringer," she said. "He doesn't put them in a cooler."

"Well, Mr. Dew does it his way; I do it mine."

"He bangs 'em on the head before he cleans them," she said. "I don't like that part."

"Me neither," Jack said as they went back to their poles. "This way, they just go to sleep and then they die."

"Are the other ones dead already?" she asked him as he stuck another piece of cheese on her line.

"Yes ma'am, they are," he answered.

"Are we gonna eat them for dinner?"

"Yes, ma'am," he told her. "We'll take them home and clean them and your mom'll fry them up for dinner. We'll fry 'em up whole and eat them off the bone. That's the best way."

"Can I eat the one I caught?"

"You bet. That's your fish."

He helped her cast her line and they sat back down on the bank.

"Can we go hunting next?" she asked him. "I wanna eat something else."

He looked at her and she looked so flat out cute and angelic, but her smile was pure carnivore.

"I'm not much for hunting, Little Bit," he told her.

"Mr. Dew brings us some deer meat when he goes hunting," she said. "It's good."

"It is good. I don't mind eating it; I just don't care to kill it," he said.

"But we're hunting fish," she said.

"That's different somehow," he said.

She was quiet for a minute and they sat there and watched their lines.

"You killed that possum in the mud room," she said after a bit.

"That's different, too," he told her.

"How come?"

Jack sighed and looked at her, tried to think of an answer that would satisfy her.

"How'd you do on that book report yesterday?" was what he came up with.

A little while later, Becca chattered away at Jack as he cleaned the fish out by the woodshed, using a cutting board that he'd used for cleaning fish since he was at least fifteen. Then Becca ran off with her bag of fish guts and Jack washed out the cooler and headed to the house.

Emma was at the kitchen table with a glass of tea and a book.

"Hey," she said as he came in.

"Hey," he said back.

"How'd you do?" she asked him.

"Got six good ones," he told her as he took the bucket of fish to the sink. "Becca caught her first catfish, too."

Emma smiled big.

"Where is she?"

Jack turned on the faucet and started washing his hands.

"She's out looking for some of your special needs cats so she can feed them some innards."

Emma walked over to the stove and lifted the lid off a pot.

"Well, I'm making some corn chowder for lunch," she said. "It'll be ready in about twenty minutes."

"Sounds good," he said.

Emma sat back down at the table and Jack poured a glass of tea and joined her.

"That little girl's something else," Jack said. Emma smiled. "You know she's got a boyfriend? When did first-graders start having boyfriends and girlfriends?"

"Oh come on," Emma said. "You didn't have crushes on girls when you were six?"

"No, I did not," he said. "I had a crush on Mary Tyler Moore."

Emma grinned at him.

"Well, at least you had good taste," she said.

"I did. Until I hit puberty, then it all went to pieces," he said. "Thirteen-year-olds don't have the sense God gave Republicans."

"Yeah, well, when Becca turns thirteen, I'm locking her in the house," Emma said.

"I'd say you'd better. She's gonna be a beauty," Jack said. "I don't envy you going through puberty with her. Crap, I barely lived through yours."

"You were barely here for mine," Emma said indignantly.

"Please. From the time you were twelve until you graduated high school, every time I came home I had to listen to her rant about you and whatever boy," he said.

Emma rolled her eyes.

"It's a fact," Jack said. "She could spend a good thirty minutes on the dangers of raging hormones and rampaging whatnots."

"What whatnots?" she asked him.

"How do I know?" Jack asked back. "But she knew all about 'em. I just sympathized with her and tried to pay attention to whether I needed to stomp somebody for something."

"Well, you didn't. Aside from a little making-out here and there, I was a pretty level-headed kid," Emma said. "I was a ... well, Trevor was my first."

Jack got instantly uncomfortable with the conversation and wished he hadn't started the thing. A few weeks ago, the obvious fact that Emma had been with anybody wouldn't have meant much to him if he'd thought about it. Now it brought a bitter taste to his mouth. It also made him want to ask if Trevor was her last and he wasn't about to do that.

"You dated anybody since?" he asked anyway.

Emma's eyes dipped down to the Formica tabletop.

"No," she said.

"Why not?" he asked her, while he told himself to shut up.

Emma opened her mouth and looked at him a second, then shut it again and looked away, out the kitchen window. He saw her swallow before she spoke.

"I found out that I couldn't settle," she said. "When I was growing up ... I grew up with an ideal. I had this man in my head."

She glanced at him and looked away again.

"I'm too much of a romantic to give it up, I guess," she said.

Jack had a hard time not asking her about her ideal, but he didn't really want to know. He knew he couldn't have her, but he didn't want to hear about the type of man who could.

"Well," he said instead. "As far as I can tell, no true romantic has any business messing around with love."

Emma looked at him as she ran a finger up and down her glass. He stood up and pushed in his chair.

"Is that why you've never been married?" she asked him. "Because you don't believe in love?"

She looked almost sad and he wanted to tell her that it was crap and he'd just made it up.

"No," he said. "I just didn't have any idea what it was."

He took his glass to the sink.

"I'm gonna go grab some firewood for later," he said as he headed for the door. "It'll be cold tonight."

Emma watched him go and was about to ask him to stop when the screen door slapped shut. She was so sick and tired of keeping herself to herself, of being torn between saving her dignity and saving herself from regret later over things left unsaid.

She knew the last thing he'd want to hear was that she was foolish enough to love him, but she had this horrible feeling that she would get up the nerve to tell him but miss her chance. It seemed like it was always right on the tip of her tongue and it took so much effort to hold it back.

Her chair scraped the floor as she jumped up and headed for the back door. She yanked it open and walked out onto the porch. Jack was halfway to the barn already, a good hundred feet away.

She jammed her hands onto her hips and spoke in a normal tone, like he was standing right there in front of her.

"Let me explain something to you, Jack," she said. "I love you. I've always loved you. And now I'm always going to love you because you're here and you're real and I know you and I'm never going to get rid of it."

She watched Jack's back as he strode to the wood shed and she felt her throat tighten up.

"You have this place on your neck, right here under your jaw," she said, touching her own. "Every time I'm within five feet of you I want to kiss it and I'm pretty sure that I would give up ten years of my life to make love to you just one time."

Emma was aggravated to feel tears heating her eyes as Jack rounded the barn and went out of sight.

"I bury my face in your shirts before I wash

them because I want to inhale you and when you talk the whole world is just the sound of your voice," she said. "I'm so angry with you for being here because everything is going to hurt. I'm scared to death that when you're gone I won't know how to be."

She felt tears drifting down her cheeks and she swiped them away.

"If you would just look at me, really look at me, without seeing that little girl or her grandmother, I think that you could love me and I think that would be the smartest thing you ever did."

Jack reappeared from around the barn, several logs under his arm, and headed toward her without looking her way. Emma angrily wiped her nose with the back of her hand.

"That's all I had to say and now I don't want to talk about it anymore so just drop it," she said.

Then she turned and headed back to the kitchen, tripping over a cat on her way in.

"Move it, Tink!"

Chapter 12

*I*T OCCURRED TO JACK several times over the following couple of weeks that time shouldn't seem to move so slowly to someone whose time was so limited.

Usually, it felt like time was speeding up on him, trying to rob him of the opportunity to savor whatever amount he had left. But once he'd ingeniously figured out that he was in love with Emma, the effort of not showing it made every minute creep by at the speed of mountains growing.

It also seemed to him that the house was shrinking. Every time he turned around, there she was. He spent an unusual amount of time looking at the floor or the walls or out the window so she wouldn't have a chance to read it on his face.

He also had a hard time walking across a room or helping with the dishes without brushing up against her. When she would accidentally touch his hand, like when she was reaching for something at the table, and he would have to bite his tongue to keep from saying, "Put down the damn butter; I love you."

His only respite from the effort of shutting up came when she was upstairs writing. He was glad she was working because it was what he wanted her to do. But he was also glad because it gave him a few hours here and there to think, to feel halfway like himself. Otherwise, he just tried to find more stuff to fix or build and if it didn't need fixing or building he either broke it or tore it down.

For her part, Emma almost resented her time spent writing. It meant time away from Jack and she was so conscious of the sneakiness of time that she swore she could hear it swishing past her ear like a bullet.

So, eighteen times a day, she would run downstairs for a glass of tea, a cup of coffee or a breath of fresh air, depending on where Jack was at the moment, then get verbally chased back upstairs to "go be productive, dammit."

Fortunately, she was pretty sure he took it

as generic timewasting and overall meandering, rather than the need to be with him that it was. The highlights of her day were the shared chores, mealtimes and their now-traditional time on the back porch after dinner, during all of which she tried not to stare at him more than she could explain if asked.

At night, after everyone had gone to bed, she would lie in Grandma's big white iron bed, offering God deals and praying for one more month, one more week, one more day to memorize the way Jack smelled and looked and sounded.

Emma had taken possession of Grandma's little writing table from downstairs and set it up next to one of the windows in her room. It afforded her good light and a view of the back yard. She'd arranged her laptop and her notebooks and her Ball jar of pens just the way she'd always had them. Sitting down at the desk for the first time had felt like going back in time.

She'd spent her first week at home re-reading her manuscript, hating most of it and loving the rest. It surprised her how much her opinion of her own writing had changed and she wondered if that was due to maturity, loss or both.

In any event, she was tempted to either trash or put away *The Cricket Jar* and move on to something new. That temptation was particularly keen the day she heard Jack and Becca's voices come through her open window and she'd looked out to see them feeding the chickens together in the back yard.

She'd watched them for several minutes and thought how much they must look like she and Jack back when she was small. She couldn't recall them ever feeding the chickens together, but he hadn't ignored her entirely. She couldn't hear what Becca and Jack were saying, but they were chatting while they worked and as Emma watched, she thought of a story about a girl. A girl who loved a man who only came home once a year.

But then she'd remembered that she didn't exactly know the end of that story. She also felt a very strong desire to try to finish a book before that ending did come, something she could hand to Jack and thank him for. Something that he could read and maybe tell her was good. She was pretty sure that if no one else ever read the thing, she'd be okay with that as long as Jack approved.

So she'd stuck with *The Cricket Jar* and from that day forward, she worked more diligently.

Once she started actually writing, instead of editing or rewriting what she'd written so many years ago, she gradually remembered what it was for her to write.

There had been a time when writing was her

air and she could have stopped breathing more easily than she could have stopped writing. She had remembered feeling it, but it had been years since she'd recalled the feeling itself, the sense of being at home among the words, of dwelling in the story.

When she'd been younger, she had gotten lost for hours on end nearly every day. There were times when she'd felt more like a biographer than a storyteller, as though the characters were telling her what had happened and she was just jotting it down. She discovered the story as she wrote and as she wrote she discovered things about her that she hadn't known until she'd read them on paper.

Writing again, after so many years without, was like a reunion with someone who had once been a constant friend.

Always, she felt the pressure of time on the back of her head, keeping her mind focused on her work as much as possible, even when she knew Jack was right outside or just downstairs. She wrote several hours every day and edited ruthlessly the next, always feeling like the literature-major she was writing for was reading over her shoulder.

One day in the middle of November, Emma was at her desk, struggling to separate the stupid from the worth saving, when she heard the muffled sound of Jack's voice from downstairs. Since

Becca was still at school, she discerned quite happily that he must be calling her.

When she got down to the kitchen, she saw his bottom half sticking out from under the sink.

"Did you call me?" She asked him, not noticing any part of the fact that he was just lying there right in front of her or that there was a patch of stomach exposed where the tails of his flannel shirt had opened up.

"Yeah," he said from the cupboard. "I've got to use two hands for this. Can you grab that flashlight and get under here?"

She was glad he couldn't see her face, because she was pretty sure she'd given herself some kind of psychic sunburn staring at him like that. She was also pretty sure that nobody else on the planet was ridiculous enough to think that being invited under the kitchen sink could in any way be alluring.

"Uh, sure," she said, with as much nonchalance as she could falsify.

She grabbed the flashlight off of the counter, got down on her hands and knees next to his legs and poked her upper half into the cupboard. She flipped onto her back on the other side of the pipe from him and turned on the flashlight.

Jack was holding a bowl-shaped piece of metal up to the drain opening with one hand and holding a tube of something in the other.

"Just shine that right up here at the drain,"

Jack said. "I can't see what I'm doing here."

She poked the light up where he said.

"I got the sink trap cleaned out," Jack said. "I just need to get this glued back up and we're good to go."

Emma had always thought that the cupboard under the kitchen sink was huge, but upon further reflection she felt like they were crammed into a shoebox. The sound of his breathing seemed far too intimate and close and she realized she was having a little trouble with her own.

Despite the fact that the cupboard doors were open, Emma couldn't help thinking she might kill the both of them with carbon dioxide poisoning if she didn't stop breathing so shallowly. She tried to distract herself by making up new cuss words in her head.

"Little bit to the left," Jack said.

The light was just a little shaky and Jack looked over at Emma. Her eyes were big and she was breathing through her mouth. Her lips were open just a little and they were so close, less than a foot away. Jack found himself staring at them and wondering if he could get away with kissing her by claiming it must have been the tumor.

"You alright?" he asked her.

"Yeah, sure," she said. "Why?"

"Can you try to hold it a little steadier?" he asked.

"Sure," she told him and willed the flash-

183 Dawn Lee McKenna 183

light not to tap against the pipe.

She watched him squeeze some greenish goop along the rim of the bowl.

"What is that?" she asked as though she cared.

"Gorilla Snot," he said.

"Okay," she said.

"During Reconstruction, they used it to put the country back together."

A small dollop of the stuff fell onto his cheek.

"Crap. Get that off me before it glues my face shut," he said.

Emma turned her head this way and then that.

"We took everything out," she said. "Hold on."

She was all set to shimmy back out when he stopped her.

"Just use my shirt," he said.

Emma turned over on her stomach, pulled his collar up a bit and wiped the goop off with it. The flashlight went hither and yon.

"Thank you," Jack told her and tried not to look at her face. She smelled like shampoo and he could feel her breath on his face and he was pretty sure that her leaning over him in a kitchen cabinet made him more nervous than the first day of boot camp had.

Emma turned back onto her back and pointed the light somewhat at Jack's hands. It was like trying to focus on a firefly.

"Are you okay?" he asked her again as he finished gluing the rim. "Maybe you should cut back on the caffeine."

"I'm just a little claustrophobic," she said.

"Since when? You used to read in the closet under the stairs."

"I was smaller then," she said.

"Not by much," he told her. He put the tube down and continued holding the bowl up there.

"I'm done," he said. "I just need to hold it in place a minute. You can go ahead out."

Emma thanked God, Jesus and Gorilla Snot as she scooted on out and stood.

"How long do you have to hold it?" she asked him.

"Couple of minutes," he said.

Emma figured that ought to be enough time for her to get normal and she opened the fridge.

"Do you want some tea?" she asked him.

"Oh yeah," he said with evident certainty.

Emma poured them each a glass, sat down, then snuck a few seconds of holding her tea up to her hot face before Jack came out of the cupboard.

"Thank you for fixing the sink," she said as he put his things back in the toolbox.

"Yep," he said, his back to her.

"When can I run the water?" she asked him.

"Few minutes," he said back and she wondered if he was annoyed with her for some reason.

Then she wondered if he knew.

"Okay. Good," she said. "I was thinking of making some chocolate chip raisin cookies."

"That sounds good," he said and closed up the toolbox.

Emma watched him as he came to the table and picked up his tea without looking at her. She got a sick feeling in her stomach, a small swirling of certainty that she'd made him uncomfortable and that meant he knew.

"Do you want some lunch?" she asked him, hoping he would look at her. She wanted him to smile at her, say something sarcastic and show her he didn't have a clue, to keep her from throwing up on Grandma's kitchen table.

But he swallowed the last of his tea and took the glass to the sink.

"No. Thanks. I grabbed a sandwich earlier," he said to the sink.

He turned around and looked at the kitchen doorway instead of looking at her.

"I've gotta run, anyway," he said. "I told Brother Fillmore I'd help him mend his fence."

He headed out of the kitchen without once looking at her.

"See you," he said on his way out.

"See you," she said back and sat there long after she heard the front door close, wondering if she could pack a few things and move somewhere before he got back.

Jack's boots crunched along on the gravel as he walked out of Miss Margret's driveway at a fairly good stomp and turned onto the road.

He had no destination in mind and Brother Fillmore wasn't expecting him just yet. He just needed to get away.

What he really wanted was to get away from himself and from all the noise going on in his head about Emma, about finally loving someone when he was almost out of time, about loving a woman he couldn't have and had no right to need.

She was Miss Margret's grandchild. She was Daniel's little girl. He'd seen her sometimes, the way she'd looked at him when she was young, when she didn't think he saw her staring. He'd known she saw him as some kind of absentee father figure and he'd wondered if that was a small part of what had kept him leaving.

Not telling her how he felt added to the weight of not telling her the truth about why he had never been able to come home for good. He'd already decided that he would tell her one day, that he would break a promise to Miss Margret for the first time in his life and ask her forgiveness later.

For once, he wished he could know for sure when he was dying. He wasn't inclined to give in to cowardice, but he'd prefer to tell Emma about what had happened no sooner than five minutes before he left this earth.

He wasn't sure which secret was harder to hide; the one about the past or the one about the present. But as each day passed, pretending to Emma that he saw her as nothing more than the daughter of his dead best friend felt more and more like lying. He wondered if he should do so much lying when he was pretty close to looking God in the eye.

At the same time, he wondered if he had the right to make Emma so uncomfortable and the back-and-forthing in his head just made him angry. He stopped walking, picked up a small rock and threw it at the pear tree that marked the beginning of Brother Fillmore's property line.

He should just go on to Brother Fillmore's and hammer nails and pull wire fencing taut until he didn't have to think anymore. Or maybe he should head up the road a little further and have a beer with Dew first to mud the cracks in his head.

He put his fists on his hips and stood there in the middle of the road, staring down at the clay and gravel. Then he kicked at a clod of hardened orange clay.

"Dammitall," he said, then turned around and stomped back down the road.

Chapter 13

EMMA WAS ON HER knees on the counter, looking for something in the top cupboard, when he showed up in the kitchen doorway. She looked over her shoulder at him.

"I thought you went to Brother Fillmore's," she said.

"What are you doing?" he said by way of not answering.

"Looking for the raisins," she said.

"I need to talk to you about something," he said.

"Okay," she said back. She thought he sounded almost angry.

"Could you get down first?" he asked.

Emma already knew she wasn't going to like whatever he had on his mind. In fact, she was pretty sure she knew what it was. He may not know she loved him, but he'd picked up on the fact that she sure wanted him. Now he was going to give her some kind of speech about that and she didn't want to hear it.

So she closed the cupboard and turned around, but she didn't get down. Instead, she sat on the counter, because it somehow made her feel better to be taller than she was, like his words wouldn't hurt so much or her embarrassment wouldn't be so obvious. She sat on her hands, too, so she wouldn't feel quite so compelled to cover her face.

He watched her sit and looked at her a second, then looked past her somewhere. He seemed nervous or agitated more than angry, she realized. Somehow, that made it worse, like she'd not only freaked him out but also burdened him with the task of trying to be diplomatic about it.

She was scared, which meant she simultaneously wanted to run out the back door and punch him in the face.

"I'm going to say something to you and I don't want you to say one thing," he said. "Then I'm going to walk right back out that door and we're never going to speak of it again, do you hear me?"

"Jack, you don't need to—"

"Quiet, please," he interrupted politely. "You don't know what I need to."

Emma felt the tears of forthcoming humiliation and she blinked them back, but she didn't say anything, just swallowed and waited for it.

"I love you, Emma," he said.

"I know that," she said quietly. She thought then that the only thing worse than someone telling you they didn't love you was them telling you they did.

"No, Emma," he said and huffed out a sigh. "I'm telling you that I love you."

Emma blinked a few times. Her brain was still trying to process what he was saying, because it couldn't possibly be what she thought she'd heard. She didn't even open her mouth.

Jack sighed again and looked around the kitchen for a minute before he met her eye.

"I'm sorry," he said. "But I just couldn't stand the idea of being gone and you never knowing."

Emma just sat and stared at him.

"Try to look a little less horrified, Emma," he told her.

"I'm not horrified, Jack. Dumbstruck maybe."

"Well. That's all I had to say," he said. "We don't ever have to mention it again. It doesn't have to change anything, but if you think it does, I can leave."

"Jack, are you blind?" she blurted out.

"No, I'm not blind," he snapped. "You think I don't see the look on your face?"

She put a hand on her chest, pretty sure she was going to faint right off the counter.

"Jack, ever since I was a little girl—"

Jack held up a hand.

"Please shut up," he said quietly. "Just this once, I beg you."

"Let me talk," she said.

"You don't need to, Emma," he told her, shaking his head. "I know you've always seen me as an uncle or a father figure. I've been trying not to tell you for weeks, but it just wouldn't keep."

"Jack, I've been trying not to tell you for twenty years."

He stood there and squinted at her, like he was trying to put her pieces together and figure out what she was.

"Tell me what?" he asked her.

"Jack, I've always loved you," she couldn't believe she said. "I was in love with you when you got here."

Jack stared at her like she'd just thrown a live animal in his face. Emma had a momentary fear that she'd imagined everything she'd thought he said and just blurted her truth out with no provocation whatsoever.

"What the hell for?" he asked her, as if

she'd said she was thinking of becoming an exotic dancer.

"What do you mean what—why not?" she asked him.

All he could do for a minute was stare. At least a hundred reasons came to mind and all of them fought for egress at once. It took him a minute to sort the key points and put them together.

"Well, let's set Miss Margret and your Daddy and our whole lifetime aside for just a second," he said. "I'm almost sixty years old, Emma and you're barely over thirty."

"So what? When you get within three feet of me, I can't even breathe," she said.

He was quiet for a moment, just looked at her.

"Are you serious?" he finally said.

"Are you?" she asked him back.

"Serious as hell," he barely said.

Emma actually felt faint, so much so that she curled her fingers over the edge of the counter and hung on. She'd dreamed so long of him saying he loved her, without once ever thinking it would actually happen. She honestly couldn't help feeling that she might be having some kind of psychotic episode.

"Excuse me," he said, like he'd called the wrong number, and walked right out the back door.

Emma was so startled by it that she couldn't

move. When she'd first figured out that he had meant what she'd thought he'd meant, her first reactions had been astonishment and then joy.

But when someone told you they loved you and you told them you loved them back, they were supposed to be happy about it. They weren't supposed to look like you'd just stolen their car and they weren't supposed to just walk out the door.

Jack stood in the middle of the back yard, his hands on his hips and his eyes on the back fence, and wondered what the hell.

He hadn't known what to expect. He'd thought it likely that she would just stare at him in a stricken sort of way and then he would leave. He'd thought it was also likely that she would be so kind and apologetic and understanding that he'd wish he'd never told her.

His imagination wasn't wild enough to have thrown out the possibility that she would say what she'd said. At no time in the thirty-something years he'd known her did he ever get the idea she might feel something for him besides family affection.

He'd just wanted it said. He'd just wanted to tell her and have that be the end of it. The re-alization that he was capable of loving someone had just been too surprising, too much of a relief to keep to himself. He'd thought about just telling Dew or Gina, but it wouldn't have relieved him much at all to tell someone who already thought he loved the woman he'd married.

He'd hurt a lot of women in his life, with his inability to either commit or leave them alone soon enough for it not to matter. But Emma ... he'd suggested this whole thing, this marriage thing, so that he could help her. He'd never meant to hurt her, but how could she not be hurt? And how could he have been so damn blind?

He walked over to a tree stump by the chicken coop and sat, rubbed his face with both hands. Loving him was just about the worst thing that Emma could do. But as he sat there, it began to sink in that he'd just taken the last chance he had to love someone and that someone actually loved him back.

He sat there for a few minutes longer before he realized that him walking out like that probably hadn't been the smoothest or kindest thing he'd ever done and he got up and headed back to the house to find her.

He didn't have to look far. She startled the crap out of him by being right where he'd left her, sitting on top of the kitchen counter.

When she looked up at him, he saw that she'd been crying and he wanted to punch himself for it. He thought about going over there and hugging her, but he walked over to the table and leaned on it instead. He looked at her with what he hoped was some kind of apology on his face.

"I'm sorry, Emma," he said. "I shouldn't have just walked out like that."

"It's okay," she told him.

"Is that why you've been crying?" he asked her.

Emma swallowed hard before she answered.

"No. I'm scared because I don't know what you're thinking," she said. "And because I'm afraid you'll leave."

Jack looked at her and thought that few things had ever seemed quite so urgent as making her not look like that.

"No. No, I'm not leaving," he said and he saw her shoulders relax just a little. "That conversation just didn't go any of the ways that I was prepared for."

"Did you really not have any idea?" she asked.

"Emma, if I had, it would have scared me so bad that I would have been gone a long time ago," he said.

She nodded and looked down at the floor and he took a deep breath and sighed.

"I can't believe how badly I've screwed this up," he finally said.

She looked up at him.

"What do you mean?"

"Emma, I never would have done all this,

getting married ... I wouldn't have done any of it if I thought for one minute that you felt that way," he said. "I would not intentionally 'cause you pain."

"You just gave me the one thing I've wanted my whole life, Jack," she said.

"I'm dying, Emma. Remember?" he asked her gently.

"You're dying anyway, Jack. It was already going to hurt." she told him just as quietly. "At least you love me."

Jack looked at her and she thought he just looked so sad.

"I'm so sorry," he said again.

"Jack, I knew what I was doing when I said 'yes,'" she said. "I was ready for you to leave me with nothing. But now you're telling me you love me."

"I do."

"I can keep that. It's mine," she said.

They stared at each other a moment.

"You should come down off that counter now," he said.

Emma chewed on her bottom lip for a second, thinking about that.

"I would have to jump and then I'd look stupid," she said.

Jack took a step forward, put his hands on her hips and lifted her down. Emma was eyeball-to-chest with him and couldn't help noticing that spot on his neck was just right there, inches away. She wasn't yet convinced enough that she wasn't hallucinating everything he'd said, so she avoided kissing his neck by staring at the pocket of his flannel shirt.

"What are we going to do now, Emma?" he said quietly and she could feel the breath of his words in her hair.

"I'd like to just plonk my head right there," she said, putting a finger on his collarbone.

"You should do that then," he said. So she did.

She laid her right cheek on his chest, the same place she'd put her head when they had danced that day at the barbecue. But this time she felt that it was real and that maybe she had a right to be there.

She took a slow, deep breath and took in the smell of him, felt the fabric of his shirt move against her face as he gently wrapped his arms around her.

They stood there like that for what seemed to her like an hour and she tried to put a name to a feeling that whispered just beneath all the noise of love and disbelief and gratitude and longing.

Then she realized that, despite the fact that she lived in the same house in which she'd been born, his chest felt more like home than any place she'd ever known.

"Thank you," she breathed out and she wasn't sure if she was talking to God or Jack or both.

She felt Jack's arms leave her and then one rough finger gently lifted her chin so that she was looking into his face. She didn't even know she was crying until he kissed a tear from the corner of her left eye.

Then he slid one hand alongside her face and slipped his fingers into her hair and when she finally had the nerve to look him in the eye she felt like she wasn't standing on her own feet, but floating just a few inches above the floor, being pulled into a tunnel with crystal-blue walls.

His face moved closer and she dropped her eyes to his mouth. As it dipped toward her, she stared at every crack and line of his lips and she could almost feel him already.

"You guys, guess what?!"

Emma's heart flipped and skittered across the linoleum and Jack spun around and leaned against the counter next to her, one hand on his chest. Becca dropped her backpack on the table with a thunk.

"What, baby?" Emma croaked out.

"I won the fifty-yard dash in P.E. today!" Becca said, grinning. "First place!"

"That's great, sweetie," Emma said as Becca brushed past them to get to the fridge.

Just then there was a knock at the front

door.

"I'll get it," Becca hollered as she grabbed an apple and ran out of the kitchen. Emma and Jack looked at each other.

"You know, we're married," Emma said. "We probably don't need to worry about her catching us kissing."

Jack stared at her for a minute and she suddenly felt like she'd been underwater too long.

"Maybe so," Jack said. "But something tells me we should probably practice stopping first."

He was three feet away from her, but Emma could have sworn he'd touched her.

"Well," she said quietly, then tried to laugh. "I have been storing it up for about twenty years. Beware the raging whatnots."

Jack felt something warm move from his feet all the way up to his neck.

"Sugar, I'm not the least bit afraid of your whatnots," he said evenly, and it sounded almost like a threat.

Emma felt her cheeks redden on the spot.

"Hey Jack," Becca said from the doorway and Jack jumped just a hair. "Brother Fillmore's out front for you."

Jack sighed and pushed away from the counter.

"Well," Jack said. "Okay then."

He patted Becca on the head as he went past.

"Good grief almighty," he said and went out the kitchen door with Becca trailing behind him.

Emma turned around and laid her forehead on the counter.

"Jiminy crickets," she said.

Emma spent the next few hours trying to remember how to walk, talk and breathe with her mouth closed.

She was unusually monosyllabic whenever Becca asked her a question or told her about something going on at school and she managed to burn two out of five sheets of cookies.

She was thrilled when Becca decided to go play Barbies, only because it gave her the privacy and lack of conversation she needed to climb all over her own thoughts or, more accurately, the repeating of one single thought; *he actually loves me.*

She thanked God no fewer than two-hundred and nine times, pinched herself no fewer than five and when she went out to feed the chickens, she told each hen individually that Jack loved her. They seemed to agree that this was startling and commenced to discuss it amongst themselves when she headed back inside.

But once she heard Jack come back through the front door, Emma found herself suddenly nervous and mute. Jack had gone upstairs to shower while Emma finished cooking dinner. The sound of the water running above her head filled her mind with thoughts and pictures that left her standing in the middle of the room with a spatula in her hand, looking stupid and trying to remember what she was supposed to be doing.

When he came back down in clean jeans, bare feet and her favorite white button-down shirt with the tails hanging down, she was grateful that he seemed almost to be ignoring her, because when he did look at her she was pretty sure he was reading her mind. She was glad he kept the knowledge to himself.

It was even worse when he did speak to her; everything he said sounded like a euphemism for something else and every look he gave her seemed like a promise of something else as well.

She realized that this should have made her happy and excited but it scared her as badly as if a passenger plane had just crashed in the back yard. The entire time she was cooking dinner, all Emma could think was that at some point, Jack was going to touch her and most likely, she was going to touch him back.

After years of daydreaming and pretending and not even hopeful wishing, it seemed like the reality of it would be a little too much for her or the universe at large to deal with. At one point she got so caught up with worrying about how and when it would happen and whether she'd keel over dead and miss the whole thing that she'd mashed the potatoes halfway to soup before she caught what she was doing.

Dinner itself wasn't much better, although the glass of blackberry wine Emma snuck while setting the table had calmed her nerves a great deal. While Becca chattered brightly about the cats, a boy named Ethan who had thrown up at school and the upcoming holidays, Jack took Emma apart one piece at a time.

He insisted on staring at her through most of the meal and she could tell by the way he tried not to smile that he knew he was her undoing. But eventually the wine seemed to ooze over her brain and she found herself calming down just a little and even trying to turn the tables a bit.

It had been a very long time since she'd flirted with anyone, but she figured she could still come across with a few smoldering looks and insinuations of her own. Apparently she could, because Jack had buttered his roll three times before he actually bit into it.

When the phone rang in the hallway, Emma felt like she'd taken her first breath in the last five minutes.

"Mommy?" Becca called from the hall. "Miss Regina wants to know if I can spend the night. Allie's over there for the weekend."

"Yes," Emma almost screamed.

Jack looked at her before he let out a big breath.

"Praise God," he said. "Go pack that child's pajamas."

Emma helped Becca gather her things and kissed her goodnight, then stuttered something to Jack about taking a shower, leaving him downstairs to wait for Regina. While she was in there, Emma noticed that it took her five minutes to shave her legs on an ordinary day, but fifteen to shave them tonight. She couldn't remember any time ever before when smooth kneecaps had seemed so integral to her future happiness.

She was finally forced to come out of the shower when the hot water ran out, then spent an inordinate amount of time trying to figure out what she should wear. A sexy nightie would be silly and she didn't own one anyway, but she didn't think going downstairs in her bathrobe was such a great idea, either.

She threw on her weathered old Dallas Cowboys jersey and some shorts in an attempt to convince one or both of them that she wasn't precisely expecting anything, but then she realized that if he was, he'd think she wasn't and then they wouldn't, so the jersey went onto the closet floor.

She finally decided on a huge white button-down shirt that she liked to sleep in at night. It covered more than most of her nightgowns, and she'd worn such shirts around the house before since Jack had been home. She felt satisfied that she looked neither eager nor entirely devoid of eagerness. But when it came time to actually go downstairs, she managed to get herself freaked out anew.

She had no idea how either one of them would start a conversation now that they were alone. She suddenly realized that she didn't know what to say or how to act. So she found herself dying to fly downstairs, but standing around in her room instead. This frustrated her greatly, so she went into the bathroom to stand around.

Jack poured two glasses of wine and took them into the living room.

He'd figured that they'd better have some sort of segue between where they'd been and where they were undoubtedly headed, so he had in mind to have something of a little date right there in the living room.

The water pipes had stopped groaning ten minutes ago, so he knew she'd been out of the shower for a while and would be downstairs any second. He wanted it to be at least a little romantic, so he turned off all the lights except for one lamp and started rifling through his small pile of CDs.

He'd take her on a real date soon; maybe take her up to Eufaula to the River City Grill for some Cajun seafood. They could go tomorrow if she liked, but he didn't think anything else was going to wait that long. He also couldn't see the benefit of tossing her into the truck and running her over to Waffle House just so they could say they went out before they stayed in.

They'd gotten married two months before he told her he loved her and had been married for those two months before the idea of making love ever came up. They'd done everything inside out so far; he figured their first date could wait.

As soon as he'd thought it, he stopped short with a CD in his hand. The idea of making love hadn't actually come up. It had seemed like the natural and downright inevitable next step. The tension between them all day had certainly given him the impression that the first chance they got would be the one they took. But now that he thought about it, he hadn't come right out and said anything to her about it, nor she to him.

He looked over toward the stairs. She'd been out of the shower for a good long time, really. He'd assumed that she was doing all those

206 🌸 *See You*

things women do, with things that smell good and things that look good, when they're getting ready to make love. But now he was kind of wondering if she'd gone to bed.

He tapped the CD against his hand and considered the situation. Maybe she'd gotten scared. It was also possible that he hadn't made his intentions as clear as he'd thought; but he didn't see how anybody could miss it.

Deciding she'd be down in a minute, he opened up the case for his favorite Van Morrison CD, popped it into the player and hit "Pause." He'd been listening to the album the other day and heard "Tupelo Honey" and it had made him think of her. He wanted to dance to it with her.

He stood there and had a few sips of his wine and considered going upstairs. Maybe she was getting ready. Maybe she was asleep. Maybe she was actually waiting on him and wondering what *his* problem was.

He'd never had much trouble reading women; in fact, he figured he'd read them too well and they had been too easy for him to use, even as he meant to be kind. But he'd never tried to read Emma Lee Maxwell in that way.

With that thought came the realization that he was thinking about going up to Miss Margret's bedroom to either yank her granddaughter out of bed or join her in it. The thought made him feel like he'd come suddenly and fully out from under the effects of an all-day drunk. He didn't quite feel ashamed, but he did feel like he ought to.

He was just thinking about drinking both glasses of wine and going to his room when she showed up in the living room doorway. Her hair was still a little damp and she was wearing one of her big old men's shirts that hung down to her knees. She looked a little nervous and a little unsure, and so tiny and pretty that he wanted to wrap himself around her.

"Hey," he said quietly.

"Hey," she said back.

They stood there and stared at each other for a second and he remembered the wine. He picked up the glasses and held one out to her.

"I thought maybe you'd like to have a glass of wine," he said.

Emma smiled.

"Okay," she said, and came to take the glass he offered.

As they sipped their wine, Jack felt himself coming back to himself. It was as though wanting her to be comfortable washed his own uncertainty away.

He leaned over and gave her a kiss on the forehead, then turned on the CD. He took her glass from her, put the glasses on the coffee table and held out his hand.

"Let's do that slow dance over again, Emma Lee," he said.

She smiled again, almost gratefully, and he pulled her to him as his song came on.

"This is pretty," she said. "What is it?"

"'Tupelo Honey,'" Jack told her. "One of my favorites. I had it on the other day and it made me think of you."

Emma smiled again and rested her head on his chest. After all the nerves she'd endured all evening, it surprised her that she suddenly felt calm, almost comforted.

"Emma, we can stop right here and pretend everything is just the way it was," he said. "It's not too late to change your mind."

"Of course it is," she said. "It's always been too late."

Jack held her just far enough away from his chest to look at her. He stared at her a moment, like he was about to ask her something.

"Well, then it's my intention to make love to you," he said instead.

All day long, she had pretty much figured that was a given. But him saying it right out loud like that made her feel like she was standing in the path of a runaway horse.

Jack looked at her standing there with her mouth hanging open just a little and his brain started coming unwound.

"Or not," he said. "If we're not ready for that quite yet."

Emma felt her face redden and she sudden-

ly felt like she'd asked someone on a date, sure of
acceptance, and then been turned down flat. He
read it as just plain fear of jumping into something too different too suddenly.

"Don't panic," Jack said, pulling her closer.
"Let's just dance."

Emma put her face into his shirt, more to
hide herself than for anything else. She could feel
Jack's heart pounding underneath her cheek and
it took her a minute to be able to speak.

"Jack, are you having second thoughts?
About how you feel?"

It took him a second to answer her, during
which time she thought about running out the
front door.

"Emma, I feel so many things that I can't get
them untangled," he said.

"What do you mean?"

Jack let out a whoosh of air.

"I mean that for the last two weeks, I've gotten used to the idea of loving you and I got okay
with it, because nobody knew and nothing was
going to come of it," he said. "But now here we are
and one minute, all I can think about is throwing you down on this rug and the next minute I
feel like I need to apologize to somebody for that."

Emma's brain sorted through all that to
settle on the one thing that mattered.

"But you love me?" she asked into his shirt.

"Yes, Emma," he said, sighing into her neck.

"Right in front of God, I love you."

"Okay," she said, and she could breathe again. "Jack, if we weren't both raised in this house, if you had just met me somewhere, what would you want right now?"

"That would be the rug, Emma, no question," he said quietly. "But we are who we are and we can't help how that makes this a little complicated."

Jack stopped and let go of her, cupped her face and made her look at him.

"What do you want, Emma?" he asked her. "Don't think about what you should say, just give me the first honest answer that comes to mind."

"Are you sure you want honest?' she asked.

"No."

"Well," she said. "We can slow down or not, but I think I might have some kind of organ failure if you don't at least finally kiss me."

She tried to hold his gaze, but she suddenly felt naked and had to look down at his collar.

"Oh, I can kiss you," he said quietly.

"I don't doubt that for a second," she said.

Jack tilted her head up and Emma had a sudden flash of a memory, of a time when she was fourteen or fifteen and had been sitting on the porch, thinking what it would be like if Jack kissed her. Her imagination had been so unexpectedly vivid that it scared her and she'd had to play two games of rummy with Grandma just to straighten herself out.

But when Jack finally kissed her it was nothing like she expected. He kissed her gently at first and then he kissed her for real and it was so much more than physical sensation.

Emma tasted the man she'd loved most of her life and he was at once completely strange and entirely familiar. She mentally threw her arms wide and let herself fall into a pool of warmth and softness, intensity and need, homecoming and blackberry wine.

After a moment, he pulled away, took her hand and they began dancing again.

"Do you want to wait, Emma?" he asked her after a moment.

"I've probably never wanted anything less in my life," she said.

"Good thing," he said.

Emma looked up at him and she wondered if the look in her eyes was the same as in his, a mixture of gratitude and resignation, want and peace. It was almost too frank, too honest to tolerate for long and Emma found herself wanting to get out from under the weight of it for just a moment.

"You know, I almost feel sorry for you," she said with half a grin.

"Why's that?' he asked her.

"I don't think you understand the severity with which I've wanted you all these years, Jack," she said. "I can't decide whether to savor you or devour you."

One side of Jack's mouth lifted up in half a grin and he winked at her. Banter was good; he could still handle banter.

"Is that a fact?" he asked her. "Well, you're in luck, darlin'. One of the benefits of being with an older man is that we'll have time for both."

Emma felt all of her swagger and confidence drop down to her feet somewhere.

"Well," she managed. "Okey-dokey."

He gently pulled her closer and she put her face into his neck and breathed him in.

"Jack?" she said.

"Yes, Emma?"

"It is okay isn't it?" she asked. "For you to … for us to make love?"

She felt a vibration in his chest and knew he was trying not to laugh.

"Yes, Emma, it is okay."

"Are you sure?"

"Well, if you like, I can take a quick nap while you go Google it," he told her.

"Shut up," she said into his collar, but she smiled.

They danced in silence for a moment, then she lifted her head and looked at that spot she loved right below his jaw, the one she'd wanted to kiss since the day he'd come home. Her hand tightened on the back of his neck and she put her lips on his throat and kissed it.

Jack cleared his throat as the song ended.

"Emma, I believe I'm going to take you upstairs now," he said quietly.

A few minutes later, they stood in the middle of her room. The only light was a hint of moon coming through the white lace curtains and a glow from the lamp in the hall.

Jack reached up and tucked a stray strand of hair behind her ear, then cupped her face with his hands. He looked at her for a long moment before he spoke.

"I never saw you coming, Emma Lee," he said. "But I do love you."

Emma felt hot tears spring up in her eyes and she didn't bother blinking them away.

"It's about time, Jack," she said.

Somewhere around 3 a.m., rain falling onto the tin roof woke Emma from her sleep. She blinked up at the ceiling and for just a moment she thought that maybe she'd been dreaming, but then she heard the gentle sound of breathing beside her.

She turned her head on the pillow and saw Jack's face just inches from hers and felt a wave of relief and gratitude that almost overwhelmed her. She turned onto her side to face him and watched him sleep for a long time, listening to his breath going in and out and feeling the warmth of him against her.

She went over the day in her head repeatedly, seeing and hearing Jack tell her for the first time that he loved her and feeling the amazement well up in her chest again. As she felt herself drifting, she realized that she had been so preoccupied and overjoyed at the idea that Jack was hers that it had been almost twelve hours since she'd thought about the fact that he was dying.

One more miracle and I'll never ask You for another thing, she thought as she fell asleep again.

Chapter 14

THE NEXT MORNING, Emma woke up alone and panicked for just a moment. She had a sickening thought that she'd imagined everything, until the faint scent of Jack reached her from the other pillow.

The sun was already most of the way risen and she got out of bed and pulled on a pair of jeans and a sweater. She felt a little lump of dread deep in her stomach, a gnawing feeling that Jack might have thought everything over and decided he regretted it all.

She made a passable effort at brushing her hair, put more enthusiasm into brushing her teeth, and then went on downstairs.

She could smell coffee, but the kitchen was empty when she got there. She got her mug down from the cupboard and poured herself a cup and was stirring the sugar in when Jack came through the back door.

She glanced up at him as he crossed the kitchen with his own empty mug in his hand.

"Hey," he said quietly.

"Hey," she said back and looked back down at her coffee, stirred what didn't need stirring. She felt awkward and shy and just a little bit afraid.

Out of the corner of her eye, she saw Jack come over to the counter. She sipped her coffee and tried to think of what she should say as he fixed himself another cup.

"You missed a beautiful sunrise, lazing around in bed," he said.

"Did I?" she asked.

He'd thought about waking her up to show her, but instead he'd sat on the porch alone, wondering if everything would be terribly awkward in the light of day. He touched her shoulder and turned her around to face him.

She looked so pretty. He reached out and gently rubbed his knuckles across her cheek. He didn't see any sorry on her face, just something that looked a little like relief and something else that looked an awful lot like love.

"Good morning," he told her.

"Good morning," she said, finally smiling.

He gave her a gentle kiss and she tasted like coffee and toothpaste. He remembered her, not from twenty years ago, but from last night.

He gave her a kiss on the forehead and headed for the door.

"Come outside with me and see this sky."

"It's cold," she said, but picked up her mug and followed.

"Don't be a sissy," he told her as he opened the door.

The sky was indeed beautiful, eighty different shades of pink and lavender and blue. Emma took a sip of her coffee and leaned up against the porch rail.

Jack came up behind her and put an arm around her waist.

"An unusual thing happened this morning, Emma," he said. "It took a few minutes for me to put my finger on what it was."

"What was it?" she asked him.

"I woke up happy," he said.

That afternoon, while Jack and Becca were taking some eggs and a pound cake over to Brother Fillmore's, Emma hung some sheets on the line. It was a bright day and a fairly assertive breeze was blowing. Emma hated that it would soon be too cold and dreary to hang the laundry on the line.

She hung the flat sheet from her bed and smoothed it out; it made her think of last night and she started smiling. At first it was a small and privately pleased smile, but it soon overtook her entire face as she put her nose up to the sheet, closed her eyes and remembered.

Jack Canfield loved her. Last night, the love of her life had made love to her and it was sweeter, more overwhelming and more intense than anything she had ever known outside of giving birth.

It was so unlikely as to be ridiculous, but he loved her.

Emma threw the sheet up in the air so it billowed over her head and couldn't stop herself from running in place for just a second. She wished there was such a thing as grass angels, because she wanted to throw herself down on her back and make some.

She contented herself with jumping up and down, twirling around a few times and laughing out loud, then checked to make sure no one was looking. Ed sat a few feet away and seemed ready to ask if she was alright and that was enough to embarrass her just a little.

But not enough to keep her from swinging around the clothesline pole a couple of times.

Jack was halfway across the hall, an armload of hanging clothes over one arm and his favorite pillow under the other, when Becca came running up the stairs and stopped.

"Hey, Jack," she said.

"Hey, Little Bit," he said back.

"What are you doing?" she asked him.

"Uh, I'm moving my stuff into the other room," he said. "Into your Mom's room."

"Oh. I thought you said you had to sleep in your room because you snored," she said.

"Yeah, well. I got over that," he said.

"That's good," she said. "I used to pee the bed, but I got over that, too."

"Well, that's good, too," Jack answered.

"I hope you guys aren't gonna be as noisy as Miss Regina and Mr. Dew," she said.

"Do what?" Jack managed.

"Miss Regina told Allie it's 'cause they have a lot of tickle fights," she said.

Jack looked down at the floor a second before he answered.

"Well, I'm not real ticklish," he said to her.

"Mommy is," Becca said. "She says Great-Grandma used to be able to tickle her from across the room, just by pretending she was."

"Is that a fact?" Jack asked. "I'll have to give that a try some time."

"I'm starving," Becca said and spun around and headed back down the stairs.

Jack stood there for a second, then headed for Emma's room.

Emma was on her back across the bed, holding a pillow over her face. He couldn't hear her laughing, but he could see her stomach bouncing.

He hung his clothes up in the space she'd made for him and threw his pillow at her head.

"Of course, I think you suck right now," he said.

He heard a snort from under the pillow.

"You know, I can move my stuff right back across that hall," he said.

Emma took the pillows off of her face.

"No, you will not," she said.

Jack looked at her lying there and smiled.

"Okay, maybe not."

He picked his Dopp kit up off of the bed and looked around.

"Where would you like me to put my bathroom stuff?" he asked her.

"Wherever you want," she said. "I mean, it's supposed to be your room, too."

Jack tapped his fingers on the leather bag and looked at her a minute.

"Strange," he said finally.

"A little strange," she said, nodding. "But good."

"Yes. Good," he said.

He went into the bathroom, took his cologne and deodorant out of his Dopp kit and opened the medicine cabinet. He paused for a second or two before setting them inside, then took a pink plastic disk off of the shelf and leaned up against the bedroom doorway.

Emma had put his pillow on the bed and was pulling the quilt up over it.

"I don't want to come across as jealous and overbearing," he said, "but please take fewer than seven seconds to explain why you're on the pill."

Emma turned around and looked at him holding up her birth control pills. She sat down on the bed and smiled before she spoke.

"I had some trouble with my cycle," she said. "So they put me on a low-dose pill."

"Thank you," he said simply and went to put them back. "Your answer pleases me greatly."

Emma smiled as he came back into the bedroom.

"Emma, I've never been in love with a woman in my life, though I did try," he said. "Now I'm in love with a woman I've known almost *all* my life. It might take me a bit to figure out how to be."

"That's okay," she said and tried to give him a grin. "As long as you're in love with me."

"I am that, Emma," he told her.

He reached into his duffel and pulled out a rather large automatic pistol.

"Why do you have a gun?" she asked him, surprised she was surprised.

"Because I'm a Marine," he said, pulling a magazine from his bag. "And because I'm from Alabama. Does it bother you, Emma?"

"No, not with you," she said.

He looked around, then put the gun and clip on the top shelf of the closet.

"Don't worry, it's got a trigger lock and it's unloaded," he said.

He closed the closet door and stood by the bed.

"Do you know how to shoot?" he asked her.

"No," she said. "But that's one thing I wouldn't mind learning."

"You will," he said.

He sat down on the bed and pulled her onto his lap.

"We'll get used to this, sugar," he said. "Although that might happen faster if you take Miss Margret's needlepoint pillow off this bed."

"Why?" she asked, smiling.

"Because," he said. "If I had seen it last night, I might not have had the ability to amaze and astonish you like I did."

"It's a pillow, Jack."

"It's her pillow. On her bed," he added. "Where I have just recently undertaken having relations with her granddaughter."

Emma laughed at him.

"I can't help thinking she's gonna walk in on us and beat me within an inch of my life."

"Want to hear something nuts?" Emma asked him, smiling. "Miss Mary told me something at the barbecue. She said Grandma told her the only man who'd ever be good enough for me was the one she raised."

Jack felt like she'd just punched him in the chest. Then they both looked toward the door as they heard Becca calling Emma from downstairs.

"Really," Emma said, standing up. "Isn't it funny the way God does things sometimes?"

Jack watched Emma walk out of the room.

"Yeah," he said quietly. "God's a really goofy guy."

Thanksgiving Day was cool and clear and smelled of damp leaves and wood smoke.

Most years, Emma and Becca went to Regina and Dew's to celebrate the holiday, but after some discussion, Jack said he'd prefer to have a small Thanksgiving at home and then head to Regina and Dew's later for football.

So it was just the four of them for dinner, counting Brother Fillmore, who was always an honored guest at somebody's house. Nevertheless, Emma cooked for twenty, as she really didn't know any other way to cook Thanksgiving. When

Grandma had been alive, there had always been lots of friends and neighbors over.

Emma was finishing setting the kitchen table when Jack, Becca and Brother Fillmore came in from the living room.

"Things sure do smell good in here, Emma Lee," Brother Fillmore said as he went to stand behind one of the chairs.

"Thank you, Brother Fillmore," she said.

"I helped bake Great Grandma's pumpkin and apple pies," Becca said.

"She did," Emma said. "Grandma would be proud."

Jack leaned over to look at the gravy Emma was setting on the table.

"Is that Miss Margret's gravy, too?" he asked.

"Well, no, "Emma said with an apologetic shrug. "My gravy's actually better, but we don't speak of it."

"I'm surprised an asteroid didn't just come flying through that window on you," he said and kissed her temple.

"Everybody sit," Emma said and sat down as Jack pulled out her chair.

"Lord, we thank Thee for this, Thy bounty," Brother Fillmore prayed once everyone had joined hands. "We thank Thee, too, for family and for the love of good friends. We ask that You will sanctify this food to our bodies and our bodies to Your glory. In Jesus' name we pray, Amen."

Everyone echoed his "Amen" and let go of each other's hands.

"Emma Lee, this sure is a beautiful feast," Brother Fillmore said.

"Thank you," she told him.

Emma smiled as everyone passed around the turkey, mashed potatoes, stuffing and other fixings. She had been especially meticulous about her cooking this year. Although she didn't want to be maudlin on her second-favorite holiday, she couldn't help but know that if the doctors were to be believed, this would be Jack's last Thanksgiving. To her mind, that made it the most important Thanksgiving.

So she'd taken great care with her seasoning, tasting as she cooked to be sure there was just the right amount of sugar in the glazed carrots, the perfect ratio of apples to celery in the stuffing. She wanted everything to be as perfect as possible for Jack and as she watched him taste everything and proclaim it amazing, she felt like she'd accomplished something more important than good food.

Later on, after some pie and a game of Scrabble with Brother Fillmore, they saw him home and continued on to the Porters' for more but different pies and the all-important Iron Bowl, the annual rivalry game between Alabama and Auburn. In Alabama, the Iron Bowl had all the importance of aliens landing in the middle of Birmingham.

Dew and Regina's house was packed to the rafters with every iteration of relative and the noise level was almost painful, yet somehow joyous. Even the littlest children had a Tide cap, shirt or socks on, though most of them never saw the game.

This year, it was a night game. The youngest kids were either in bed or shoved into the dining room to play board games by kick-off and it was just as well. The game was of the nail-biting, screaming, chair-vacating variety, dramatic and exciting, even for an Iron Bowl.

Jack enjoyed it immensely, and enjoyed the camaraderie and fun that went with it. It had been a long time since he'd been much of a social person and he'd forgotten that he wasn't a complete loner.

The only thing that marred his night was the realization that the most exciting Iron Bowl he'd ever seen, with a record-breaking 55-44 score for 'Bama, was also the last Iron Bowl he would see. He put the thought out of his mind and enjoyed the evening for what it was.

Later that night, he awoke from a dream he couldn't remember, even immediately after. Emma was curled up behind him, her face on his back and her knees tucked in behind his. Her arm was around his chest and when he woke he was holding her hand in both of his.

He'd never really thought before about the

intimacy of just sleeping with someone. Maybe it was because of the vulnerability of sleep or maybe it was just because it was Emma, but he thought that the simple act of sleeping with her was as intimate and honest as anything he'd ever done.

That Saturday, Jack, Emma and Becca went to the Christmas tree lot by the True Value and chose two Christmas trees. One was an impressive and fragrant specimen, the other the most pathetic and forlorn example they could find, in honor of Charlie Brown.

They set the Charlie Brown tree up on a table in the hall and Becca insisted on decorating it herself as Jack and Emma set up the big tree in the living room. Jack had brought down the boxes of decorations from the attic and, after they strung the lights, they opened up a lifetime's collection of ornaments.

Most of the decorations were made by Miss Margret and reflected several different crafting phases she'd been through. There were little plastic canvas reindeer, cross-stitched Santa faces and misshapen gift boxes made from painted clay. But Grandma's favorites had been the ornaments the children had made, Daniel and Jack and, later on, Emma.

Emma lifted the top from the box and un-

228

See You

folded the tissue paper that covered the cardboard dividers. The first ornament she pulled out was a small plaster of Paris disc with her father's handprint on it, made when he was seven years old. It was painted red and green and "Daniel 1964" was scrawled on the back in block letters.

She smiled and hung it on one of the branches, then reached into the compartment next to it to lift out her favorite. It was almost identical to the first, but on the back, in much smaller, neater writing, was "Merry Christmas Miss Margret from Jack 1964."

Emma brushed her thumb across the writing, as she often had.

"I got my first Christmas present that year," said Jack quietly. "In this house."

"Your first?" Emma asked him.

"That I can recall. My daddy didn't believe in Christmas," Jack said. "Or anything else, for that matter. But he was only too happy to let me come stay over here Christmas Eve. It was just the three of us. You know how she always liked us to open one present on Christmas Eve. Hers was the first gift I remember getting."

"What was it?" she asked as she handed him his own handprint.

"A Bible," he said and hung the handprint up near the top. "Same one I have now."

Emma smiled and Jack reached into the box of ornaments.

"Well, looky here," he said, smiling.

He held up a clear, plastic ball with a cut-out picture of nine-year old Emma in it. She was grinning, showing a missing tooth.

"Augh," Emma said, smiling.

She reached into the box as Jack hung her ornament on the tree.

"Why'd you stop going to church, Emma?" he asked without looking at her.

She was a little startled by the question and felt a bit put on the spot.

"I didn't, not really," she said. "I just don't go to First Baptist anymore. I only went there because of Grandma. But there's a really cool church that we go to. I just haven't been in a few months."

"Why not?" he asked her.

"I don't know. Laziness," she said. "And it's all the way in Eufaula."

"We should go," Jack said quietly, hanging a papier-mâché candy cane that Daniel had made.

"Do you want to?" Emma asked.

"Yeah."

"Okay," she said, smiling a little. "It's nothing like First Baptist. The music's a lot more contemporary. I don't know ... will you like that?"

Jack smiled over at her.

"I have every album Third Day ever made," he said, smiling. "There I go, crawling out of your pigeon hole again. I went to First Baptist because of her."

"Do you want to go tomorrow?"

"I do," he said.

"Well, okay then," she said.

They hung a few more ornaments in silence.

"It's your birthday next week," he said.

"Yes, it is," she said, startled that he remembered.

"I'm just full of surprises, aren't I?" he asked her. "What do you want for your birthday, Emma Lee?"

She thought about it for a moment.

"A day with you," she said.

"Consider it promised," he said back.

Jack let Emma drive them the thirty miles or so to Eufaula. He'd been letting her drive more and more and she knew he wondered if he really should be driving at all.

She ought not to have worried much about whether Jack would like the church, a non-denominational, fairly new church that was located in what used to be a skating rink. He seemed to like everything just fine, from the young pastor with the blue jeans and dry sense of humor to the very contemporary, sometimes loud music.

At the end of the service, Jack took her hand as everyone bowed their heads to pray. Emma snuck a quick look at Jack and saw that a tear was hanging from the tip of his nose. She wondered if his prayers were anything like hers. She had prayed what she always prayed. *Please let me keep this man.*

Chapter 15

THE MORNING OF Emma's birthday, Jack had started out being especially nice, letting Emma sleep in while he got Becca ready for school and walked her out to the school bus. But then he ruined everything by announcing at the kitchen table that he was going to teach her how to change the oil in the truck.

"But it's my birthday," she said to him.

"Which is relevant to what?"

"Which is relevant to how much I don't want to do it," she said.

"I feel all kinds of bad about that," he said.

Two hours later, Jack stood over Emma's feet, listening to her under the truck, mumbling things he probably didn't need a translator for. As he stood there with his hands on his hips, he listened to what seemed like an unnecessary amount of clanking and pondered her ankles.

She'd looked so cute, in old jeans and one of his flannel shirts, that he'd almost told her he'd changed his mind and she could do whatever she wanted with her day. Now, he was a little sorry that he hadn't; she was a pain in the neck to teach something she didn't want to learn.

But as he stared down at her legs poking out from under the truck, he had to admit that she was somewhat adorable when she was frustrated or angry. Today she was all three and he started thinking about skipping lunch.

"Crap!" she yelled from under the truck.

"Now what?" he asked her.

"It's this stupid—" she started off, then dribbled off into a bunch of stuff he couldn't exactly understand, punctuated by a lot of jerking and kicking from her boots. A few seconds later, the oil filter came flying out from under the side of the truck.

"I can't get it back on there!" she yelled.

He stood there, looking down at her feet while she drummed them on the blanket he'd folded up and put down there for her.

"What seems to be the problem?" he asked her.

"What's the problem?" she yelled.

Jack couldn't help smiling.

"I'll tell you what the stupid problem is, you jerk," she said.

She commenced with what looked like a sincere effort to scoot out from under the truck, but which really just amounted to a bunch of foot-scissoring, since her knees were under the truck.

Jack started to laugh, then bent down and yanked on the blanket, pulling her out from under the truck. She had black smudges all over her face and looked like she was going to bite something.

"Screw it," he said. "Twenty bucks at Pep Boys. I need to take you upstairs."

"Right now?" she asked, still scowling as he pulled her up onto her feet.

"Well, it's a little too late to have done it already," he said as he pulled her toward the house.

That evening, the three of them had a quiet dinner and then Becca presented Emma with a rather convex chocolate cake that she and Jack had managed to put together, and a book that Becca had made out of construction paper and ribbon.

In the book were crayon drawings of beaches and flowers and chickens and other things that Emma particularly liked, including a picture of Jack in his Crimson Tide cap. Emma attempted not to cry and pulled Becca in for a hug.

"You're the most awesome creature, Joybug," she said.

Becca sat down and Jack pulled a tiny, gift-wrapped box out of his shirt pocket and set it down in front of her. Emma looked at him and smiled before carefully unwrapping it. She lifted the top away and saw a delicate white flower pendant, with leaves made of tiny bits of tourmaline.

"Jack, it's beautiful," she said. "Is that a gardenia?"

"It is," he said. "I ordered it last month from a guy that makes custom jewelry over in New Orleans."

Emma smiled at him, thinking she might start crying and blowing snot around. He smiled back, then he took the necklace out of the box, stood behind her and hung it on her neck.

"It's beautiful, Mommy," Becca said, then grabbed the box of candles. "Can I stick the candles in?"

"Yes," she said and grabbed Jack's other hand as he bent over the table and started lighting the only five candles they had in the house.

Jack sat back down and Emma saw the flames reflected in his eyes as he watched her.

"Time to make a wish, Mommy!"

"Okay," Emma said.

She looked at the candles for a second, then took a deep breath and blew them out. When she looked back over at Jack, he was still watching her. She smiled at him and he gave her a wink.

December was coming in cold and bright, with few clouds and days filled with a light that seemed to make every color somehow more true.

If anything, Jack seemed to be having fewer headaches and Emma settled back into her writing with a focus afforded by not feeling a need to check on him quite so much. When Emma took breaks or once Becca was in bed, she and Jack spent their time alternately flirting with each other and arguing their opinions on literature.

Their one agreement was on the best poem ever written; both of them would defend to the death that Poe's "The Raven" was uncontested. This led to an admission from Emma that she had fallen instantly and unrepentantly in love with Poe when she'd first read "Annabel Lee."

That, of course, led to some teasing from Jack, who agreed that *Annabel Lee* was a truly romantic poem, but failed to see the appeal of an opium-addicted writer who also happened to be dead. Emma tried to explain, but ended up too defensive and frustrated to be effective and settled for declaring him an infidel.

With each morning, they gradually became a little less shy about waking up in the same bed and felt a little less wary that someone was going to show up to ask them why they were. There were still awkward moments, when one or the other would come out of the shower or one or the other was the first to reach out at night. But they were slowly becoming more comfortable with their changing landscape.

One day, Jack seemed unusually quiet but insisted, each time Emma asked, that he was feeling fine. It left her distracted and worried, even more so when he announced after dinner that he was going for a short drive. Emma considered arguing the wisdom of it and he seemed to be expecting that, but she let it go.

An hour or so later, Emma sat on the swing on the front porch, wrapped in her old barn jacket, sipping coffee she didn't really need and waiting for Jack to come home. When he finally pulled in, she felt so much tension leave her muscles that she was afraid she might slide off the swing.

"Hey," Jack said as he came up the steps and crossed the porch.

"Hey," she said back.

Jack sat down beside her.

"I'm sorry if I worried you," he said.

Emma looked at his profile. He looked tired and somehow closed up and she was reminded of how unreadable he had seemed to her in the past, of how she hadn't really known him much at all. The thought made her feel uncertain, like she was walking through an unfamiliar room in the dark.

"Are you okay?" she asked him.

"Yes," he said. He didn't look at her, but he put an arm around her and gently squeezed her shoulder.

"I went to your daddy's—your parents' graves," he said.

Emma was immediately ashamed.

"I forgot," she said.

She'd never really observed the anniversary much since Grandma had passed, but she'd never forgotten it, either.

"I'm sorry. I would have gone with you," she said.

"No," he said quietly. "I haven't been there since the funeral. I wanted to go by myself."

Emma sat and watched his profile and he finally looked at her.

"It's fine," he said.

Emma handed him her coffee and he took a sip.

"What was he like?" she asked him. "Everything I've ever heard ... it seems like you two were so different."

Jack looked at her for a minute before answering.

"We were. Like night and day," he said. "I

think we became friends at first because we were about the same age when he lost his Daddy and my mother died. But we became best friends because we genuinely loved each other."

He looked away, out into the yard.

"Your Daddy got a bad rap because he was a little wild. He smoked and he drank and he had a real mouth." He looked at Emma and almost smiled. "Like you," he said.

"People always kind of expected that from me because I came from white trash, but if I wasn't on the football field, I was reading a book or studying or just having fun, not really getting into much trouble."

Emma waited for him to continue, but Jack stared down at the porch floor.

"It sounds like he must have given Grandma some grief," she said.

Jack looked at her.

"Oh, yeah, he did," Jack said. "But as much trouble as he gave her, he would have walked through fire twice for that woman. He loved her."

Jack swallowed hard and looked away for a second before he looked back at Emma.

"He was a little wild, but he was also incredibly loyal and he couldn't abide meanness," he said. "He was a wiry little guy, but he'd defend anybody that needed defending."

He took another sip of the coffee and handed it back to Emma. It was cold.

"One time when we were about fourteen, Daniel got into a fight out in the school parking lot," Jack said. "There was this big black kid. His name was Andre and he was a really quiet kid, shy. Hung out with the girls mostly. It was like '72-73, something like that and it wasn't a really good time around here for black guys, shy or otherwise."

Jack's eyes drifted back out into the yard and Emma put her coffee down so she could stuff her hands into her pockets.

"Anyway, Daniel went out in the parking lot to grab a cigarette, waiting on me to get out of football practice, and these three white boys were giving Andre a hard time, knocking his books out of his hands, pushing him around a little. I think Andre'd missed his bus and he was waiting on someone to come get him."

Jack sighed and ran a hand through his hair.

"A bunch of other kids were standing around, some of them egging it on, others just watching, not knowing what to do. When I got out there a few minutes later, Daniel was on the ground, and all three of those boys were beating on him and kicking him. It was bad," he said. "I got in there, got into it a little bit, finally got the thing broken up and everybody left. Andre was already long gone."

He looked at Emma and smiled.

"I said, 'Daniel, what the hell? Why didn't you wait for me? You had to know you were gonna get your ass beat'. And he just said, 'Andre didn't get his beat, though, did he?'"

Jack smiled again, but it was something of a sad smile.

"I may have been the good kid, but he was brave and he was kind and he had honor," Jack said. "You're a lot like him, Emma Lee."

Emma felt a hot tear roll down her cheek and Jack wiped it away with a knuckle.

"What do you think he would think about us?" she asked him.

Jack looked at her a long time before answering.

"If he had lived and all of this somehow happened anyway ... I don't know," he said. "But as it is now, I think he's probably okay with it. He would want me to take care of you."

Jack cleared his throat and looked away.

"Jack. That's not why—" she started.

"Oh, hell no," he said emphatically. "I love you because I do."

He looked at her and pulled her to him.

"Come here, dumbass," he said and wrapped his other arm around her.

Emma put an arm around his stomach and laid her head down on his chest. They sat there for some time, Jack gently rocking the swing with one foot.

"You want me to take you somewhere, Emma Lee?" he said after a while.

"Where?" she asked him.

"I don't know. Disney World, New Orleans. Somewhere," he said. "Since I didn't have sense enough to fall in love with you before we got married, I feel like you got cheated out of a wedding. Thought maybe you'd like a honeymoon or a vacation or something. We could take Becca."

Emma sat up and looked at him.

"Do you want to go somewhere?" she asked him.

"I don't need to, but I'd be happy to do it," he said.

Emma thought about it for a minute.

"Honestly, I'm happy right here," she said. "Besides...."

"Besides, what?"

"You said you wanted to be here," she told him reluctantly.

"Are you saying 'no' because you're afraid something will happen somewhere else?"

"No, I'm saying 'no' because I don't really care to go anywhere," she said. "I like us being here, where we've always been. Kind of like we're in our own little world."

"Emma, I would prefer to be here when the time comes," he said quietly. "But as long as you were there, it wouldn't really matter all that much where we were. I'd still be home."

Emma put her head back on his chest and hugged him.

"I just thought it was something you might want to do," he said.

Emma sighed into his jacket and spoke before she thought enough not to.

"To be honest, if we could do anything, I'd want to just sit here and plan the next five years of our lives," she said.

Jack's arm tightened around her shoulder and Emma instantly regretted her words.

"Jack, I'm sorry," she said. "That was such a thoughtless thing to say."

He was quiet for a minute.

"No, it wasn't," he said. "Maybe we'll do that some time. Just for fun."

A little over a week later, Jack put his hands on the sink to steady himself as he waited for the shower water to get hot.

He'd had a low-grade headache most of the day. Warmth always seemed to help, so Emma had made him a hot washcloth after lunch and he'd sat back in the recliner and dozed.

But during dinner, the headache had come back with a vengeance and he'd noticed that his sense of smell was off. For just a second, his steak had smelled of fresh-cut grass and then it hadn't smelled like anything at all.

He was glad that Emma had closed herself and Becca up in the kitchen to wrap presents, so that he could deal with the headache out of Emma's sight. He knew she knew he hurt; he just didn't want her to notice how much.

Finally, when Becca and Emma had put their packages under the tree and Emma had gone to tuck Becca into bed, he'd come upstairs to take a pain pill and a hot shower.

He took a few deep breaths as he leaned on the sink and tried to ignore the scent of cut grass again. Or maybe it was kerosene. He shook his head and reached over to see if the water was hot. The sudden motion made his head spin and he leaned over the toilet just in time to throw up.

Emma had changed into her robe and was waiting for Jack to get out of the shower so she could take hers. She was just about to sit down on the bed and brush her hair out when she heard a noise from the bathroom.

It took her a second to realize that it was retching.

"Jack?" she called to him. He didn't answer, but she heard the toilet flush and she jumped up and hurried to the bathroom.

When she opened the door, he was standing in the shower, one hand on the wall and listing just a little.

"Jack, are you okay?" she asked him.

He nodded but didn't look at her. If his head didn't hurt so much, he thought, he would feel almost angry with her. He couldn't stand the idea of appearing weak in front of anyone, least of all her.

Emma walked over to the shower. Obviously, Jack was in pain and she felt guilty that her first thought, on walking into the bathroom, was how beautiful he really was.

"Do you need a pain pill?"

"Took it," he said. "Just a little woozy."

He was standing at the end of the tub, outside the spray. He turned his back to her, putting his other hand on the wall as well.

"Maybe you should get out," she said.

"No. I want the water," he said, shaking his head. "Just getting my bearings."

Emma thought for a second, then dropped her robe and got in behind him. She put a hand on his back and wrapped her other arm around him.

"It's okay, Emma." He really wanted her to get out of the shower, get out of the bathroom. He needed her to let him alone until he could be himself.

Emma looked up at the shower head, then let go of Jack and turned the knob so the water poured through the tub faucet. Then she dropped the plug into the drain and got down on her knees to face him.

"Come here," she said. "Sit down."

He looked down at her and wished he had the heart to tell her to go.

"I'll be okay, Emma," he said through a wave of pain that tired him and fogged his vision.

"I know," she said. "Please come here."

He wanted to ask her to please leave him, but as he looked at her, so naked and honest there on her knees, she humbled him and drew him at the same time. He turned and sat down in front of her. He felt her hand on his shoulder and he put his head down and tried to breathe.

Emma dumped the shower poufs and sponges out of their Tupperware container and set it under the flow until it was half full. Then she put her hand on his chest and gently pressed.

"Lean back," she said.

He hesitated a second before he leaned back until his head was resting on her stomach. She picked up the container and slowly poured the water over his head. Then she did it again and again and again.

A little while later, Jack climbed into bed and laid down on his back, his eyes already closed.

Emma climbed in next to him and laid on her side, started running her fingers through his hair the way she sometimes did for Becca when she couldn't sleep.

"That's nice," he said.

"How's your head?" she asked him.

"S'okay," he said. "Just sleepy."

"Do you want some water or anything?" she asked. He shook his head.

"Just talk to me a minute, maybe read me something," he said. "No, "The Raven." Prove it."

"What?"

"You said you know it by heart," he said.

"I do."

"Prove it," he said, his voice almost a whisper.

Emma scooted closer to him, put her head on his shoulder as she ran her fingers through his hair, so beautiful and soft and smelling of coconut.

"'Once upon a midnight dreary, while I pondered, weak and weary,'" she started and Jack gave a little smile. "'Over many a quaint and curious volume of forgotten lore; While I nodded, nearly napping, suddenly there came a tapping; As of someone gently rapping, rapping at my chamber door...'"

Emma recited the poem almost without thinking, and as she did, her fingers brushed across the scar from Jack's surgery, just above his right ear.

She realized, as she rubbed his head, that her fingers were just a few inches or maybe even an inch away from the thing that sought to take him away, and she wondered why it was that she could be that close to it and not be able or allowed to just pluck it out.

It seemed to her that she ought to be able to reach just a few inches further and rip the thing out like the parasitic evil that it was. As she recited the poem, keeping her voice even and soft, a red hot anger burned in her chest until she thought she might just burst into flames right there in the bed.

The anger felt good, better than the fear, but then it subsided and she was left with tears falling out of the corners of her eyes and onto the sheet, as though they'd put the fire out.

Halfway through the poem, she had nothing else to be but afraid, and she tried to soothe herself, with both the poem and the sound of Jack's steady breathing.

"'And my soul from out that shadow that lies floating on the floor; Shall be lifted—nevermore,'" she finished and looked at Jack's face.

"Jack? Are you awake?" she asked quietly.

Jack continued breathing and said nothing. Emma reached over and turned out the lamp, then scooted down and rested her head on his stomach. She felt the warmth from his body, the gentle rocking as his stomach lifted and fell with his breathing, and she closed her eyes.

"Please stop dying," she whispered.

The next morning, Jack woke up slowly. His mouth felt like cotton and his eyes were gritty and unfocused.

He blinked a few times until they started to clear and saw that it was still dark outside, with just the barest indication of dawn. Then he rolled onto his side and looked at Emma's face on the pillow beside him. Her mouth was slightly open and her hair was messy and covering half her face.

He watched her for a long time, then reached out and brushed some of the hair back from her eyes.

For more than thirty years, she had been almost a niece and he had been almost a stranger. Then, with what seemed like lightning speed, she'd gone from being his spouse in name only to being his lover and the woman he loved.

But at some point last night in that bathtub, while she knelt naked and unprotected behind him, something he didn't even know existed had changed.

She'd seen him at his weakest without the slightest hint of pity on her face. Then, while she'd poured cups of water and her own strength over his head, she'd somehow become his wife. And he had become her husband.

He hadn't done anything to deserve lying there at that moment, staring at someone who loved him. But as he watched her face, he thought that maybe he'd discovered yet another definition of grace.

Chapter 16

THEY SPENT A QUIET Christmas Eve.
After going to the River City Grill in Eufaula for some shrimp and grits, they
came home and changed into some variation of
pajamas, laid a fire, turned on the radio for some
Christmas music and each of them opened one
gift.

The family tradition was for the Christmas
Eve gift to be something small. When Jack, Daniel and Emma were kids, the gift was usually
something to do, to occupy them in their rooms
while Miss Margret wrapped last-minute gifts,
baked pies and watched *White Christmas* in her

fuzzy red robe.

Jack and Emma presented Becca with a boxed set of the *Little House* books, which was received with a level of excitement and awe that made the two bookworms happy. Becca insisted that Jack and Emma's Christmas Eve gifts be the ones that she had made, and was quite proud of her wrapping, which looked like something Ed might have done.

For Emma, she'd made a bead bracelet with little snowflake charms, which Emma slipped immediately onto her wrist.

When Jack opened his gift, he pulled out an ornament that Becca had made at school. It was a round, wooden ornament, which she had hand painted in bright, primary colors. The figures circling the ornament were somewhat crude, but recognizable as Jack, Becca, Emma and even the cats on hind legs, all holding hands.

Jack proclaimed it the finest ornament he'd ever seen and made a big deal of discussing with Becca the most advantageous place to hang it on the tree. Emma watched them do it with a mixture of pride, contentment and fear. She couldn't help but wonder how it was going to feel to hang that ornament next Christmas.

She put such thoughts out of her mind as she and Becca put out milk and cookies for Santa and a carrot for the reindeer.

Then Becca begged to be allowed to sleep

with them that night and after they agreed, she scurried upstairs to read in bed, with a promise that she wouldn't come back down. Once she was gone, Emma ate most of the carrot and Jack had the milk and cookies.

When they woke up Christmas morning, Jack put forth that sleeping with Becca was like sleeping with a sack of broken boomerangs and made a show of limping downstairs to get his coffee before the child and the noise level rose simultaneously.

But Jack had what he thought was his best Christmas in years, maybe ever. It wasn't because of anything special or momentous that he could name and he didn't think it was because this Christmas was certainly his last. He was pretty sure it was because of Emma, the same Emma that he had spent more than a few Christmases with, without ever realizing how important she would become to his life at the end of it.

After breakfast and presents and the cleaning up after both, they drove over to Dew and Regina's for more noise, more presents and a table loaded to breaking with ham, collards, black-eyed peas, sweet potatoes, homemade rolls and a dozen other ways to put home on a plate and feed it to someone.

Everyone had a great time, eating too much, settling squabbles between kids and starting squabbles with adults. Emma and Jack enjoyed it immensely and the only moment that Emma was anything other than happy was the moment she realized that she resented Regina just a little bit.

Regina had been teasing Dew, pretending to find fault with the fact that he gave her a weirder sweater every year, reliable as Christmas itself, and she'd said she had about forty of them in her closet to prove it.

Emma had laughed along with everyone else, but what she'd thought was that Regina was awfully fortunate to have forty years of sweaters from her man. She knew Regina adored Dew and she doubted that she took him for granted, but for just a moment, Emma had resented her all the same.

Becca was sound asleep before they even pulled into the driveway and Emma gathered their gifts while Jack gathered Becca. As Emma watched Jack carry the child upstairs, she noticed how quiet their house was in comparison to the Porters'. It wasn't the first time she'd noticed it; it had been a remarkable difference all of her life.

But watching Jack take Becca upstairs to bed, she noticed that the silence tonight was the absence of other children, the lack of brothers or sisters to whisper to Becca about the gifts, the day, the fun. As the only child to a widowed woman, Emma had felt comfortable living alone with

Becca, until just then, and she thought for the first time about the possibility of having a child with Jack.

But she had no idea how she would start that conversation and she knew Christmas wasn't the time, so when Jack came back downstairs, she told him to come into the kitchen with her for one last gift.

She grabbed his hand and pulled him behind her, pulled a chair out from the table and told him to sit. Then she told him to close his eyes.

"What's on your mind, Emma?" he asked her, grinning.

"Just a little something I thought of," Emma said, going into the pantry. "I was going to give it to you last night, but Becca had her heart set on giving you your Christmas Eve present."

She came out of the pantry with a quart jar of sliced peaches and opened them up and grabbed a fork before going to the table.

"Why are my eyes closed?" Jack asked her.

"Because," Emma told him and sat down on his lap facing him. "Keep them closed and open your mouth."

"You're frightening me," he said, but he put his hands on her waist.

"Just do it," Emma said, laughing.

She speared a slice of peach and held it over her other palm.

"Open your mouth, Jack," she said.

He did and Emma put the peach into his mouth. He smiled and chewed.

"Can I open my eyes now?" he asked her.

"No, not yet."

"You're giving me peaches for Christmas?"

Emma picked up the jar, speared another slice and held it over the jar to catch the drips.

"Open," she said. He did and she put the peach in his mouth.

"Just taste it, Jack. Really taste it," she said quietly.

"Okay. What is it?" he asked her.

"It's summer," she said. "These are the peaches we canned the first week you were home."

Jack slowly chewed and swallowed the peach, opened his eyes and looked at her for a minute. Then he reached into the jar, took out a slice of peach and put it into Emma's mouth.

"Sure seems like that was a long time ago, doesn't it?" he asked her.

Emma swallowed before answering him.

"Like a long time ago and like last week," she said. "Everything is so different."

"Yes," Jack said and ran his clean hand through her hair. "Thank God."

"Yes," she said.

They ate the entire jar of peaches that night. Jack couldn't help thinking that it reminded him of taking communion, but instead of the flesh of

Christ it was the love of a woman, and the taste of the time he'd spent with her.

A few weeks after Christmas came Becca's birthday. As much as Emma had always disliked having a birthday in December, Becca disliked having hers in January even more. She was somewhat jealous of the friends who were able to have pool parties for their birthdays, whether or not they had pools at their disposal.

Becca was, however, entirely enthralled when she woke up to find there was snow on the ground. Snow that stuck in that part of Alabama was only slightly more common than having neighbors from New Jersey and generally regarded more kindly.

All plans for board games and Pin the Tail on the Donkey were abandoned in the face of such serendipity and everyone made makeshift sleds out of cardboard boxes, deflated pool floats and even one genuine inner tube.

A large assortment of Porter minors was in attendance, as well as a smattering of kids from school and their parents and it became hard to tell kid from adult based on behavior. Everyone attacked the back yard with reckless abandon, or at least as reckless as a slightly sloping property would allow.

By late afternoon, the snow had melted away and most of the younger kids and a good portion of the adults went inside for hot chocolate, more food and warmer play. Dew and Jack got the idea to throw together a football game and Emma was invited to join.

Never having played the game, she was going to decline and just sit and watch, but she was compelled to accept when Jack seemed to find the idea of her playing hilarious. It was for that reason that Emma was glad when she was picked to be on Dew's team. She was certain that her playing was no more ridiculous than Regina, who had traded her stilettos for a pair of Jack's rain boots and was standing there in a bright purple sweater covered in pink snowflakes.

As everyone was taking off coats and rolling up sleeves, Emma took Jack aside.

"Should you be playing football?" she asked him. "Getting tackled and stuff?"

"I'd play football with a pipe sticking out of my head, Emma Lee," Jack said. "And right this minute, I cannot tell you how badly I want to play."

He saw the worry in her eyes and felt badly for it, but he just patted her on the head.

"It'll be fine," he said gently and walked over to the others.

Emma had every intention of keeping her eye on Jack and making sure he didn't get hurt.

Nevertheless, she spent most of the first half trying not to get run over and attempting to perfect a form of tackle that Jack named the "wear-down takedown". She was rarely able knock anyone down; instead, she just rode their backs until they either wore out or made a touchdown.

At the beginning of the game, Regina and Dew had a set-to over Dew's strategy of placing one of their teenaged grandkids in opposition to Regina. Regina insisted it was against the rules, since "You know I ain't gonna mow down no grandbabies!" but by an hour into the game, everyone was so agitated with competition that everybody was fair game. It may have been a backyard game, but it was still football in Alabama.

Emma had almost forgotten her worry over Jack; she was having too much fun watching him do something he obviously loved, something she'd never seen him do.

By halftime, the score was 28-21 in favor of Jack's team, all familial sentiment had been suspended and Dew's team had the ball. Jack took a look at the scrimmage line and smiled at Emma, who was positioned opposite him. They might have only half a team each, but Jack knew this play. He and Dew had run it many a time.

"Don't you do it, Emma," he said quietly.

"Do what?"

"Don't you let Dew slip you that ball. I will take it from you."

"You'll have to catch me first," she said defiantly. "I might be little, but I'm fast."

"Is that a fact?" he asked her. "This is football, lady. I won't go easy on you because you're a midget."

"Fair enough," she said. "I won't go easy on you because of your age, either."

"Y'all shut up over there," Dew yelled.

"You shut up, Dew!" Regina yelled down the line, then pointed her finger at her grandson Todd, who was hunkered down in front of her. "You get that ball, boy, you better throw it on the ground! Don't you make Nana chase you down."

At the snap, Dew feigned a pass, then spun around and tossed the ball to Emma, but the feint was pretty much pointless, as Jack was running straight for her. For a second, Emma almost threw the ball at him, but then she took off.

She made it a good ten yards or so before she felt a bus hit her back and Jack threw her to the ground. She did manage to hold onto the football, but at great expense to her chest.

She rolled over onto her back under Jack, gasping for air and wishing she didn't have breasts.

"Second-team All-Conference for the SEC, two years running," he said quietly. "I will catch you. Every single time."

Emma spat a bit of cold dirt out of her mouth.

"That's actually kinda hot," she said.

Jack sighed and dropped his head onto her chest.

"You have no business playing football," he said.

"Hey, man," Dew said calmly from above them. "Get off my little running back so I don't have to stomp you."

Jack's team ended up winning by seven points and the players all dragged themselves into the house, walking off various minor injuries. Most of the school kids and their parents drifted off for home, leaving Becca and the Porter kids to play Uno in the dining room while the adults watched a playoff game on TV.

Emma had had plenty of football for one day, but she stuck around for the opportunity to curl up next to Jack on the couch, watch him have fun and get an occasional wink or kiss.

At halftime, Jack found Becca snoring on the dining room table and carried her upstairs and Emma went into the kitchen to refill her tea. She heard Regina holler at the kids to clean up and get their shoes on, then Regina came into the kitchen.

"Are you leaving, Regina?" she asked her. "It's only halftime."

"We can watch the game at home," Regina said, putting her tea glass in the sink.

"But Jack and Dew are having fun," Emma said.

"Please," Regina said, hugging Emma. "I been in love with the same man for forty years. I know when it's time to get out somebody's house."

Chapter 17

EMMA HAD STARTED taking pictures.

She'd been looking at pictures of Jack all her life; they were everywhere, all over the house. There was Jack the little boy, Jack the high-school football star, Jack and Daniel fishing and building the chicken coop and standing next to girls in shiny pastel dresses and platform shoes.

There were pictures of Jack and Grandma, too, back when Grandma's hair was almost black. Jack in his graduation gown and cap and Grandma, already round, wearing a light blue polyester dress with a little bolero jacket. Jack in his dress blues, the day he graduated boot camp, with an arm around Grandma's shoulder. She even had one picture of Jack the groom, slow dancing with his new wife, Emma. Regina had emailed it to her and she'd printed it out and tacked it to the corkboard over her desk.

Emma had even recently found, in a cardboard box full of loose photographs, a picture of Jack that she had never seen. He was sitting on the back porch steps with a plate of barbecue in one hand. He was about thirty-five years old, his beautiful hair was cut way too short and he already had variety of lines alongside his mouth and at the corners of his eyes. He was pointing his finger and talking and Emma knew that he was saying that the best way to dream was to either read a book or write one.

She knew that because he was talking to her. There she was sitting on the other end of the step, thirteen years old and feeling self-conscious in the long, flowered skirt that Grandma had made her wear to church. She was in bare feet and had her arms wrapped around her knees.

She didn't know if it was maturity or memory, but even looking at her profile, Emma could see the adoration on her own face. She wondered why Jack never noticed and she couldn't help but wonder if Grandma had seen it, looking through the lens of her Polaroid camera. If she had, she'd loved Emma too tenderly to let her know.

After she found that photograph, she started taking pictures of her own. They were always candid shots of something going on, never posed and never too obviously meant to capture Jack.

She took pictures of Jack and Becca hanging a tire swing on one of the pecan trees, pictures of Jack and Dew with a nine-pound bass and pictures of Jack and Brother Fillmore staring at a chess board on a cold January afternoon.

What Emma really wanted was to take hundreds of pictures of Jack, close up and from every angle. Jack in every mood, Jack in every light. Just Jack, looking at the camera, looking at her. She wanted a record of every expression, every line on his face.

But she never asked him to just sit and pose for a picture. She knew that if she did, he would know exactly what she was doing and that he would feel a little bit like he was already dead.

Emma added two handfuls of knick-knacks to the assortment on the coffee table, sprayed some furniture polish onto a rag and started wiping down the bookcase. Ed and his tongue sat watching her from Ed's "blankie", an old, short bathrobe of Emma's that he had adopted as a kitten and still dragged from room to room.

Emma sneezed three times in quick succession, tiny, squeaky sounds like Ed might have made. She rubbed at her nose, flipped the rag over and was wiping the other end of the shelf when Jack came in from the kitchen eating an apple.

"Washer's fixed," he said.

"Thanks," she said and gave him a quick smile. "I'm just doing a little spring cleaning."

"In February?" he asked her.

"Well. I needed a break from the book," she said.

"How's it coming?"

"Good, I think," she answered. "I wrote almost two-thousand words this morning."

"Good words?" he asked her.

"I hope so," she said.

Jack started sifting through the knick-knacks on the table as he chewed his apple.

"When are you gonna let me read that thing?" he asked her.

Emma paused just a second in her polishing but she didn't turn around. She'd been about to make a remark about giving it to him for their anniversary, but she thought it might be unkind.

"Well, how about if I finish up the month and then you can start reading?" she asked instead. "That way, you should have a good dozen chapters to read before you catch up to me."

"That sounds fair," he said. "But for the

next three weeks, I expect to see you working, not rearranging knick-knacks or talking to your idiot cat."

"My idiot cat hangs out with you now almost as much as he does me," she said.

"Only until I catch him at it," Jack said. "You putting all this stuff back up there?"

"Yeah, why?"

"Emma," he said and Emma turned around to see him holding up a dusty plastic figurine, a pair of flamenco dancers with costumes made of fabric.

"What?" she asked him.

"For a lady that watches an awful lot of HGTV, you don't redecorate much," he answered.

"I like this house the way it is," she said.

"Is that right?" he asked her. "Aside from Becca's room, I don't think anything's changed here in the last nine years."

"So?"

"So when are you going to start making this house yours?" he asked her.

"What's wrong with it?"

"Nothing's wrong with it," he said. "As long as the plastic flamenco dancers are on the bookcase because you like plastic flamenco dancers."

Emma felt her back getting up just a bit.

"Grandma got that when she and Miss Mary went to Spain," she said. "It was important to her."

"It's not important to her anymore, Emma," Jack said quietly.

Emma put a fist on her hip.

"Well, maybe it's still important to me," she said.

"Why?" he asked.

"Because it was hers," she said.

Jack threw a hand around the room.

"It's all hers, Emma," he said. "Every single thing that was in this room when she died is still here. Maybe you threw out the TV Guide or something, but this place is exactly like she left it."

Emma couldn't understand why this seemed to bother him, especially since he hadn't really said anything about it before, other than a little teasing about the place being outdated.

"I like her things being here," she said. "I like it being the way it's always been."

"But it's still her house," Jack said. "And it should be your house."

"If it's my house, then I get to decide what it looks like," she shot back.

"Tell me how much you like that orange recliner, Emma," he said, irritation creeping into his voice. "I seem to remember you teasing her all the time that that thing was the most hideous chair you'd ever seen."

"It's comfortable."

"It's ugly. And you know what, Emma? She thought it was ugly, too," Jack said. "She got it because it was short enough for her feet to reach the floor and it was on sale."

"So?"

"So why don't you just keep a few things around that you do like and start making this your house?"

Emma felt her eyes start to sting.

"It's *our* house," she said.

"Then make it our house," he said quietly.

"What do you want me to do with it?" she asked.

"I don't care," he said. "Whatever you want. I just don't want you to … to stay stuck."

"I'm not stuck."

"Then what are you Emma? You're either stuck or you're scared or you're guilty or something," he said. "She doesn't care what you do with the flamenco dancers or the rooster wallpaper or the seven-hundred butter tubs in the pantry. She's not going to get mad at you."

"Jack, I don't think she's going to be mad at me," Emma said, starting to get angry.

"Then why are you acting like you don't want to offend her?" Jack asked. "What are you so sorry for? She lived a good, long life."

It took a moment for Emma to be sure she wouldn't either yell or cry.

"I know that," she said.

"Are you gonna do this with me, too, Emma?" he asked her more gently. "You gonna keep my cologne on the dresser and my tooth-brush by the sink?"

His words were like a glass of cold tea thrown right in her face, because she had every intention of doing just that. His words brought a picture to her mind of their toothbrushes in the Ball jar in the bathroom, hers changing periodically and his never at all.

She saw it and felt her heart break for her future self, who would want nothing more than for her husband to need a new toothbrush.

"Don't do it, Emma. Don't hang my stuff around you like some kind of shroud and don't you dare apologize to me for something you didn't do."

Emma couldn't stand to look at him just then, to let him see her future in her eyes. She looked away, looked at Ed sitting on his blank-ie watching them, his tongue hanging out like he was trying to taste their intentions. Emma wiped her nose like she had dust in it, then looked back up at Jack.

"Let me explain something to you, Jack," she said evenly. "I'll rearrange the furniture and paint and put away some of Grandma's things if you want me to. But I like the rooster wallpaper and I'll keep what I want to keep. And for the re-cord, I will do and feel whatever I please when you're gone. You do not get to tell me how to live my life without you."

"I'm not trying to hurt you, Emma," he said. "I love you."

"I love you, too," she said. "But if you touch those flamenco dancers or throw out one bottle of cologne, I will kick your sorry ass all over this house."

She threw down her rag and walked off to the bathroom to pretend to pee.

Jack looked after her for a minute, then set the flamenco dancers back on the shelf.

A few days later, Jack walked up the stairs and through the open door to the bedroom to get Emma. She was at her computer and didn't look up as he came in. Ed sat on the desk staring at nothing, which apparently was about three feet away.

"Hey," Jack said.

Emma jumped a little and turned around.

"Hey," she said back and she sounded a little nervous.

As he walked over to the desk, she sat up straight, looking like she was trying to get bigger somehow so she could block his view of the screen.

"What are you doing?" he asked.

Emma glanced back at the screen before answering.

"Just piddling. Reading," she said. She pushed the "Sleep" button on her keyboard and the screen went dark.

"Gina's out front," he said as he got to the desk. "She says you're going up to Montgomery to Sam's Club."

"Oh, yeah. I forgot," Emma answered.

"So what are you reading?" Jack asked as he pushed the sleep button again.

A medical site came on the screen, a page about brain tumors. Jack read a little of it, then looked at Emma. She looked like she'd been caught shoplifting.

"Just keeping up with things. Asking questions," she said. "I've been doing it since you told me."

Jack leaned against the desk and folded his arms across his chest.

"Why don't you just ask me?" he asked her.

"Because we don't really talk about it. You don't want to talk about it. So I look things up. I go to research sites. I read the forums," she said and then shrugged. "I ask questions."

Jack sighed and rubbed a hand over his face. He felt suddenly exhausted, like the tumors weighed a hundred pounds each and he'd just picked them up off the floor.

"What do you want to know, Emma?"

She looked surprised by the question.

"Jack, you have a brain tumor," she said. "I

want to know everything."

Jack nodded and looked past her out the window.

"I want to know what I'm supposed to do," she said. "I want to know the latest research. I want to know what other people are going through."

Jack looked back at her and the urgency on her face made him feel like he'd failed her. He didn't know if he felt like he failed her because they didn't talk about it or because he had the damn tumors in the first place. He felt a slow-burning but well-remembered anger building and he tried to push it away.

"Jack, I know you said that they can't do anything other than monitor you, but I'd still feel a lot better if you were going to the doctor anyway," Emma said.

Jack almost snapped back that it wasn't about how much better *she* felt, but of course, it was. He was angry with her for wanting and wondering things she had every right to want and wonder. It angered him that she couldn't leave it alone and it hurt him that he was angry with her at all.

"Emma, all they can do is take more MRIs and tell me bigger, more, the same. It won't change anything and it won't accomplish anything other than wasting several hours of my time."

"But the neurologist in Bethesda told you

to see this guy in Montgomery once a month," Emma said.

"What else was he supposed to say, Emma? 'You're set for unlimited refills, but there's nothing else I can do, so don't come back'?"

"I don't know," Emma said.

"Look, I'm sorry that I don't have any good answers for you," Jack said. "I'm sorry that there *are* no good answers. I know it bothers you that we don't talk about it and I guess that's unfair. But I spent two years talking about it and now I just want to deal with it as best I can."

Emma looked down at the floor a minute and tried to choose her words carefully.

"I just feel like we're dealing with it separately," she finally said.

"We are," Jack said. "We're together in every other way, Emma, but the truth is that this will end very differently for each of us and I don't think either one of us can help the other prepare for it. Not really."

Emma's eyes filled and she felt the sting of something very like rejection. She looked down at the floor again so he wouldn't see her face, but she needn't have bothered.

"Gina's waiting out front, baby," he said, and kissed her temple before heading for the door. "You need to get going."

"Okay, see you," Emma said but he was already out the door.

Emma let the front door close behind her and walked out to Regina's little yellow Kia sedan. Emma could see Regina's niece Darcy in the back, head gently bobbing while she listened to her headphones. Darcy was a sweet girl of thirteen and had been living with Dew and Gina for the last two years.

Her father was Dew's youngest brother and had become a wonderful single father when his girlfriend had up and disappeared. Now Victor was working on an oil rig to help support them, and only made it home every few months.

Regina had her window open and was singing along to a hip-hop song on the radio when Emma walked up to the window.

"Hey, girl. You ready?" Regina asked her.

"Hey, Regina," Emma said. "Um, I'm really sorry, but I don't think I'm going to go."

"Why not?" Regina asked her.

"It just turned out not to be a good day for it," Emma answered. "I should have called you but I forgot we were even going."

"What's the matter?"

"Nothing, I'm just a little behind," Emma lied.

"Mm-hm, then what's your face doing on your chest?" Regina said back. "Jack do something to make you mad?"

"No," Emma said, shaking her head. "No, not at all."

"You do something to make him mad?"

Emma was trying to figure out how to answer that, which was pretty much an answer in its own right.

"What'd you do?" Regina asked, smiling.

"I just asked some questions that didn't have any easy answers," Emma said, hoping that would be enough.

"Lemme tell you something, girl," Regina said. "Jackson's the nicest guy I've ever known 'sides Dew and he'd kill or die for anybody close to him. But he's never been real good at saying things he doesn't want to say. Sometimes you gotta pull Jack out of himself kickin' and screamin'."

"He's usually pretty open," Emma said. "It's just one of those days."

"Ah, he'll be alright," Regina said. "Bake him something, then give him some good lovin'."

Emma smiled at this woman, who had babysat her when she was little and helped her learn how to walk in heels, and was now trying to help her love one of her own best friends.

"I'm sorry about Sam's Club," she said.

"It's alright," Regina said. "I got Darcy with me. She stayed home from school 'cause the Red Menace staged a coup this morning."

Regina started up her car.

"I'll see you later, girl," she said.

"Be careful, Regina," Emma said.

"Please. Those Montgomery people need to just stay out my way," Regina told her.

Emma watched Regina drive off, then went into the house to apologize or something.

Jack grunted as he slammed the axe down on the last of what had been a log, then he kicked at the pieces until they fell from the stump to the grass, joining the remnants of the log before. He picked up another piece of firewood, laid it on the stump and started over, whacking the log in half, then commencing to chop the piece that didn't roll off onto the ground.

When that chunk was in many smaller bits, he kicked those bits off of the stump and replaced them with yet another log. Then he took a deep breath, raised the axe over his head and swung it down with all of his strength.

"Jack?"

Jack had just been about to swing the axe back up, but lowered it and looked over at Emma. She looked scared.

"I thought you went with Gina," he said, slightly out of breath.

"No," she said.

Jack didn't want to look at her looking scared. He turned and straightened the chunk of wood on the stump.

"I'm sorry I was an ass upstairs, Emma," he said to the stump. "But please go back in the house."

"No," she said again.

"I'm not good company right now," he said, lifting the axe and slamming it back down.

Emma watched him swing the axe and waited for it to miss its target and slice through Jack's leg. He was swinging in anger, almost recklessly, and it scared her.

She knew that many people with Jack's type of tumor went through behavioral changes and unexpected mood swings and she wasn't sure if she was looking at Jack being angry or looking at Jack going through something new in his disease.

"Could you just stop for a minute?" she asked him and she couldn't help it sounding urgent.

"Emma, everything's fine out here," he said. "Just go inside."

He kicked another bunch of scraps from the stump, then paused to catch his breath.

"Please," he said.

"Jack, I'm sorry I upset you—" she started.

"You didn't upset me!" he snapped, and slammed the axe into the stump before he turned around.

"This upsets me!" he yelled, slapping the

heel of his hand against his head. "This upsets me!"

Emma stood there with her mouth open as he stalked toward her.

"Do you have any idea what it's like to not get a moment's peace from your enemy because it's right there inside you?" he said. "I can't punch it and I can't shoot it and I can't get away from it for even five minutes so I can breathe, because it's just so relentlessly *there*!"

He stopped an arm's length from her.

"I'm so sick and tired of not being alone in my own body and I'm so sick and tired of knowing that my dying isn't just about me anymore," he yelled. "I'm sick of asking God to explain why He's punishing me."

"You think God's punishing you because you have a brain tumor?" Emma asked him.

"No, Emma, I think God's punishing me by showing me a life I cannot keep!" Jack yelled.

"Punishing you for what?" Emma asked.

Jack looked at her and his face was so tight with anguish that she wanted to look away, but didn't.

"Pick something, Emma," Jack answered. "There's just so damn much to choose from."

"Jack, neither one of us believes that God is cruel and you know it," she said firmly. "You're seeing it as punishment and I'm seeing it as a gift."

"A gift?" Jack was back to yelling. "How is it a gift, Emma Lee? How is it a gift for God to show me at the last minute what I could have had?"

Emma swallowed and took a breath. She had had this same conversation with God.

"But it's not the last minute. It's been almost six months!" Emma said. "Jack, what if He just wanted to give us what's left of a life He meant us to have all along?"

Jack looked at her and she could see him thinking. She could also see him resisting everything she'd said.

"What if it's not punishment, Jack?" she asked. "Maybe we took some wrong turns or made some wrong choices and He got you here anyway before it was too late. That doesn't seem like punishment. That seems like love."

Emma saw tears well up in Jack's eyes just before he looked down at the ground. She stepped closer, put her hands on his face and made him look at her.

"Jack, you have every right to be angry, but I'm just so grateful."

"I'm going to leave you, Emma," he said. "I'm going to leave you alone."

"I was alone, Jack. Now I'm not," she said. "And I won't be alone again, not really."

"Emma, every time I look at you, I see it in your face," Jack said. "I see you believing that if we pray hard enough and you love me hard enough, I'll just keep living."

Jack took her hands from his face and squeezed them, then let them go.

"I can honestly say I would do anything for you, Emma," he said. "And I wish you would ask me to walk through fire, because I could do that for you, but the one thing you need me to do I cannot do. I can't stay."

"Jack, there's always a chance—" she started.

Jack held up a hand and walked away from her

"Listen to me. I could do more chemo and more radiation and more surgery, and all that might get me more time, but it'll be time in bed, time sick as a dog," he said. "More time, but less life."

She tried not to let her eyes fill but they did anyway. She tried not to let him see, but he did anyway, too.

"Damn it!" Jack yelled, then spun away to yell at the back yard. "Damn it, damn it, damn it!"

Jack sat down hard on the ground with his back to her. Emma made herself not cry and went to stand behind him.

"Emma, you said when I first told you about this that I seemed so calm," Jack said. "I wasn't calm, I was just resigned. I went through all the shock and I went through all the anger and then after a while I almost didn't mind dying so much because I really didn't have any other plans."

Emma saw his back hitch up, heard him choke it back. She thought about what Regina had said, about pulling Jack out of himself kicking and screaming.

"Emma, I'm only going to say this one time and then I hope neither one of us ever mentions it again," he said. "I don't want to die. I want to stay right here."

She sat down in the grass behind him and put her arms around him, put her head on his back. After a moment, he began to cry and she wrapped her legs around his body, too and let him.

When he was quiet again, they just stayed there like that for more than an hour, him sitting in silence with his thoughts and her with her body wrapped around him like a suit of armor.

Chapter 18

"WHAT DO YOU CALL a cow with two legs?" Becca asked.

Jack pulled the blanket up over her chest and sat down on the side of the bed.

"I don't know," he said. "What do you call a cow with two legs?"

"Lean beef," Becca answered and grinned at herself. "What do you call a cow with no legs?"

"What?" Jack asked.

"Ground beef."

Jack rolled his eyes and smiled at her.

"You're lucky I have such a sophisticated sense of humor," Jack told her.

He tucked her decrepit bunny under the covers.

"Do you think God has a sense of humor?" Becca asked him.

"Oh, I know He does," Jack said. "That's why He gave us the ability to laugh. I've known Him to be kind of hilarious Himself at times."

"Really?"

"It's a fact," Jack said.

He took the *Little House* book they'd been reading from her hand and put it on the nightstand.

"You want to know a secret?" he asked her. "I've never told anybody, ever."

"Yeah."

"When I was a kid, I used to tell God knock-knock jokes," Jack said. "I know for a fact that He thought it was funny because we both knew He'd already heard 'em all. And who tells God knock-knock jokes, anyway, right? I figured He needed the laugh."

Becca grinned at him.

"You don't do it anymore?" she asked him.

"No. Not in a long time," Jack answered.

"Why not?"

Jack thought about that. How did he tell her that, somewhere along the line, he'd figured he'd lost the privilege of cracking God up?

"I just ran out of knock-knock jokes, I guess," he said.

"But if He's heard 'em all anyway, what difference does it make?"

"You'll make a fine philosopher one day, kiddo," he said. "Say your prayers."

Becca closed her eyes and Jack could see her lips moving just a bit as she prayed. He heard a rustling sound from the hallway and turned to look. Ed was dragging Emma's bathrobe past the doorway with some difficulty, evidently headed for their room.

Jack shook his head and then a flash of memory came to his mind. He looked at the doorway and remembered lying in his own bed, which was positioned in just this same way relative to his door. He remembered opening his eyes and seeing little Emma Lee standing there, four years old.

She was wearing light green pajamas with little horses on them and just by standing there, rubbing the sleep out of her big eyes, she had laid a weight on top of a burden of conviction he already couldn't stand.

Miss Margret had shown up then with a glass of juice in her hand, and gently pushed Emma away from the door.

"Emma Lee, you go on downstairs," she'd said. "Uncle Jack doesn't feel well. You go on and I'll come fix your breakfast in a minute."

Emma had held Jack's gaze for just a moment longer before she moved on down the hall, and Jack had rolled over to face the wall and wished he could will himself to just stop breathing.

He was going to have to talk to Emma about that soon. But not tonight.

"Amen," Becca said.

Jack flinched a bit, then looked back down at Becca.

"Amen," he said and reached over and turned off her lamp.

"See you, Jack," Becca said sleepily.

"See you, Little Bit."

A few days later, late on a Friday afternoon, Jack sat in the hideous orange recliner reading *Light in August*. Over the winter months, he had undertaken rereading his favorite Faulkners and he had saved his favorite for last. If he didn't drop dead beforehand, he planned to revisit Erskine Caldwell next.

"Hey."

Jack looked up to see Emma leaning in the doorway to the living room, her hands behind her back.

"Hey," he told her back.

"So, I was thinking," she said. "Tomorrow's Valentine's Day."

"Please be advised that I am already aware

of this," Jack told her.

He stuck a finger in his book to hold his place and winked at her.

"I bet you think that means I'll let you get to home base with me, don't you?"

Emma smiled at him.

"Actually, remember when you asked me if I'd like to go somewhere?" she asked him. "You know, take a little trip?"

Jack closed the book on his lap.

"Yeah."

"I'd really like to go to the beach. Just over-night," she said. "We don't have to, but would that be okay?"

"Yes," he said enthusiastically.

"When do you want to go?"

"Now, doofus," he said, getting up. "Go pack us a bag and I'll ask Gina to send one of the kids to feed the animals."

Emma grinned as he walked toward her.

"Yeah?"

"Yeah," he said. "Move it."

"Are you bringing Faulkner?" she asked him.

"On Valentine's Day?" he asked her. "What kind of simpleton do you take me for?"

"Well, actually," she said, pulling a black binder from behind her back, "I thought you might want to do *some* reading."

Jack stopped in front of her and looked at the binder.

"Is that *The Cricket Jar*?" he asked her quietly.

"Well, three-quarters of it anyway," she said.

"That's a fine thing, Emma." He stuck a knuckle under her chin and kissed her. "I'm proud of you."

"It's not Faulkner," she said.

"Screw Faulkner; he sucks," Jack said. "Pack it. Pack me a bathing suit, too."

Emma crinkled her eyebrows at him as he pulled his cell phone out of his back pocket.

"It's February, Jack."

"*Carpe diem*, sugar," he said, dialing. "Go pack. Don't forget the offspring."

They had already been in the truck for thirty minutes before they remembered that the snowbirds would have descended on the beach for the winter and they might not be able to find a place to stay.

Jack got on Emma's cell phone and thirteen calls later, Miss Mary's dead husband Carl's cousin on his mother's side let him know that their rental house was empty until Tuesday. Jack gave the man his credit card number and the man told him the key would be under the stone flamingo on the back deck.

With all the bathroom stops, it took them

five hours to get to the beach and Jack proclaimed that, if they ever managed another trip, Emma and Becca would both be provided with catheters.

After a quick run into Publix for some groceries, they eventually made it to their accommodation. It was one of the more downtrodden little houses on that stretch of beach, but it was right on the sand and it suited them just fine.

They had a quick dinner of soup and sandwiches, then Emma went to tuck Becca into bed and Jack went off to take a shower. When he got out, Emma was nowhere to be found inside, so he walked out onto the deck. He was surprised to find she wasn't there.

He was also surprised to see a whole lot of lightning just offshore, a little unusual this time of year. The ocean breeze had also picked up substantially since they'd arrived. It took a minute for his eyes to adjust to the darkness, but he finally spotted Emma standing at the water line, looking out at the sea.

"Now what?" he asked himself.

He cupped his hands next to his mouth and yelled.

"Hey!" he called, but she didn't turn. "Hey!"

Emma looked over her shoulder at him and smiled as big as he'd ever seen her smile.

"Hey! Come on," she yelled back, waving him to her.

Jack sighed and stepped back through the sliding-glass door to put on his jacket and grab hers. When he was almost to her he called to her again.

"Hey Forrest! Come in outa the damn lightning!"

Emma turned and smiled at him.

"No! Look at it, Jack, isn't it beautiful?"

He held her jacket up and she slipped it into it.

"Yeah, but it would be awfully ironic if I end up having to bury *you*," he said.

"Oh, quit whining," she said and looked back at the ocean. "Have you ever seen anything more beautiful than a storm at sea?"

"Yes," Jack said, wrapping her up from behind. "But she's being an idiot right now so I'm not naming names."

They stood there and watched the occasional streaks of light, saw them reflected for just a few seconds in the breaks just offshore.

"I used to love it when we'd get real thunderstorms during the summer," she said.

"Yeah, me too," Jack said. "I remember one time when we were about sixteen, Daniel and I snuck out and went bodysurfing. It was like four in the afternoon and the beach was almost deserted except for the surfers. The waves were amazing. The lightning was everywhere and the rain felt like somebody was shooting a thousand darts at us."

"I loved bodysurfing," Emma said. "I still do. It's like climbing into a washing machine."

"Yeah, nothing like it," Jack said. "Miss Margret was so pissed at us, though. She came running out to the beach, red in the face from yelling. I never knew you could throw a teenaged boy up a flight of stairs."

Emma laughed.

"You remember the year I was home on leave and we all came down? Dew and Gina and their kids, Miss Margret of course." Jack said. "We had that huge water spout. I guess you were about ten."

"I was eight," Emma said. "I remember."

They'd set up picnic tables on the concrete patio under the house they'd rented and when the water spout had formed, it had been as dark as night. Emma had been that thrilling combination of fascinated and frightened, but Jack had been just a few feet away across the table from her, and because he was she'd known that nothing bad would happen to her.

Now they stood there watching another storm, and she felt the strength of his arms around her and the warmth of his body behind her, and she still felt almost invincible because he was there.

"It was beautiful and scary at the same time," she said.

Jack knew she had been there, but he

couldn't remember where she'd been when the water spout appeared and the sky went dark. He knew she'd just been a child then, but he found it hard now to imagine being completely unaware of her.

"Yes, it was," Jack said. "We've all had some good times down here over the years."

He felt her shiver in his arms and he turned her around to face him.

"Let's go inside, it's getting cold out here."

"No, not yet," she said, and pulled him by the hand. "Let's just sit out here for a little while."

She sat down on the sand and wrapped her arms around her knees. He sat down behind her and wrapped his arms around her.

"You're trying to get us both fried," he said.

"You have to try to imagine the romance of it all," she said, laughing.

"'And neither the angels in Heaven above; Nor the demons down under the sea," Jack recited, "Can ever dissever my soul from the soul; Of the beautiful Emma Lee.'"

"Sexy," Emma said. "I don't know what Edgar would think about you changing the name, though."

"I think he'd understand," Jack said. "And I don't have to try to imagine the romance of anything, Miss Emma."

The lightning was starting to strike less frequently and further out to sea.

"You know, Jack, I'd give anything to have

been born twenty years earlier," Emma said quietly. "I'd have pursued you every day of your life until you loved me."

Jack pulled her against him and kissed her hair.

"You wouldn't have to, Emma," he said. "If I hadn't watched you grow up, I believe I would have recognized you straightaway."

It was close to midnight when they finally went to bed, huddling close together under the covers until their bodies had generated enough heat beneath the blankets to make the air there tolerable.

When Emma remarked to Jack that it had become Valentine's Day, they decided silently and mutually to postpone sleep for making love. It was a lovemaking that had more tenderness than need and more care than passion; it was instead sweet, quiet and languid.

Afterwards, Jack looked down into Emma's face as her eyelids drooped and fluttered and he wished his own sleepiness hadn't left him all of a sudden. He found it remarkably soothing, drifting away with her.

He carefully moved away from her, turned the lamp on and picked up her manuscript from the nightstand.

"What are you doing?" she asked him.

"I'm gonna read just a little," he said. "Do you want me to go out to the living room?"

She rolled over onto her stomach and turned her head to face him. The one eye he could see was wide open and she looked nervous.

"No," she said.

He opened the binder and sat up to lean back against the headboard.

"'I was eight years old the day I saw my Daddy get run over and killed by an ice cream truck," he read aloud. "'There's something bizarre about watching somebody die to the tune of Pop Goes the Weasel and, truth be told, I haven't had a Nutty Buddy since.'"

He looked over at her and smiled. She wasn't smiling.

"This isn't going to be the type of book I was expecting, is it?"

"What were you expecting?" she asked him.

"I don't know," he said and turned back to the pages.

"'Getting run over by an ice cream truck is something of an accomplishment, since you could easily avoid it just by jogging along ahead of it,'" he continued. "'But the fact is that Daddy was out cold; he'd stumbled out into the street just previously, nearly unconscious already from a two-by-four administered by my Mama.'"

"Stop," Emma said. "Don't read it out loud."

"Why not?" he asked her.

"Because if you hate it, I don't want to have to hear it in your voice."

"Don't be scared, Emma," he said gently.

"'*So I suppose that Mama was as much a contributing factor as the ice cream truck and Daddy really couldn't take much credit at all, but then he'd never been known for his achievements.*'"

"Huh," he said to Emma.

"Huh, what?" Emma asked and he could tell she almost didn't want an answer.

"Huh it surprises me," he said. "It's very different from the other stuff you've written."

"Is that bad?" she asked him.

"No, it's exciting and intriguing," he said.

Her one eye blinked a few times and he leaned over and kissed her forehead.

"Go to sleep, Emma," he said. "Leave me alone."

She looked at him a minute, then closed her eyes. He went back to his reading, silently now, and in a few minutes, he heard the steady breathing of sleep.

Twenty or so pages later, he slipped out of bed and took the manuscript with him to the kitchen. He made himself a cup of coffee as quietly as he could, then sat down at the kitchen table to read.

It was almost four-thirty by the time he came back into the bedroom. He set the manuscript down on the dresser and slid carefully back into bed. Emma was still on her stomach, just as he'd left her. He reached out and brushed a lock of hair out of her face.

"That's my girl," he whispered.

Emma was surprised to find she was the first one to wake up. Jack seemed to have some kind of bet with the sun and was usually on his second cup of coffee when she woke up at six-thirty. Today, she'd slept in and he was on his back snoring softly beside her, one hand on her arm and his other arm across his face.

Emma often wondered if he got up so early because of his years in the Marine Corps or if it was because he didn't want to waste any time. She propped herself up on an elbow and watched Jack for a minute and she prayed what she always prayed: *Please.* God knew what she was asking and they were down to shorthand now.

She got out of bed carefully and went into the kitchen to make the coffee. While it brewed, she opened the sliding glass door and breathed deeply of the slightly salty air. If she closed her eyes and ignored the brisk temperature, it could be any of the summers that she had come here with Grandma. They had loved this ocean together.

Once the coffee had brewed, Emma fixed two

cups and carried them into the bedroom. As she walked past Becca's room, she saw that Becca was sleeping on her stomach, mouth wide open, with her bunny clutched in her hand.

Emma set Jack's coffee down on the night-stand and moved the manuscript to the dresser, then sat down on the side of the bed. The sun was just starting to lighten the sky.

"Hey, Jack," Emma said quietly.

His eyes opened immediately and that, she knew, was from thirty years in the Marine Corps.

"Good morning," Emma said. "I brought you coffee."

"It is imperative that you go away," Jack said, closing his eyes again.

"Are you hurting?" Emma asked him.

"No, I just went to bed, I think."

"Why?" Emma asked him.

"I was up all night reading your book, goof-ball."

"Yeah?" she asked, and she felt like spiders were skittering along her intestines.

"Yeah," he said and opened his eyes again. "And don't you dare look so stricken."

He started to sit up and Emma got off the bed to get out of his way. He swung his legs over the side and stood up, and Emma almost wished she was the type of woman to tell her girlfriends how fine a picture her man was, standing there in his light blue boxers with his hair every which

way. But then, she really didn't have any girlfriends other than Gina and telling Gina would
just be too weird.

"So?" Emma asked him once she got her
head straight.

"So, I'm going to drink my coffee in the
shower and then I'll talk to you about it," he said.

He took the cup from her and took a big
swallow.

"Is it bad?" Emma asked him.

He looked at her without a hint of a smile.

"Emma, you know it's not," he said quietly.
"Now, take your coffee and go look at the ocean
so I can wake up."

He walked into the bathroom and turned on
the shower and Emma took her coffee and headed out onto the deck.

There was no sign of the storm from last
night; the sky was almost devoid of clouds and
the air smelled new and promising. It was surprisingly warm, still cool enough for a sweater,
but beautiful for February all the same.

Every time Emma came to the beach, she
felt like she was coming home and she wondered what it would be like to just stay. Then she
couldn't help wondering what it would be like to
say, "Jack, let's retire here one day. Let's come
one day and not leave."

She was glad that they had come, not just
so they could enjoy this day, but because every

time she returned, a small part of Jack would still be here for her.

Emma was on her second cup when Jack came outside with his own. He had changed into tan cargo pants and his blue denim shirt with the tails left out and he smelled of unfamiliar, complimentary shampoo when he sat down next to her on the old wicker loveseat.

"Man, that's beautiful," he said of the pink sky. "Kiss me."

Emma did and then sat there and watched his profile while he took a drink of his coffee. Finally, he scooted over and turned a little to face her.

"I want you to forget for just a minute that I love you," he said.

"Why?" she asked.

"Because you doubt yourself too much to tell the difference between love and admiration," he said. "Emma, I don't know if you're going to be successful. I don't know if you'll be a bestselling author or one of those small writers who does just well enough to eke out a living. But I do know that you will keep writing."

He tucked a finger under her chin and lifted her face.

"You will keep writing," he repeated. "Because it is your one thing."

"I can't tell if you like the book or not," she said nervously.

He turned to face her fully then.

"Emma, ten pages into that thing, I forgot you wrote it," he said. "I love it for what it is, completely separate from loving you. But I think it made me love you more. There's something remarkably unexpected about respecting someone so much, someone that you eat and sleep and argue with. I have that respect for you."

Emma stared at him and found she couldn't speak. Then the tears flowed down her cheeks before she'd noticed she was about to cry them. Jack set his coffee down on the end table and put a hand on the back of her neck

"Why are you so stunned, Emma Lee? You knew it," he said. "Deep down somewhere, you already knew it."

Emma had no idea what she would say if she could say it, so she put her head on Jack's chest, tucked her nose into her spot and quietly wept.

The day got into the low sixties and provided pure, glorious sunshine. They wasted not a minute of it.

After breakfast, Jack and Emma and Becca dragged a variety of beach chairs, towels and sand toys out onto the beach. Then they spent all day pretending that the day was just one of many and yet savoring it at the same time.

A middle-aged French-Canadian couple was staying next door with their three grandchildren, a girl just a bit older than Becca and twin boys just a bit younger. The kids helped Jack and Becca build a sandcastle that turned out to be pretty much a sand hovel, but they enjoyed it all the same.

Later, the kids played tag with the waves, with only the Canadian children venturing deeper than their ankles, and Jack asked the husband if he would take some pictures of him with his family. The man took several pictures of Jack and Emma and Becca together, a few of Jack and Becca and, after she ran off, some of just Jack and Emma.

"You know, Emma," Jack had said after the man went back to his beach chair, "You'll never have any pictures of us together if you're always the one holding the camera."

Then he'd kissed her on the forehead and gone off to toss a ball with the kids and Emma had blushed just a little at the thought that Jack had known all along. She didn't really care about being caught, since he didn't seem to mind catching her. He was also right and now she had pictures that she knew would be her most prized.

Late in the afternoon, the husband, who turned out to be Frederick, walked up to them as they sat in their beach chairs watching the seagulls making gang signs at each other. Frederick had taken off his Orange Beach tee shirt and was wearing just his red Hawaiian trunks. He slapped his pretty impressive and hairy chest as he stopped next to Jack's chair.

"Now we go in!" he said with just a trace of French to his words.

"Now?" Jack asked.

Earlier, they had had quite the conversation about swimming at this time of year. His wife Helene wanted no part of it, but Frederick insisted that the water was tolerable by the afternoon.

"Yes, the sun has been warming the water all day," Frederick said. "It will be good now."

Jack looked at Emma.

"That's all you, Jack," she said.

Though Jack had changed into trunks and a tee shirt earlier, Becca and Emma had been convinced by thorough and repeated toe-dipping that their suits could stay in the suitcase.

"Oh, but we will do it correctly," Frederick said, "As I did with my father. Come."

Jack and Emma got up and followed him over to the Canadians' blanket, where Helene was taking a bottle and some Dixie cups out of their cooler.

"Unfortunately, I have no brandy, but we are in the south of course, so I got this," he said, holding up the bottle of Southern Comfort. "You like this?"

"Well, sir, I apologize on behalf of all Alabamians, but I've never had it," he said. "I've never been much of a liquor man."

"Well, we will make it do," Frederick said. "We go in quickly and come out quickly and we drink to warm ourselves. I did this with my father every year."

Jack pulled off his tee shirt and tossed it to Becca, who had gathered with the other kids.

"Let's give it a whirl," Jack said.

Emma followed them to the shoreline and Helene was right behind her with the open bottle and the Dixie cups. She had a beautiful smile and it was big; obviously, she was used to her husband's ideas about fun.

"You can't walk in and you can't go halfway or you won't go in at all," said Frederick. "You run and you jump in completely. Then you get the hell out."

"Jack, that water is freezing," Emma said, but she couldn't help laughing.

Jack grinned at Emma and shook his head.

"Seize the day, Emma, and shake it til it throws up," he said.

"Ready?" Frederick asked with a big grin.

"Let's do it," Jack said.

Then as Frederick ran for the water, Jack picked Emma up and threw her over his shoulder and started walking.

"Jack! Don't you take me in that water!" Emma screamed.

"I'm not," he said and threw her in like a large bag of chum.

Emma hit the water butt first and sank the three feet to the bottom. The water was so cold it felt hot and she was sure her heart had stopped before her butt bounced off the sandy bottom. She shot to her feet within a second and a half.

"Is it too cold for me to go in, baby?" Jack called to her, his hands on his hips.

Frederick laughed, but all Emma could do was suck in a great deal of air. Jack charged in and dove, landing a few feet behind Emma. He was back on his feet in a heartbeat and waded after Emma as she started for the shore. The water was only up to her thighs, but it felt like piranha were munching on her legs.

Jack scooped Emma up in his arms and kept on going.

"C'mon, Emma, quit loitering," he said and carried her back onto the sand, where Frederick was taking his towel from one of his grandsons.

"She will hate you now, almost forever," Frederick said.

Emma just nodded at Jack, as he laughed and wrapped a towel around her. She wanted to be naked, her clothes hurt that much.

"Drink, hurry," Frederick said and Helene handed them their Dixie cups half-filled with Southern Comfort.

They all downed their drinks in one go, except for Emma, who choked up a bit and had to take a second swallow.

"Oh, no, I don't know what to say, my friends," said Frederick. His face said it all, with his lower lip hanging almost to his chin.

Jack coughed a couple of times, then smacked his chest with his fist.

"You have awful alcohol," said Frederick.

"I agree," Jack said.

"Let's try another," Frederick said.

Helene poured him another half cup and Jack only accepted another because he was too busy swallowing his spit to say "no." Emma held her cup out readily. Her towel was doing her no good at all over her wet khakis and sweatshirt.

They all choked down their drinks and emitted various gasps and snarls. Helene took their empty cups and Frederick stuck the bottle in the sand at Jack's feet.

"You may keep this, Jack," he said. "It's horrible."

Jack laughed and turned and rubbed Emma's shoulders vigorously over her towel.

"You okay, Emma Lee?" he asked her, smiling.

After two hefty shots of Southern Comfort, Emma was finally able to speak.

"Do not rub me," she said evenly.

Jack laughed and looked at Frederick.

"You're right, almost forever," he said.

"I'm going to go take a hot shower and think about how much you suck," Emma said. "Thank you for the horrible alcohol, Frederick."

"You're welcome," Frederick said with a big smile.

Emma was still standing in the shower many minutes later, thinking about being spiteful enough to use all the hot water. However, whether out of love or a decent buzz, she was starting to see the humor of the thing and had to admit that Jack having genuine fun was worth quite a lot.

She had just turned the hot water up another notch when Jack stepped into the shower with a plastic Happy Meal cup in his hand.

"You know, this stuff's not half bad once your tongue dies," Jack said.

"You're still drinking it?" she asked, smiling.

"No, I just started again."

"Where's Becca?" she asked him, worried what Becca would think about the communal shower.

"That's a cool thing," said Jack. "They invited her over for pizza and video games so we could have dinner alone on Valentine's. That's okay, right?"

"Yeah," Emma said. "They seem like good people."

She took the cup from him and took a tentative sip, which was a bonafide error.

"No, it's still awful," she said.

Jack picked up the shampoo.

"Turn around, I want to wash your hair," Jack said.

"What? Why?"

"I just feel like it. Turn around."

Emma turned to face the spray, then had to back up onto Jack's feet because their drink was getting watered down. She wasn't sure, but she hypothesized that hot Southern Comfort was worse than the usual.

Jack poured some shampoo onto her head and started rubbing it in with both hands. Emma dribbled a little of the liquor, trying to take a drink while Jack bounced her head around a bit.

"You forgive me yet?" Jack asked her.

"No. Yes," she said. "But you deserve to be shunned for at least a day."

Jack leaned into her and put his mouth right up against her ear.

"Do you think you can shun me tonight, Emma Lee?" he said, soft and low.

"Yes," Emma said, smiling, but she knew a lie when she heard one.

Jack kissed the side of her neck.

"Go ahead, Emma," he said and kissed her just below her ear. "Do it."

"Aaah, my eyeballs!" Emma yelled, as suds

ran down her face and into the Happy Meal cup.

Jack tried swiping at the suds coming down her forehead, but suds from his hands went into her eyes instead.

"Jack," she cried, slapping at his hand.

Jack put his hand on the back of her head and pushed her and the Happy Meal cup under the spray.

"Bernadette!" Jack sang and slapped a palm to his heart.

He had found the small selection of CDs in the living room cabinet and been ecstatic to find a classic Four Tops collection. Emma had had to turn it down twice, since Becca had dragged herself straight to bed after coming home. Jack had been singing and dancing for three songs now, but had become downright animated when "Bernadette" came on.

"Come on, Emma, this is one of the all-time best Valentine's songs," Jack said.

"No, I just like watching you," Emma said from the couch, and that she did. He was feeling pretty loose and he had just enough funk to pull it off without looking the least bit silly.

"No, baby, not this song," he said and pulled her up off of the couch.

Jack apparently knew every word of the

song and he sang along as he did a little bump and grind with her. Emma was okay with that and almost held her own until he decided to twirl her a time or two. He was smooth, but she'd had a hair more to drink since the shower and was barely twirl-able.

Jack smiled and pulled her back to him.

"I'll teach you to dance yet, baby," he said.

"Not tonight," she laughed.

"Maybe not," he conceded. "Too much alcohol tonight. But that stuff's really not so bad once you get past how crappy it tastes and the way it scrapes the sides off your throat on the way down."

Emma smiled and wrapped her arms around his waist as they danced, mostly.

"You're sexy," she said.

"I know. It's completely intentional," he said and smiled at her.

Emma knew he was half-drunk. They both were and it wasn't something they were used to being. But as she looked at the relaxed and happy smile that spread from one side of his face to the other, the way his laugh lines deepened and the crow's feet at the corners of his eyes crinkled up, she thought that she'd never imagined him looking quite so content and beautiful.

They could hear the waves foaming up onto the sand, just under the wind, as they lay together in the hammock on the deck.

Jack had suggested they try it out and once they'd gotten in, they either weren't motivated enough or coordinated enough to get back out, so they'd been there for over an hour. Jack had his arms wrapped around Emma, but she was glad they'd grabbed the throw from the couch on the way out. The empty Southern Comfort bottle sat on the deck floor next to them.

"Emma, I had designs to make love to you again tonight, but I sense that it'll have to be postponed," Jack said, his speech lazy and his voice low.

"That's okay," Emma said. "I'm good."

"I am feeling downright comforted though, aren't you?"

"Yeah," she said. "I think we might have over-relaxed ourselves just a little, though."

"Most likely. Although, this would be an opportune time for you to ply my virtues, with me so defenseless and all."

Emma considered and then discarded the idea without a great deal of regret.

"No, this is good, just this," she said.

"Okey-dokey," he said.

They lay there quietly for a few minutes, then Emma turned to face him, using a great deal of caution. She wasn't positive they'd be able to get up if the hammock dumped them out onto the deck.

"But since you're so relaxed, I want you to make a deal with me," she said.

"That sounds awful," he said, smiling.

"Jack."

"Okay, baby, what?"

She waited until he was looking at her.

"Name it and it's yours, Emma Lee," he said.

"Jack, I won't ever mention research or studies or anything again," Emma said.

Jack's smile faded.

"Okay," he said cautiously.

"But if you ... if we're still together on our anniversary, I want you to see the doctor in Montgomery."

Jack looked at her for what seemed like a long time.

"I will do that for you, Emma," he said.

"You will?" she asked.

"Yes," he said. "I will."

Emma scooted up a bit and kissed him.

"I love you, Jack," she said.

"As you should," he said. "It would be rude not to when I love you so completely, Emma Lee."

Chapter 19

JACK AND EMMA HAD woken up in the hammock the next morning, and had an inordinate amount of trouble getting out of it. This was due largely to having at least two cramps per muscle. Their slight hangovers from the Southern Comfort were a contributing factor as well, and they quickly amended their friendly opinions of it.

Once they'd recovered sufficiently to drive, they'd said their goodbyes to the Canadians and to the ocean and reluctantly headed home, back to Locust Grove and their normal lives.

Their first night home, Jack had his first really bad episode in weeks, though the headaches were almost a constant. It had started just after dinner, while Emma was doing their laundry from the trip and Becca and Jack were playing a game of Cribbage.

After getting Jack every medication he had and a glass of tap water, Becca had watched in silence as he took the pills he needed and reassured her twice that he would be alright. Then she had crawled up into his lap and laid her head on his chest, in the very same spot where Emma liked to lay hers.

Jack had leaned back against the back of the couch with his arms around her and his eyes closed and Becca had petted his cheek without saying a word. Then she had started singing "What a Friend We Have in Jesus," which she'd been learning in Sunday school. She sang it softly, in something close to a whisper, and Jack had felt like his soul was breaking.

Later, Emma had taken a hot washrag to Jack and taken Becca up to bed.

"Is Jack going to die soon?" Becca had asked after Emma had tucked her in.

It had taken Emma a moment to answer, partly because she didn't know the answer, partly because she didn't know which of many answers to give and partly because the question itself made it hard to speak.

"I don't know, Joybug," she had finally said.

Becca had stared up at the ceiling for a moment before she spoke again.

"Maybe Jesus will come back before Jack dies and then he won't have to," she said.

Emma had had that same thought more than once. She'd always been a little afraid of the idea of the rapture, positive that she would never feel ready to go, but at that moment she had to admit that if trumpets started blaring from the skies, she would throw herself down on her face in gratitude and relief, then gather her two people and go.

"That would be good," she had answered.

Becca had spent another moment gathering her thoughts.

"If he does die, when I get to Heaven, I'm gonna hug Jesus and then I'm gonna go find Jack," she had said.

At that, Emma had been done and undone. She swallowed hard, but the tears slid down her cheeks anyway. She nodded at Becca.

"Me, too," she had managed to say.

"Don't be sad, Mommy," Becca had said. "He's gonna have a lot of fun there."

"I know. I'll just miss him," Emma said tightly then and wondered how her little girl had managed to become so wise.

"Don't worry. I promised Jack I would keep you company," Becca had said then.

All Emma could do was nod, lean down and let Becca hug her neck. Then she'd gone back downstairs and sat down on the couch. Jack had laid down with his head on her lap and the washrag on his forehead and she'd rubbed his head until they both fell asleep.

They spent the next few days going about their normal business. Emma went back to work on her book with a fresh purpose and a growing sense of confidence that she hadn't had before the beach. Jack spent most of his time preparing the garden beds for spring planting.

The Friday morning after they got home from the beach, Jack and Becca engaged in what was now a weekday ritual of drinking coffee and Ovaltine respectively while they waited at the road for the bus. Then Jack said "See you, Little Bit" and Becca said "See you, Jack" and he watched her ride off down the road.

He walked up the porch steps, gave Blackie the fat old cat his morning scowl, and headed inside. He went into the kitchen and was rinsing his coffee cup at the sink when he heard a sound coming through the kitchen window, which Emma had opened to let in what was almost a spring breeze.

Jack turned the water off and listened and heard the sound again; it was like choking but not. He leaned closer to the window and looked outside and saw Emma down by the chicken coop, sitting on the edge of one of the raised beds with her back to him.

She was hunched over a little and after a

moment he realized she was crying. He dropped the cup into the sink and walked out the back door.

He stopped a few feet behind the raised bed. She wasn't just crying, she was weeping and it scared him.

"Emma Lee?" he said to her.

Emma startled and looked over her shoulder at him. He'd never seen her look so wretched. Her eyes were red and swollen, her face covered in tears. She didn't speak, just choked out another sob and turned away again.

He moved closer to her, alongside her, and saw that she had something bundled up in the skirt of the apron she liked to use when she fed the chickens and gathered eggs. She had whatever she had wrapped up tight and pulled close to her chest.

"Emma, baby, what is it?" he asked her softly.

Emma looked up at him then, tilting her head a little.

"Jack—" she started, then looked back down, laying her face on her bundle. Her crying scraped at his insides and he knelt down in front of her.

At first he thought she was holding one of her beloved hens, but then he saw a little bit of the brown, striped fur and when he reached out and gently pulled a corner of the apron away, he saw the face, the eyes half-closed and the tip of the tongue still poking out.

"I shouldn't have let him sleep on the porch last night," Emma said. "But he wouldn't come in and I just wanted to hurry up and go to bed and I left him."

"Emma—" Jack started, but she stopped him with another heart wrenching sob as she put her face down into her apron again.

"I never should have left him out here," she cried. "He was so dumb. He shouldn't be outside all night by himself."

Jack thought, with a twinge of apology to Miss Margret, that it should have been the fat old one, who slept outside all the time, had nothing to offer any human being other than hissing or scratching. He wished it was the fat old one.

"Emma, he's slept outside lots of times," Jack said. "It's not your fault, baby."

"Of course it is, Jack," she said into her apron. "I'm supposed to protect him!"

Jack laid a hand on Emma's head and her crying became quieter after a minute. Then she looked up at him.

"Please help me, Jack," she said softly, her face collapsing. "I think my heart is breaking."

Jack sat down next to Emma, untied the strings around her waist, and then lifted the loop over her head.

"Let me have him, baby," he said gently and

carefully took Ed from her arms.

He turned away from Emma just a bit and pulled the bottom of the apron from over Ed's body. He hadn't really expected to see anything; he had assumed that Ed had just died, but the poor little cat had been savaged. His abdomen was a mess, the fur matted with blood that was still slightly tacky.

Jack gently touched the cat's belly, opening the wounds just a bit. Ed hadn't been killed for food, he had just been killed and it had been awful; it had been angry and mean.

"What happened to him, Jack?" Emma asked from behind him.

"I don't know, Emma," he answered. "Maybe a possum. Maybe a coyote."

He looked over his shoulder at her.

"Have you seen any coyotes around here the last couple of years?" he asked her.

"No," Emma said, shaking her head. "Brother Fillmore killed one about five or six years ago, but I've never seen one."

Jack covered Ed back up again and turned to face her.

"I'm sorry, Emma Lee," he said.

She was looking at him like he could somehow fix it and he wanted to tell her that he would. He wanted to make everything on her face go away, to turn time back to last night and yank up the idiot cat who had somehow managed to become his friend.

Emma looked down into his lap at her cat and as Jack watched her lower lip tremble, he thought that maybe the hardest thing about loving someone was the certainty of failing them.

They agreed that they should wait for Becca to get home from school before they buried Ed, so Emma found some work to do while Jack dug a small grave in an area beyond the orchard that they had always called the "cemetery," on account of the several cats, occasional chickens and one rabbit buried there.

After Becca got home, Jack explained what happened, then they wrapped Ed in his bathrobe and buried him with a few words, a cross made of branches and a handful of winter honeysuckle.

A little while later, Emma sat at the kitchen table with Becca in her lap, not sipping the hot tea that had grown cold. Jack came in with his handgun, stood on his toes to take a tin off of the shelf over the back door, and put the gun up in its place.

He turned and told Becca that she wasn't to climb a chair, not even to look at it, but he knew that even with a chair she'd never reach it.

Emma didn't say a word. In fact, outside of comforting Becca, Jack doubted that Emma had said seven words since the morning.

After Jack got Becca tucked in, he found Emma on the back porch with both hands wrapped around a cup of hot Ovaltine. She was fresh from the shower, her hair still damp on the collar of her robe. Jack went and sat beside her in his chair.

He watched her profile for a long time and waited for her to say something, but she didn't.

"It wasn't your fault, Emma," he finally said.

She looked at him, her face almost expressionless.

"Yes, it was," she said quietly. "He didn't want to stay out all night, he just wanted to stay out a little longer. But I didn't want to wait and I didn't want to come out here and get him, so I closed the door and went upstairs."

Jack knew he wouldn't argue her out of that; she was going to have to change her own mind, so he let her talk.

"I did what I wanted and I let him down," she said.

She opened her mouth to say something else, then looked back out into the dark. It was a couple of minutes before she spoke again.

"Why do you suppose it is that we love people more after they're dead?" she asked him. "Maybe not more, but better."

Jack didn't understand the change in topic. He thought she was about to go off on something about him and he was going to squash that quick, but she spoke first.

"What did Regina tell you about when Grandma died?" she asked him without looking.

The question was so unexpected that it took him a second to catch up with the turn in the conversation.

"Not much," he answered. "Just that she had a massive stroke, probably a few of them, sometime during the night. That Gina found her when she came over in the morning to take her to Home Depot."

He paused a second, feeling his throat tighten up at the memory of that phone call.

"That she died just after she got to the hospital," he said.

"You know, I had just gone back to Mobile a couple of months before then," Emma said. "I wasn't sure I was going to go back to school, but Trevor was there, so I went back. We'd only been together about a year and he'd gotten a job there because I was there."

The last thing Jack wanted to hear about at the moment was Trevor Hollings, who still beckoned for a beating, but he just let her talk.

Emma looked back at him and although he had an idea where the conversation was headed, he really couldn't say for sure what she was feeling, her face was that blank. He wasn't used to that and he didn't like it.

"She didn't want me to go. She wanted me to come back home for good," Emma said. "But I was so intent on chasing something that wasn't here."

"Emma, it's not your fault she had a stroke," Jack told her. "One thing had nothing to do with the other."

Emma looked at him and she wanted to stop talking. She looked at Jack's face and she wanted to spare this person she loved, this man who had loved Grandma just as much as she did. But the weight of it, the weight she'd dragged around for ten years, it pushed the words out of her, with no regard for thoughtfulness.

"Maybe so, Jack," she said. "But it's my fault she was alone and it's my fault that—"

Jack waited for her to finish.

"What, Emma?" he finally asked her quietly.

"She was in the bathroom when it happened," Emma said. "Apparently she fell against the door, against that mirror on the back of the door, and it broke."

Emma's voice caught and Jack was glad because he had already heard enough to know that he would want to un-know anything she said after.

"Regina said that when she found Grandma ... when she found her, it was obvious that she had been crawling around on that broken glass for some time," Emma said. "I don't know, I guess she couldn't reach the door knob from the floor or maybe the stroke, maybe she just didn't know how to get out."

Emma looked at Jack's face then and saw the pain that she had put there. She'd thought she'd cried herself dry over Ed, but at the look of dawning despair in Jack's eyes, her own eyes quickly filled and then overflowed.

"I'm sorry, Jack," she said.

Jack wanted to walk down to Gina's and demand to know why she hadn't told him this, but he already knew the answer. It would have served no purpose, and she loved him too much to hurt him without reason.

He wanted to ask Emma why she hadn't told him, either, but he knew the answer to that, too. They'd barely been within ten feet of each other the day of the funeral and then he'd been gone. He hadn't known what to say to her, how to look her grief in the eye or share his own.

"That wasn't your fault, either, Emma," he said, trying to keep his voice even.

"No? What if she called out, Jack?" Emma asked him. "What if she called for help? What if she even called me? I've always wondered if she wished I was there."

That last bit undid him. What if she had wished *he* was there?

"It does you no good to wonder any such

thing, Emma," he told her just a little sharply. "You won't figure it out and it wouldn't change anything to know."

"She didn't want me to go, Jack," Emma said. "She cried her eyes out when I left again and I only saw her one time after, when I came home for her birthday."

"Emma, she wanted you to grow up and start your life, all parents do," Jack told her and he couldn't help the hint of irritation in his voice. His own guilt, his own absence was freshly pricking him.

"Yes, she did, Jack, but she wanted me to do it here, not somewhere else," Emma said.

She said it with the urgency of someone who needed to convince someone else of something vitally important. Jack knew she wanted him to agree with her, to let her know that she had rightfully convicted herself all these years.

Jack rubbed a hand over his face and Emma stood up and put her cup down, jammed her hands into the pockets of her robe.

"I needed that woman my whole life and she was here for me," Emma said. "And the one time she finally needed me for something—the one time—I was off somewhere else, chasing something else. And she was here crawling around on broken glass all night like she didn't have anybody!"

Jack jumped up out of the chair and stepped

toward her, registering that he'd scared her, but too late to change it.

"You shut up and listen to me, Emma Lee," he said quietly, grabbing her shoulders. "This isn't yours. It doesn't belong to you. It just happened, and you carrying it around with you is pointless. She would tell you that."

"I let her down, Jack," Emma said.

"She knew you loved her, Emma," Jack said.

He watched her look away out into the yard and he wondered who he was talking to, her or himself. He'd had no idea she'd been feeling this way all this time and he wondered at the fact that they had both been burdened with the weight of so much guilt and both of them guilty over the same woman. Only, Emma had had the courage to finally tell it.

He felt his shock and his resentment dissipate slowly, like a vapor, and he pulled her to him and tucked her head into her spot.

"We loved her, Emma and she knew it," he said.

After a minute, Emma took her hands out of her pockets and wrapped her arms around him.

"Everything hurts," she said quietly.

He put his face down into her neck and sighed, then breathed her in. He had nothing to say. She was right; sometimes everything did.

The next day was Saturday and Emma spent most of it doing what always healed her; she wrote.

After breakfast, Jack and Becca had gone to get Dew and head to the river for a day of fishing. Emma sat down at her desk with her coffee and lost herself in a world that she had at least some say in, even if that world and the people in it sometimes took her by surprise.

Now and then, she accidentally looked around to see what her buddy Ed was doing and found him gone. It was then that she would get up for some coffee or a glass of tea and walk around a little until she thought she could focus again.

On her fourth such walkabout, in the afternoon, Emma came back into the bedroom and Grandma's needlepoint pillow caught her eye. She had moved it some time ago, setting it on a small stool in the corner, the one she used to get at things on the shelf in the closet.

She walked over to it and ran a finger over and around the stitching. Emma wasn't sure when Grandma had made it, but she knew that it had been when her father and Jack were still living here. She traced the stitching around one of the gardenia blossoms and thought about the quiet pride that Grandma had taken in doing something well, whether it was needlepoint or laundry.

Like the wallpaper in this room. That little old woman had run up and down the ladder, wrestled the strips of paper and straightened out all of the wrinkles on her own, with Emma just running to get more water for the adhesive when needed.

Emma walked over to the wall and ran her hand down the paper, which had faded quite a bit since that day. Grandma had always insisted on lots of fresh air and sunlight. Emma felt something brush against her finger and saw that there was a small, ragged tear at one of the seams.

She picked at it just a little with her fingernail and saw the mint green paint underneath. She had forgotten what had been on the walls before the wallpaper.

She picked at the tear with her thumbnail until it was just big enough to pull on, then slowly, gingerly pulled a ragged strip of the wallpaper from the wall.

As she did it, she couldn't help feeling that she was vandalizing, that she was doing something very wrong. The sweet tea got stirred with the Kool-Aid spoon, the potato salad went into the potato salad bowl. Underwear was hung on the line with the crotch facing the sun and Grandma's bedroom had pink posy wallpaper.

These were the things that she'd always thought had to be true, the things that made things right. But they didn't, really. They just made things seem to stay the same, which felt right, but maybe the rightness of it was an illusion.

Rolling the toilet paper under rather than over wouldn't bring her back early from Mobile, just like keeping everything the way it looked in 2002 wouldn't freeze Jack in time and keep him with her forever.

Emma ran her hand along the wall again, felt the seams that Grandma had run her hand over as she made sure they laid smooth against the wall. Then she pulled another ragged strip of it from the wall.

Grandma had also put great emphasis on the value of finishing, regardless of what was being done. Finish and enjoy it, then move on to something else. Grandma didn't care about the wallpaper anymore; she'd already moved on.

Jack was sitting on the back porch, his boots up on the rail and a cold glass of tea held up to the side of his head.

They'd had a good day of fishing, even though they hadn't caught much. But an hour or so ago, his head had started hurting and the hooks didn't seem to be able to stay where he saw them, so he'd sent Dew off with their few fish and brought Becca on home.

She'd gone down to the creek, which was more of a trickle this time of year, to set the rest of their worms free. The creek was just beyond the back tree line, a couple hundred yards out the back yard, and in July the blackberries down there would be so abundant that you could almost smell them from the porch.

He'd gone inside and taken his pain pill, then brought his tea out here to wait on Becca and relief. The light seemed too bright and when he looked at his boot, there seemed to be another one just behind it. It made him slightly nauseous and he took another sip of tea, partly to quench his thirst and partly to make himself stop looking at his boot.

Emma came out the screen door with a glass of tea of her own and took the hand that Jack held up for her. She kissed the back of it and her lips were cold from the tea.

"Hey, how was fishing?" she asked him.

"Good enough," Jack answered.

"Do I need to cook fish tonight?" she asked him.

"Naw, we just caught a few scrawny ones," Jack said. "Dew took 'em to the kids."

"Where's Becca?"

Jack looked up at her and squinted against the afternoon sun, which made everything look bleached out and the things on the sides of his vision look like they might not really be there.

"She went down to the creek to liberate the worms," he said.

Emma watched him as he pinched the bridge of his nose and squeezed his eyes shut a second.

"Are you okay?" she asked.

"Yeah, just the usual," he said.

"Do you need your meds?"

"No, I took them just a few minutes ago."

Emma ran a hand through his hair at the side of his head, her fingers gliding through the soft strands of coal black and silvery gray. Jack took her hand and tugged until she bent over, then he kissed her.

"What have you been doing all day?" he asked her.

Emma settled herself in her chair and tucked a foot under her butt.

"I got some writing done," she said. "Did a load of laundry, took down some wallpaper."

Jack looked over at her and she gave him a little smile.

"What wallpaper?" he asked her.

"In our room," she said. "I got it started, anyway."

"Is that a fact?" he asked and looked back out at the yard.

He saw Becca was coming back from the creek. She was still about a hundred yards from the house and way out there, with nothing but sunlight and one small tree, she looked even smaller than usual.

Jack looked back at Emma and managed a smile.

"What are you gonna do when you get it all down?" he asked her.

"I'm going to take you to Home Depot so you can pick out the paint," she said, smiling.

"You don't want me to pick out paint," he said, glancing back out at the yard. "I'd probably paint it camo."

Becca was walking with some real purpose, but not the kind of hurry that every kid was in just because they were going somewhere. He wondered for a second if maybe she'd scraped herself down at the creek.

"You can paint it whatever you like, Jack," Emma was saying. "Since you'll be doing most of the painting. I suck at it generally."

Jack watched Becca. She was walking a little slower, and as he watched her he saw that she glanced over toward the tree line to his right, which separated their property from the pasture belonging to the old Franklin place.

"I can do that, Emma," he said distractedly.

He looked to see what Becca kept looking at and then he saw it come out of the trees. It was a dirty light brown with maybe some gray in it and it was sort of staggering along close to the tree line. Its gait was off, there was something stiff and uncoordinated about it, like it was hurt or lame or healing from something.

He vaguely heard Emma saying something about getting new paint brushes as he stood up to get a better look. The animal was gradually moving farther away from the tree line and further into the back yard. It was just about abreast of Becca and maybe a hundred feet away.

"Jack? What's that over there by the trees?" he heard Emma ask.

Jack took his eyes from it to look at Becca, who had slowed down considerably, taking almost tentative steps as she kept her eyes on the animal, who was now ahead of her by about twenty feet and still angling inward.

"Jack, is that a coyote following her?" Emma asked, this time the fear plain in her voice.

It wasn't a coyote, Jack could see now. It was a dog, and it wasn't following her, it was flanking her. Just then, Becca broke into a run.

"Jack!" she screamed. "Jack!"

Jack flew to the back door, yanked it open and jumped to grab the gun from the shelf. He popped the safety as he ran back out. Becca was still running and calling him and the dog had slowed a bit, almost lurching, like one side of him had been frozen.

Emma had just hit the grass from the back steps and Jack jumped the steps and ran past her.

"Get your ass back on the porch!" he yelled

at her and she froze.

He ran about ten feet, then stopped to take aim at the dog, who had stopped to look at him. The dog was about fifty feet away from where Jack stood, and it would have been an easy shot on a normal day, but when he looked through the sights the dog just seemed to shimmy and vibrate. Jack started running toward Becca and in what there was of his peripheral vision, he saw the dog roll its head, and tremble and then focus on Becca again.

"Get in the tree!" he yelled at Becca, who had just passed the small ornamental pear that stood in the middle of the yard. "Get up the tree!"

Becca stopped, confused, then turned and ran back toward the tree. Jack ran faster than he could ever remember running as the dog started coming in at a sharper angle. Jack's heart slammed against his chest as he watched Becca trying to get some purchase on the trunk, the lowest limb just a little too high for her to get a firm grip.

Jack tasted bile coming up in his throat as he saw Becca's little feet trying to scramble up the trunk and then falling down to the ground. She looked over her shoulder at the dog and the sheer terror on her face made him want to throw up, much more than the throbbing in his head did.

He beat the dog by about thirty feet and scooped Becca up and shoved her onto the "V" at the lowest limb and the trunk. It was only about five feet up, but it was enough.

He spun on the dog and pointed the gun at it and the dog stopped lurching, started stepping from one side to the other. Jack knew he could hit it from here, but he wasn't sure where. Both the gun and the dog were moving, transposing themselves over themselves. Jack squeezed his eyes shut for just a second, but when he opened them, nothing was clearer.

He wasn't even sure he was really aiming directly at the dog. He needed it to come closer. He needed to know he could kill and not wound. The last thing he wanted was for the dog to be able to make it back to the trees.

He forced his breathing to slow, forced his heart to start slowing down, too. He stared at the dog, listening to the sound of his breath coming out of his mouth and Becca's soft crying coming from behind him. Then he heard the growling.

The dog took a few more sideways steps, then a few tentative steps toward Jack. Jack tried to make his eyes work properly and he could see that the dog was tilting his head back and forth in an odd, not-dog way, almost like he was trying to shake water out of his ear. A low, steady growl came from his mouth, but it had a wet sound to it, almost like gargling.

The dog circled a little to its right, coming around Jack as he also came closer. Jack followed it with the gun. The dog moved with that odd frozen gait that reminded Jack now of one of those shopping carts with stiff wheels that always pull to one side.

Once the dog was about twenty feet away, Jack could see that its face and jaw were wet and matted. The dog stopped advancing again and went back to its side stepping, its growl lower and more menacing.

Jack looked over his shoulder at Becca, whose eyes were wide and fixed on him.

"Becca, look away," he said and heard the dog growl a bit louder.

"Now!" he yelled at her and the dog barked once. Becca turned her head, pushed her face up against the trunk of the tree.

When Jack turned back around, the dog was about ten feet away. It stopped when Jack met its eye.

Jack looked into the dog's eyes and he saw the ferocity and the wildness there, and beneath that fear, and beneath that something like sadness, but maybe that was just his interpretation.

This dog may have torn Ed apart like he wasn't anyone important, but he hadn't asked to be this way. He'd probably been someone's best friend once, maybe he had even loved a woman or a child. But something was eating away at his brain, poisoning and consuming it and changing everything.

The dog lowered his head and took a few

cautious steps forward. His wet, gurgling growl was quieter, but more threatening.

"It'll be alright," Jack said quietly and shot him between the eyes.

After Jack carried Becca up to porch and sat down, she had curled into his lap and clung to him so tightly it hurt, but he wrapped his arms around her and held her while Emma called Animal Control. When they got there, he took Becca inside and they got some water while they waited for the men to leave with the dog.

Jack remembered that he had left his weapon on the end table on the porch and he went back out to get it. He removed the clip and put the trigger lock back on and was tucking it into the back of his jeans when Becca came out the screen door.

He watched her walk to the steps and look out toward the pear tree, then she sat down on the top step. He went over and sat down next to her.

"It's really sad," Becca told him. "That he was sick."

"Yes," he said.

She looked over at him.

"Do you think it hurt when you shot him?" she asked.

"I hope not," he said. "I don't think so."

She looked out at the tree again for a minute

before turning back to him.

"I knew you would get me," she said.

Jack felt an ache in his throat at the way she looked at him.

"I'll always get you, Little Bit," he said.

She looked back out at the yard for a while, which he appreciated.

"Jack?" she asked after a few minutes.

"Yeah," he answered and she looked back at him.

"Would it be okay if you were my daddy?"

He held her gaze for a minute before he realized he was holding his breath.

"What do you mean?" he asked her.

She looked down at the step and picked at a chip of gray paint.

"Well, I'm used to calling you Jack and everything, so I might not be able to get used to calling you Daddy," she said quietly and then looked at him. "But if *I* knew you were and *you* knew you were that would be okay enough for us, right?"

Jack wasn't even certain that his heart was beating just then. He looked her in the eyes and saw so much trust, so much belief in truly simple truths.

"Yes," he said finally. "That would be okay enough for us."

Becca looked at him for a minute.

"Okay then," she said.

She got up and brushed the paint off of her

hand.

"I'm going to go wash my hands."

Jack heard the screen door slap shut behind him as he looked out into the yard. His vision blurred a little as his eyes filled and he blinked them clear again.

"Damn everything," he whispered to himself.

She reminded him so much of her mother when she was little and he supposed he must have paid at least a little more attention to Emma than he gave himself credit for. He hoped that he had.

His whole life, or at least the parts that counted, had been centered on a woman and a little girl. First Miss Margret and Emma, now Emma and Becca. When he thought about it, he'd really just come full circle.

He heard the screen door again and Emma came and sat down beside him.

"Hey, dinner's ready," she said quietly.

"Okay," he said to the yard.

"You okay?" she asked him.

"Yeah, just … it's been some kind of day," he said.

"Yeah," Emma said.

She grabbed his hand and held it in her lap.

"It was good having so much time to write today, though," she said. "It made me feel better."

He looked at her and gave her a smile.

"Of course it did," he told her. "It's your one thing."

Emma smiled at him and he looked back out into the yard for a minute.

"Emma, I think I know what my one thing is."

"What is it?" she asked him.

"I love the women who live in this house."

Chapter 20

ARCH CAME IN WARM and moist and it looked like spring might stop in early.

Emma pored over her seed catalogs, going through an annual selection process that was intricate and complicated and as ingrained in her as her fear of heights or her right-handedness.

She and Grandma had always spent the winter months comparing the attributes of one variety of lettuce to seventeen others, getting titillated by a new type of sweet corn or tomato and adding it to the old standards and then, as Spring approached, winnowing their list by at least half. For Emma, the entire process was a form of entertainment, a more tangible version of daydreaming.

Jack finished turning over the raised beds, though the loose and loamy soil didn't need much of it, and followed Emma around Holdham's Nursery while she collected peat pots and grow-light bulbs and a new trowel.

For several days, Jack and Emma and Becca spent a great deal of their time poking seeds into little pots and squares. While it was relaxing in its way, Jack found it too advantageous for contemplation and he caught himself thinking too much and in too many metaphors and clichés.

Doing the same tasks in the same place that he had done them with Miss Margret, and doing now with two generations of her offspring, had a continuity to it that made him at once content and overly conscious of the passage of time.

As he gently stuck each seed into its dirt, he couldn't help wondering, with each new variety of vegetable, if he would be at the table when it was eaten.

He also found himself thinking about the seed that was a lie. The way what grew from it looked one way in the light but was an entirely different thing beneath the soil, and how overgrown and fruitless it could all become if left untended.

He thought, too, of the courage and trust that Emma had shown, laying her imagined guilt and wrongdoing before him and inviting him to indict her for it.

After a few days of working by her side, sleeping by her side and thinking, he was fed up with secrets and cowardice. She could hate him if she needed to, but he needed her to be able to feel that, at some point, he had been honest with her.

It was a Thursday morning when he put Becca on the bus and knew that he would go now and talk to Emma. He didn't want it to be in the house. He could already feel himself trapping himself; he didn't want to be closed in. But he didn't want to talk to her on the back porch, either, the place that was their special, quiet place to be together. Even if she forgave him, the back porch would never feel quite the same.

So when he came back up the driveway from the road, he was relieved to see her on the front porch feeding Blackie, Tink and the other cat, the one who was there so seldom that he could never remember its name.

Relieved and scared at the same time, because he knew he would not walk past her, would not walk into that house without saying what he didn't want to say.

When he came up the steps and she looked over and smiled at him, he just couldn't manage to smile back. He thought for a second about waiting, about having one more day before she looked at him differently and she couldn't smile, either, but he knew he was past changing his mind.

But he did tell her "Good morning" back and he let her slide her arms around him and he did stand there for just a minute, running a hand through her hair and looking at her loving him. Then he kissed her softly at the corner of her mouth.

"Sit down," he said.

He saw the question appear immediately on her face, but she didn't ask it.

"I need to talk to you," he said, and led her to her Grandma's old white rocker.

She sat down, looking too small in bare feet and the dress she'd married him in. He squatted down in front of her and took both of her hands from her lap.

"I need to tell you about something," he said, "and I really need you to not ask me any questions or say anything until I get it all out."

He said this without the usual humor with which he usually begged her to let him say his piece. He saw by the wary look on her face that she understood nothing was going to be funny.

"First, I need to tell you that I love you," he said. "I need you to understand that I love you and I honor you and I've never wanted to be anything other than honest with you. Do you understand this, Emma Lee?"

She nodded and he saw her lower eyelids twitch just a little, like she was expecting to be slapped.

"Don't be scared, Emma," he said. "I'm scared, but don't be scared."

He kissed the back of one of her hands, then put them both back in her lap and went to lean back against the porch rail in front of her. The porch was only about six feet wide, but she suddenly seemed very far away.

"It's going to take me a few minutes to explain, to tell you everything, and I know you'll be thinking all kinds of things and maybe you'll have questions," he said. "But please just let me get it all out first. Can you do that for me, baby?"

"Yes," she said in a hushed voice.

He looked across the porch at her and her eyes were so big, so cautious. She was waiting to be hurt someway and he was going to do that. He looked down at the floor and took a few slow breaths and made himself be man enough to hurt her. Then he looked up and started talking.

"When your Mama and Daddy died, I was stationed at Beaufort. My six years were almost up and I was thinking about getting out, going to graduate school," he said. "I was thinking about teaching literature, maybe. I know the story you've always heard is that I was away when they died, that I came home for the funeral, but that's not true. I was here. I had a week's leave."

He could tell by the look on her face that he wasn't talking about any of the things that she might have expected.

"There was a screw-up with my transport and it ended up taking me almost twenty hours to get here. I usually flew back then, but I hated flying. I got in at seven o'clock in the evening and Miss Margret called Daniel and Michelle over. I was so tired. I'd been up for more than 24 hours and I was so damn tired."

He looked off to the side yard and felt that tired again, thought about how close a long time ago could seem.

"All I wanted to do was go to bed, but it was the Fourth of July and your mama wanted to go over to the river and watch the fireworks from there, have a little picnic," Jack said, still looking out into the yard. "So Miss Margret packed us up some food and we took your daddy's Jeep soft-top over to the river. We took the top off and took the picnic basket and went over to the old McNab place, where that bluff is."

"Anyway, we watched the fireworks. I was falling asleep in the middle of it all. Daniel and Michelle, they were drinking some shine Daniel'd brought with them. They were starting to ... they were a little drunk and they were young and they were getting kind of randy, so I told them I wanted to go."

He stopped for a second. He would have given most anything to stop there. But he looked her right in the eye and went on.

"I was way too tired, but Daniel was too drunk and Michelle never learned to drive a stick, so I drove."

He saw her understand and he saw her lips part and that she was going to say something. He held up a hand.

"Please," he said softly. "Don't."

He breathed in and breathed out again slowly, then he went on.

"Daniel was in the back seat and your mom was in the front. Daniel was teasing her, playing around. He wasn't wearing his seat belt and he kept leaning up front and teasing her or kicking the back of the seat."

"I was probably driving a little too fast because I was getting mad and because I was tired. I just wanted to get back," he said. "Just as I was turning onto the dirt road out there I turned around to yell at Daniel. I guess it was hitting the gravel, I don't know. I took it too sharp or too fast and then I over-corrected. The Jeep flipped twice and I hit the side of my head on the steering wheel. I blacked out."

Emma wanted him to stop or slow down, or something. She had imagined that night many times, especially as a kid, walking or riding her bike down that same dirt road. She had wondered how it had happened, what it had been like, and had pictured it many different ways. But none of those pictures had Jack in them and she was having trouble now trying to get her mind to insert him there.

"I came to and the first thing—" He swallowed hard. "There was this overwhelming smell of blood and moonshine. Your mom had been holding the picnic basket in her lap and the jar of shine was broken. It was on her seat. It was on me."

Jack could smell the shine and the blood and feel the pain in his head, things he had had to chase away for years afterward, whenever they tried to drag him back.

"I looked over at your mother and I could see she was dead. Her eyes were open," he said, then swallowed hard and looked away from Emma before he continued. "I had hit my head hard, but there wasn't a drop of blood on me. I looked and we ... the Jeep was just sitting back upright in the middle of the road, like nothing had happened, like I had just stopped."

Emma could see it. She thought maybe she could smell it, too, but she could see it just as clearly as she could see Jack now. Jack, standing there gripping the porch rail, looking out to the yard with so much pain on his face. Jack then and Jack now, both of them her Jack.

"Then Miss Margret was there, pulling open my door, yelling at me could I get out, telling me I had to get out," Jack said. "She got the door open and I was so dizzy. I felt sick and I couldn't walk on my own, so she got her arms up under me and helped me stand, then she put my arm around her shoulders and she helped me walk."

He stopped then and looked at Emma, but he couldn't see what she was thinking and it scared him to try, so he looked away again.

"We got around the back of the Jeep to the other side and I saw Daniel," he said and his voice broke for the first time. "He was lying half on the road, half in the grass. There wasn't any question at all he was dead."

Jack closed his eyes then and swore he was standing there in the road, looking over at the bizarre and broken body of the man who had been his brother. He could even feel the nausea rising again. That much was real.

"I tried to stop, to go to him, and Miss Margret started screaming at me," he said and then his throat closed up.

Emma saw the tears in his eyes and she felt her own tears warming her face. She wanted to go to him, but she couldn't move. She wanted to say something but she didn't even know yet what she wanted to say.

"She kept screaming at me to come on and … that tiny woman, she got me all the way into the house, got me up the stairs and onto the bed and then she called 911."

"She thought I'd been drinking," Jack said. "She didn't realize, until the next day when I could make sense, but by then it was too late. She'd already lied to the police and the paramedics, lied to all of them."

Emma thought about how Grandma never talked about what had happened and how that had just seemed like a natural thing to her. She thought, too, about everything she knew of Grandma and how it felt like Jack was talking about someone else.

"Nobody even knew I was home. The only people who knew I was here was the Corps," Jack was saying. "Miss Margret took care of me and I stayed upstairs until the day before the funeral. Everybody assumed I'd just come home."

Jack finally made himself look at Emma, made himself face her full on.

"She left her only child lying dead on the side of the road and dragged me home. Just left him there" he said quietly. "That's who your Grandma was. That's what Miss Margret was to me."

She just looked him in the eye. He didn't think she had moved a muscle this whole time. She sat there now watching him and he wanted to look away, but he wouldn't allow himself to do it.

"You can say something now, Emma, if you need to," he said and he waited.

Emma stared at him and so many thoughts

and feelings were scrambling around inside her that she didn't know what she needed to say. It had hurt her to hear the details of her parents' deaths, though they weren't any worse than any of the ways that she had imagined the accident happening.

She hurt, but she wasn't really hurting for them. She was hurting for her Grandma and she was hurting for the man that stood there watching her, so much grief and pain and what she now recognized as resignation on his face. She hurt for the years that he had carried this with him.

She understood it all, all at once, in a flood. He had lost his future, his home, his family. He had taken them away from himself. As he stared at her, she realized that he was preparing to lose her, too and that was when she really felt pain.

"Jack, I didn't know those people," she said finally. "I don't have one single memory of either one of them."

She stopped and tried to figure out what she really wanted to say, but there was just so much and none of it enough and none of it right. She shook her head to get rid of it and just said what came out of her mouth.

"Jack, I hate that this happened to you," she said. "I hate that you're in pain and that you've been in pain. But ... I know this is selfish and awful, but I'm glad you were driving that car. I'm so sorry, but I am."

She saw the confusion on his face and something else, like she'd slapped him.

"Why, Emma?"

"Because if you hadn't been driving that car, you wouldn't be here right now," she said. "You would have moved on and maybe moved away. You would have gotten married and you would be somewhere else with some other woman. You'd be living and dying with some other woman right now and I wouldn't have you."

She watched him think, saw him trying to understand it.

"I know it's wrong, Jack," she said. "I know it's wrong to love you and not want to take all of this away from you. But I'm sorry ... I don't. I just want you to stop hating yourself for it."

Jack swallowed and blinked a few times.

"I killed your mama and daddy, Emma Lee, accident or no, and then I let Daniel take the blame for it," he said. "And I've let you love me and I have loved you and made love to you and haven't told you until now."

He looked down at her chest or her lap or somewhere before looking her in the eye again.

"Do you despise me for it?" he asked her, and it was almost a whisper.

Jack watched her get up out of the chair and he tried not to flinch as she walked across the porch. She stopped in front of him and she seemed to be looking for something in his face.

He felt like she was looking right inside him and it was too intrusive and made him feel too naked. He couldn't look her in the eye anymore and he dropped his own eyes to her chin.

Then she cupped his face in her hands and tried to make him look back up. He resisted at first, but he was just so tired, felt so wilted from it all and he finally let her lift his head.

"It doesn't change anything, Jack, not for me," she said. "You are the most honorable and beautiful man I have ever known and you are my man and I will never be done being grateful for it."

He didn't bother trying to squeeze back the tears. He felt them course down his face and he let them.

"She did what she wanted to do, Jack. Why should she lose both of her sons?" Emma asked. "And I know she wasn't sorry she did it."

"You can't know that, Emma," he whispered.

"Yes I can, because I know what it's like to love you that much," she said.

He closed his eyes and tried to breathe. Then he felt her breath on his face and he opened his eyes as she kissed him, then kissed him again.

They were whispery little kisses that he could barely feel. He closed his eyes again as her kisses landed on his lower lip like tiny drops of water from Lourdes, and for the first time in his life, he began to believe in healing.

Chapter 21

APRIL DID COME IN warm and gentle, and after the last danger of frost had passed, Jack and Emma spent most of their mornings planting one seedling after another. Emma felt less and less like writing, not because she didn't love it, but because she could feel Jack close by but not present and every hour she spent writing was an hour that she lost. Whether he was outside working on something or downstairs reading, she wanted just to be with him.

She had tried to get him to read upstairs, in the little armchair between the bed and her desk, but he had insisted that he was incapable of being in a bedroom unless he was sleeping or making love, particularly during the day.

So she worked hard instead, worked with fewer breaks and very little staring out of the window unless she could see Jack. She worked to finish, to be done and hand him the book and then be free to not be away from him so much.

She finished on a Wednesday afternoon at the end of May. Her first thought was to run downstairs and present it to him, but then she remembered that he had taken himself over to the True Value to get some wrench that wasn't anything like the other seventeen wrenches he already had.

It was also his birthday next week and she couldn't think of anything better to give him than the finished book, so she printed out the last pages and slipped the binder into her desk.

She was sitting on the front porch having some tea when Jack finally pulled into the driveway. He walked across the yard with a big, square cardboard box under his arm and she wondered how many tools and doodads he'd succumbed to.

"That's a pretty big wrench you got there," she said as he walked to the porch.

He held up a finger as he came up the steps, then dumped the box on her lap, barely slowing down to do it.

"One word comes out of your face, he goes back to the pound," Jack said and then he walked right on into the house.

Emma lifted one of the flaps open and saw a tiny kitten with brown striped fur and big, soulful eyes. The kitten looked up at her and squeaked.

"Hey, Eddie," she said, smiling.

A little while later, after Emma had helped Becca make a box bed for the kitten in her room, she walked into the kitchen to find Jack at the table, surrounded by paperwork.

"What are you doing?" she asked him.

"I need to go over some of this stuff with you," he told her. "I keep putting it off."

"What is it?" she asked him as she took out some carrots and potatoes for their dinner.

"Everything is together," he said. "I keep it in that leather box in my sock drawer."

He held up a few folded documents.

"This is the contract with the funeral home," he said. "Everything's paid for, you just need to call them. Don't let them try to talk you into adding a bunch of frills or giving me a funeral. You know what I want."

Emma chewed on the corner of her lip for a second, then went to the counter and started peeling the potatoes into the sink.

"Here's the life insurance policy. This card on here is the guy you need to call. You're the beneficiary; you have been since Miss Margret passed," Jack said, setting the papers aside and picking up another set. "This one. This is really important. Emma, look at me."

Emma looked over at him. He shook the papers a little.

"This is all the stuff you need to apply for the survivor's benefits if, you know, we get to that point," he said. "I wrote the name and number of a friend of mine right here, she works for the VA and she can help you with everything as far as that. She expects you to call."

"Jack, do we need to talk about all this now?" Emma asked him.

"When would you like to talk about it, baby?"

Emma sighed and turned back to the potatoes.

"Okay," she said.

"Okay," he said back and started pulling other papers out of the pile. "Insurance policy on the truck. We need to call and renew that next month. The Living Will. You know about that. My will. It doesn't say much. Everything goes to you, except I want Dew to have my Ole Miss championship ball and I want Gina to have my Faulkners. That woman needs to read something besides romance novels."

"Okay," Emma said and scooped the peels from the sink and dumped them into the compost bucket.

"I think that's pretty much it," he said.

"Good," she said back and started peeling carrots.

"I know it's not the sexiest conversation we've ever had, Emma, but we have to talk about stuff sometimes," Jack told her.

"I know," she said.

Jack neatened up the papers and set them aside, then drank some of his tea while he watched her a minute.

"There is one other thing, Emma," he said.

Emma sighed, but tried to do it quietly.

"Okay," she said.

He thought about his words before he spoke.

"The survivor benefits. The benefits for you, as my wife," he said. "If you get married again someday, you'll lose them."

Emma stopped peeling the carrots for a second.

"I don't really see the relevance of that, Jack," she said without turning around.

"It's something to think about," he said.

The very thought made him feel like he was swallowing a fork, but some things needed to be said.

"Emma, I'm not going to tell you to do anything that's not in your nature," he said.

"Good," she said.

"But if you meet somebody, maybe you might wait until Becca's on her own before you actually got married again," he got out.

Saying it put pictures in his head that made him want to punch himself in the face. He grabbed his glass and sucked up a chunk of ice and started chomping it. Emma turned around and looked at him, one hand on her hip.

"Meet somebody?" she asked. "Meet who?"

"How do I know?" he snapped. "Some thieving bastard I can't stand already."

Emma glared at him and he waited for poisoned darts to fly out of her eyeballs and puncture his neck.

"We're about to have our first fight," Emma said.

"No, we're not. We're not like other people, Emma, we don't have time to fight," he said. "So you tell me what's on your mind, I'll tell you you're wrong and we'll go straight to the make-up sex."

"No, we'll go ahead and fight, because you don't know what you're talking about," she said.

"I'm a realist, Emma," he said.

"No, Jack, you're a moron," she snapped.

"Why is that, Emma?" he asked her. "I'm just saying that one day you may find someone."

"I have someone," she said, slapping a carrot down onto the cutting board. "I have you."

"You have me now," he countered. "But you're a young woman. Eventually you'll need someone else."

"No, I won't, Jack," she said.

"Be realistic, Emma," he said. "How can you say that?"

Emma turned around again.

"Because I never have. I've *never* needed anyone else," she said. "You don't get it, Jack. I'm a loner. I'm fine being alone. I won't need someone, I'll need you. Nobody else can fix that."

She turned back to the counter and started cutting the carrots into chunks.

"What about having someone to love, Emma?" he asked her and the words tasted like old socks.

Emma sighed and turned around again.

"Jack, if I couldn't love anyone else before you loved me, why on earth would you think I could love someone after?"

Jack got up and stalked past her to the fridge to get more tea.

"You don't have to love him as much," he snapped. "I'm just saying that it's in your nature to love someone."

"And I will," she said. "I'll love you."

Jack put the tea back into the fridge and closed the door a little harder than he meant to.

"I'll be dead, Emma," he said.

She spun around on him, holding up the last carrot.

"So you won't be home for dinner. You'll still be my husband," she said. "The only difference between now and then is that I won't have to explain things to you so much."

She stuck the carrot into his tea and turned back around, scraping the cut vegetables from the cutting board into a baking dish.

"That was just silly," he said, then went to the sink.

He stood next to her as he rinsed the carrot and set it down on the cutting board. She didn't answer or look at him, just picked her knife back up and started cutting. He dumped his tea out and leaned against the counter and watched her, his arms folded on his chest.

"Jack, I know you think I'm wrong, but there's never going to be somebody else," she said, the frustration gone from her voice. "For me, it's not even a question. And I'm perfectly comfortable with it."

He thought about that for a minute.

"Well, I know it's selfish and immature, but I'm pretty comfortable with it myself," he said.

She looked over at him and he smiled at her. She tried not to smile back, but did anyway. She put the last carrot in the dish.

"Just love me enough to last me a while and I'll catch up with you eventually," she said.

He moved up behind her, leaned against her and wrapped his arms around her waist.

"I'll leave a light on for you, Emma Lee," he said into her neck.

She smiled and picked up the salt shaker

and started seasoning the vegetables. He kissed her neck and she tilted her head to brush him away.

"Is it time for make-up sex now?" he asked her.

"No, it is not," she said. "I'm too put out with you."

He kissed her neck again.

"It'll be okay if you're still aggravated," he said.

Emma turned around and poked him in the chest.

"I'm not in the mood to make love with you, Jack Canfield," she said.

He looked at her like she'd just spit a unicorn out of her mouth.

"That's a bald-faced lie," he said incredulously.

Emma couldn't help laughing and he laughed with her.

"Yes," she said. "But it's five in the afternoon and Becca's upstairs with your cat."

He hooked a finger through the belt loop of her jeans and tugged her to him.

"That's a shame," he said.

"Well, it is a school night," she said. "You do the dishes, I'll read her a book in the shower and we can meet upstairs by seven.

"Nah, I'm out of the mood already," he said.

"Sure you are," she said back.

The following Saturday was June 6th, Jack's fifty-seventh birthday.

He had asked for it to be a small celebration, so they had Dew and Gina and the kids over for barbecue. They grilled a pile of ribs and Emma made all of Jack's favorite side dishes, most of them from their garden, but she really went all out on his favorite cake, fresh coconut with lemon curd between the layers.

They pushed two picnic tables together out back in the shade of the apple trees and as they ate and laughed and told stories, Emma couldn't help thinking of the barbecue after their wedding and of how much had changed since then. It had been just shy of nine months but it felt like a few days and, at the same time, like half a lifetime.

Across the table, Jack stared up at the apple tree behind Emma and remembered the day he'd looked up at her through those branches and met her for the first time after knowing her for her entire life.

After they'd cleared away the lunch things, Emma brought out the cake. They settled for twenty candles and as Emma lit them, she wondered what Jack would wish for. She knew what she wished for. *Please.*

The other day, she had been working in the garden and praying. It started out as chatting more than anything else, thanking God for the good weather and the successful garden, mentioning Becca's upcoming spelling bee and reminding God to watch over Miss Mary while she had cataract surgery again.

Then, as always, it was *please. Please let me keep this man,* and as she snipped at some leaf lettuce, a question came to her, from inside her, as clear as if she'd heard it with her ears: *If I don't, will you assume it means that I just don't love you both enough?*

It wasn't unusual for her to feel God was asking her a question, but this one she had no answer for. She had thought about it off and on for a couple of days. But now, she looked at Jack sitting there with Becca on his lap, laughing at something Dew had said and she knew her answer.

No. No, it won't be because of that, she told God back.

She sat back down and everyone sang "Happy Birthday," then Jack closed his eyes, took a deep breath and blew out the candles with some help from Becca. Jack looked up and saw Emma watching and he winked at her, but he wasn't smiling.

Jack was more or less happy with his gifts. Becca had picked out a pair of slippers for him, which he couldn't imagine wearing but would. Dew and Regina had decided to be awful and bought him a Gators jersey. He threatened to wear it just to torture them with their own device, but he just couldn't bring himself to do it.

Jack was very pleased when Emma handed him the binder with *The Cricket Jar*. Emma had written him a note on the front of the first page, thanking him for making it possible for her to do her one thing. She'd done it because she didn't know that he would ever see a dedication in a published version, but she hoped he didn't know that.

After the party, Jack sat down to read while Emma cleaned up and then got Becca bathed, read to and tucked in. Then she took a long, hot shower.

She grabbed herself a glass of tea and went out onto the back porch. Jack was sipping his tea, the closed binder on his lap. The crickets were all amok out in the yard and there was a heft to the air that signaled a decent rain.

Emma stood behind Jack's chair and sipped an arm around his chest.

"Taking a break?" she asked him.

"No, I'm done," he said, and took her hand to kiss the back of it.

"You are?" she asked him. She was surprised, but not quite as nervous as that morning on the beach.

"Did you skim it?" she asked him, mostly joking.

"Don't be ridiculous, Emma" he said. "I've never skimmed a book in my life."

She sat down in her chair and took a sip of her tea and worked up her courage to ask him what he thought. She didn't need to.

"It's good, Emma Lee," he said quite seriously. "I believe it to be very, very good."

Emma felt a warmth spread from her chest to her throat. Relief and gratitude and a good deal more. His words were a benediction and a gift.

"Thank you," she said.

"So what are you going to do now?" he asked her. "You gonna send it out to some agents or publishers or something? Don't sit on it again, Emma."

"I won't," she promised. "Actually, I've been reading a lot about publishing independently. I think I want to do that."

"Good," he said, nodding. "Good."

"I have a lot of editing to do, but I want to take a little break first," she said.

He nodded again and put his chin on his fist and smiled at her.

"Actually," she said. "Would you edit it?"

"I'm not an editor, Emma," he said.

"Please," she said. She knew it was right, even though she'd just thought of it that minute. "I trust you more than anyone else in this world. And then it'll be our book."

He watched her for a moment.

"Okay, baby," he said.

"Thank you," she said back.

"I wish I could read the next ten books, Emma Lee," he said after a minute.

She looked at him and wanted to say something, but she had nothing to say that wouldn't make her cry.

"Such a short time, Emma Lee," he said. "I expect you feel God's cheated you somehow."

Emma thought about her words for a moment.

"Us being here, in the place where we've always been, doing things we've always done," she said. "It's almost like having a thirty-year marriage and a honeymoon all woven up together at the same time. Sometimes I think that later, it'll seem a little bit like we were always here together and it won't feel like it was so short."

She looked at him sitting there, leaning on his fist and watching her.

"Does that make sense?" she asked him.

"Yes," he said quietly. "But it will be short. No matter how long it ends up being, it will be short and I'm sorry."

"Jack, some people are married their whole lives and never have this ... what we have now," she said. "So who's really getting cheated?"

"You are an ever-interesting woman, Emma Lee," he said and smiled at her.

She smiled back at him and then looked

down into her tea for a bit. When she looked back over at him, he was staring out into the yard.

"Jack, I want to ask you to do something," she said. "I want to ask you to let me do something."

He looked over at her.

"What, Emma?"

She took a deep breath, trying to look like she wasn't, and let it out slowly.

"I want to try to have a baby," she said.

He just sat there and stared at her for a minute.

"No. No, Emma Lee," he said sympathetically, like she'd just told him someone had been hurt in an accident.

"Please, Jack," she said.

"Emma, think about what you're saying," he said.

"I have. I've thought about it for months."

Jack had half-expected this conversation from the first time they'd made love, but when it never happened he assumed that she didn't want more children or at least not with him, not this way. It had been a long time since he'd even wondered and he'd been relieved about that.

"Emma, assuming that you could get pregnant, I'm not leaving you alone with another child to raise."

"I'm already going to be raising a child alone, Jack," she said. "I'm okay with it. You were raised by a single mother. So was I, so was Becca until now. I know you won't be there, but I know I can do it."

"Emma, it's not just the raising," he said. "If you got pregnant *yesterday*, I still wouldn't even be there to see it born. Have you thought about that?"

Actually, she hadn't and it slammed into her chest. She'd pictured being alone with a small child after Jack was gone. She'd never really acknowledged that when that small child was still inside her, Jack would probably already be gone.

"I didn't really think about that," she admitted quietly. "But it doesn't change anything."

"Emma, I understand you wanting to have another child," he said gently. "But not now."

"Jack, there is no later," she said.

She reached over and took his hand off the arm of his chair.

"There really isn't going to be someone else, Jack," she said. "That's not sentiment or a prediction, it's a choice and it's a choice I'm happy with."

They just looked at each other for a while and she waited for him to say something.

"Please let me have this, Jack," she said. "Let me have something I can keep."

He didn't answer right away and she looked for the answer in his face but couldn't find it. His eyes watered a bit and he blinked once and cleared it away. She waited.

"Have you stopped taking the pill, Emma?" he asked softly.

"No, Jack," she said. "I wouldn't do that."

He felt bad for asking. If he'd thought about it a minute, he would have known the answer.

They sat in silence again for a minute.

"I think I need a glass of wine, Emma," he said finally and stood up. "I'm sorry, sweetheart, but I'll be right back."

Emma watched him go inside and close the screen door gently, then she looked down at the thumbnail she hadn't known she was picking to shreds.

Jack went to the cupboard and took down a wine glass and the open bottle of blackberry wine. Then he opened the cupboard again and got another glass. He poured the wine and took a long drink of his, refilled it and stood there looking out the kitchen window for a minute.

She was asking so much, but then she really wasn't. The idea of there being something else that he would have to leave, something else that he would know he was going to miss, filled him with a quiet dread. It was a lot like the feelings of foreboding he used to get in combat. Like the dread he'd felt for days last October, before he realized that something wonderful and unexpected had occurred.

He was pretty sure that letting her try to get

pregnant was a lovely, but ill-advised, idea. He was pretty sure that she didn't really understand everything that it would mean. For him, for her, for a child that she might have.

But he was also half-convinced that there really wouldn't be anyone else. He knew her well enough, with her plastic flamenco dancers and her ugly recliner, to know that even if it were possible, she would make it not so.

What if she was right? Who was he then, to tell her she could never have another child?

He stood there staring out the window and drank half of his wine before he picked up the glasses and went back outside.

Emma was leaning up against the porch rail with her arms around herself like she was cold. He held out her glass of wine and she took it. Then he kissed her on the forehead and sat back down.

"I'm sorry for leaving you like that, baby," he said. "I just needed a minute."

"It's okay," she said and took a large swallow of wine.

He took a breath, held it while he checked with himself for any last-minute thoughts, then let the air out slowly.

"Come here, Emma," he said.

She walked over to the chair and he took her glass and set it on the table next to his own. He was going to pull her onto his lap, but she sat down on the porch floor between his knees, looking up at him like he were some kind of judge that she hoped to be benevolent. Then she looked down at his leg and he was sorry that she was so scared. He put a knuckle under her chin and lifted her face, made her look at him.

"I don't know what your chances are of getting pregnant," he said. "I'm a middle-aged man and you're still going to have that pill in your system for a while aren't you?"

"Yeah, I think so," she said. "I guess."

"Your odds aren't that great, sweetheart."

"I don't believe in odds, Jack," she said and tried not to sound too hopeful or excited too soon.

He picked up one of her hands and held it.

"It's okay. You can stop taking it," he said quietly.

"Really?"

She put her forehead down on his knee for a second, then climbed onto his lap and wrapped her arms around his neck.

"I love you, Jack," she said. "Thank you."

He put his arms around her waist and held her for a second, then gently held her away from him so he could look her in the eye.

"I just need you to do one thing for me, Emma," he said. She waited. "If you do manage to get pregnant, don't tell me unless I ask."

She started to say something and then closed her mouth again.

"I just think it would be easier if I didn't know," he said. "I might change my mind later, but if I do I'll ask you."

Emma felt a sadness creep into her chest and swirl into the relief that she was feeling. She was ashamed that she had never really thought about what it would mean for him.

"Okay," she said. "But, if it does happen, I may not be able to keep it a secret, you know? I was pretty sick at first with Becca."

"We'll cross that bridge, Emma," he said and pulled her back onto his chest.

He felt her heartbeat next to his skin, felt it begin to slow down. He petted the back of her head for a minute, felt the warmth of her breaths on his neck coming more slowly.

"Emma, even if I don't want to know," he said. "I need you to understand that I would be very, very happy."

The 4th of July picnic, which was a big deal on their dirt road, was held at Dew and Gina's that year.

Every woman and half the men, from one end of the road to the other, cooked for two days in preparation. Everyone had some dish that tradition demanded; for Gina it was her mother's maple-glazed butternut squash, for Miss Mary it was her lemon chess pie. Emma made Grandma's potato salad with the little bits of sweet pickle in it.

Emma worried for days that Jack wouldn't be able to enjoy the festivities, now that she knew everything that had happened thirty July 4ths ago. She tried to think back to the few times he'd been home for the picnic, but she couldn't remember how he'd seemed and she didn't want to ask him what he was feeling, either.

But she remembered many 4th of July picnics with Grandma, and while she'd been understandably subdued at times, she'd also laughed and enjoyed the food and leaned back on the blanket and "oohed" and "ahhed" with everyone else as they watched the town fireworks off in the distance, waved her sprinklers in the air in front of her while Emma and the other kids ran with them in circles.

After a few hours at the Porters', Emma stopped worrying and watching and just enjoyed the day. There was music and dancing and far too much food. They had watermelon races and the kids threw water balloons and set rockets off far too early when it was still far too light.

Regina and Dew had taken turns now and then, walking around with their video camera and filming the goings on. Dew got a few minutes of Jack and Emma slow dancing and Emma saw Regina filming Jack and Becca in the three-legged race.

When everyone had pretty much settled down on their blankets and in their chairs along the little rise behind the barn, Regina came along and pointed the camera at Jack and Emma on their blanket, Becca standing behind Jack with her hands on his shoulders and Emma sitting between Jack's legs with his arms around her.

Before Regina moved on to the next family, Emma asked her to please send her a copy of the video and Regina promised she would. Emma knew that one day she would know exactly which places to stop the video so that she could see what she needed to see.

After Gina walked away, Jack tightened his arms around Emma's waist and pulled her closer, kissed her bare shoulder that was slightly reddened from the day in the sun.

He was glad that the headaches had started coming in the morning. They were bad, but they were usually over in a few hours and he was grateful for that today, glad that it hadn't interfered with coming here.

It was bittersweet, as it always was, but as the first fireworks appeared in the sky and he heard the faint popping and whistling off in the distance, he also felt at peace.

The next day, he told Emma they had to go to Walmart, and he bought her a video camera of her own.

One morning toward the end of the month, Emma carried a basket of clean laundry into the bedroom to put it away. Jack was still in the shower, washing away what she hoped was the last of his headache.

She set the basket down on the bed and headed for the closet to get some hangers. As she passed the desk, she saw a flash of blue in the wastebasket by her desk and bent over to take it out.

It was Jack's denim shirt. Her favorite shirt, the one he'd worn when they'd danced at their wedding party, the one that made her catch her breath at the way it mirrored the blue of his eyes and set off his beautiful black hair.

Jack came out of the bathroom with a towel around his waist and she looked up at him.

"Hey, baby," he said.

"What is this?" she asked him.

"A shirt," he answered.

"Why is it in the trash?" she asked him and the hint of anger in her voice surprised him.

"I tore a hole in it yesterday coming down out of the peach tree," he said.

Emma turned the shirt over and around in her hands and saw a jagged hole in the tail in back.

"I don't care," she said and threw it onto the

376   See You

bed. "It's my favorite. Put it away."

"I wore it all day yesterday, Emma," he said.

"Good," she said. "Hang it up."

She stalked past him to the closet and grabbed some hangers. She handed him one on her way back to the bed.

"Emma, what's going on?" he asked her. "It's dirty. It smells like sweat and peaches."

She threw the hangers down on the bed, picked the shirt back up and walked back to the closet. She took the hanger out of his hand.

"No, it smells like you and it's mine," she snapped.

"Emma, baby—" he started.

"No!" she said. She reached into the closet and ran her arm along his shirts hanging there.

"You see these? These are mine, too," she said. "You left everything to me, remember?"

She turned to face him, clutching the denim shirt to her chest and he realized that she wasn't angry with him. She was terrified. He'd seen that look before on fellow Marines; that moment when they recognized that something awful was also wholly inevitable.

"These are mine and you'll leave them alone, Jack," she said.

Jack took a step toward her and she backed up against the wall.

"Baby, what are you going to do with all of these?" he asked her gently.

"What do you think, Jack?" she snapped. "Eventually, I'll wear every single one of them and don't you dare say a thing to me about shrouds or being stuck!"

He walked up to her slowly and put his hands on her face. She tried to turn her head as tears welled up in her eyes, but he held her fast.

"It's okay, baby," he said.

"No, it's not," she said angrily and tried to blink back her tears.

"It is, Emma," he said.

"Stop, Jack!" she snapped and the tears started crawling down her face.

"Listen to me, please."

Emma clutched the shirt even tighter and tried to turn her head away. He wouldn't let go, so she looked over his shoulder instead.

"I'm so sorry, Emma Lee," he told her. "I don't mean to leave you alone."

"Stop!"

"No. I'm sorry, baby, I'm just so damned sorry," he said. "But you're strong and you're smart and you're going to be just fine."

"I'm not afraid of being without you, Jack!" she said and he hated the pain on her face. "I'm afraid of the days in between losing you and learning to live with it."

Something like the groan of shifting earth came out of her chest and he leaned to kiss her, but she pushed the shirt up into her face and cried. He let go of her face and hugged her to him tightly, let her cry into his chest for several minutes.

Finally, she pulled back against his arms and he loosened up and let her lean back against the wall.

"I'm sorry. I try so hard to make it easier for you," she said without meeting his eyes. "I try not to show you that I'm scared or that I'm mad or that I need you to stay with me. But sometimes I get so terrified that I can't even breathe and I feel like I have to wrap my arms around myself to so I don't break into pieces."

"You don't have to try to make it easier, Emma Lee," he said and brushed a palm along her hair. "It's not easy. Just let it be what it is."

She looked up at him, wrapped her free hand around one of his wrists.

"I'm sorry," she said.

"No," he said.

She took a deep breath, then pushed the shirt at his chest.

"I need to go work in the garden," she said. "Please hang that up."

He nodded and she kissed him quickly on the mouth and then walked out of the room.

He hung the shirt toward the back of the closet, then got dressed and walked over to the desk to put on the work boots sitting beside it. As he stepped into one of the boots, he looked down at Emma's little pile of notebooks, where she liked to write her notes out longhand.

He looked at them for a minute, then sat down and opened one of them to a blank page, took a pen out of the jar and began to write.

A good while later, he folded the paper and stood. He was about to stick it into the leather box where he kept his important papers, but stopped.

Then he walked over to the closet, folded the paper twice again, and slipped into the pocket of his denim shirt.

That night, Emma slipped into bed after Jack and slid over to lie on top of him. He smiled and twirled a lock of her wet hair around his finger, then Emma leaned down to kiss him. He tasted of toothpaste and she closed her eyes and lost herself in the warmth of his mouth and the sound of the rain coming in through the window.

After a few minutes, Jack rolled them both over and looked down at her and smiled. She put a finger on his lower lip and traced it along the length.

"Jack, would you do me a favor one day?" she asked him in almost a whisper.

"I'll do it now," he said.

"You can't," she said.

"Okay. What is it?"

It was a few seconds before she answered him.

"Will you ask God if you could just come back and talk to me sometimes?"

He looked at her for a moment, saw the honesty and vulnerability in her eyes and he thought maybe he had just fallen in love with her again.

He bent his head and kissed her gently on the tip of her nose, then on her right eyelid and then on her left cheek.

"Yes," he said.

Chapter 22

AUGUST WAS MERCILESS even for an Alabama summer, which was known for its hatred of all Alabama-kind.

The poor little green things in the garden beds huddled together for shade and sucked down every gallon of water that Emma and Jack poured through the hose. Even the late corn drooped in the afternoons, like it was carrying the burden of the heat on its shoulders.

Jack woke up with a headache almost every morning and sometimes they were bad and sometimes they weren't, but they'd be gone by afternoon. Then he would sit in the shade of the porch or at the kitchen table with Emma's book. He wrote his thoughts and questions in the margins with red ink, occasionally pointing out a mistake or an oddly worded sentence, or that she had said "then" seventy-five times in the last page.

On a wretchedly humid Saturday the last week of August, Jack dragged both sprinklers into the back yard and he and Emma and Becca put on their suits and played in it like they were all children, two of them like they were younger than the only actual child there.

When they'd all run themselves ragged and Becca had wandered off to get a snack, Emma laid on top of Jack under the sprinkler and painted little designs on his face with the mud, traced his laugh lines with it while he just smiled up at her, blinking his eyes against the water coming down.

Jack had flipped them both over, grabbed a handful of his own mud and stuck it into the top of her bathing suit. Then he sat up and beat his chest like some Indian brave who'd just taken her scalp.

The days became far less brutal with the arrival of September, but the first two weeks of September brought a burden of their own.

They never spoke a word about it, but Jack and Emma both tiptoed through those days like they were afraid of waking someone and they each knew the other was doing it. They made love even more than usual, got up earlier and stayed up later and didn't even leave the house except to go to church. They sought no company other than their own and even a run to the closest store to get milk seemed like a risk and an intrusion.

Jack woke up with a headache on their anniversary, but he did wake up, and he let out a breath that he thought maybe he'd been holding for fifteen days. He rolled over and put a hand on Emma's face. She opened her eyes and blinked a few times, then looked at him and smiled.

He leaned over onto her chest and buried his face in her neck and they laid like that for several minutes, Emma rubbing her hand through his hair and Jack just breathing, and grateful of it, barely feeling the throbbing in his head or the way even the faint daylight hurt his eyes.

They spent their anniversary just the way they wanted to. It was a Friday, and after they opened a hand-drawn card from Becca over breakfast and saw her off to school, Jack and Emma spent the day talking, smiling at each other a lot and finishing the white trim in the bedroom, which complimented quite nicely the dove grey paint that Jack had put up last spring.

After a quiet dinner, a roast chicken prepared with moderate success by Jack and Becca, Emma got Becca bathed and Jack told her a story, then he and Emma did the dishes together almost in silence. It was a peaceful silence, a comfortable one, accompanied by a cricket chorus and punctuated with an occasional kiss.

Then they took their blackberry wine out onto the back porch and Jack handed Emma her binder back.

"You're done finally?" Emma asked him.

"I've been done for two months, Emma," he said. "But you gave me half a book for Valentine's and I'm giving you an edited book for our anniversary. I'm an impressively romantic guy."

Emma took it and put it on the table, then got up and climbed onto his lap and leaned back against his chest.

"Do you remember my other anniversary gift?" she asked him.

"I do," he said. "I didn't forget. Go ahead and make the appointment."

"I already did," she said. "It's next Friday at ten."

Jack looked up at her and smiled.

"You're a shifty woman, Emma Lee," he said.

"You're going," she said.

"Yes, I am," he said. "A promise is a promise."

It was a promise and they were at the neurology center in Montgomery half an hour early.

Emma sat and waited anxiously with her coffee while they took Jack for an MRI, then she held Jack's hand in a death grip as they sat together in front of the doctor's desk to hear what he had to say.

He was a kind man, but all business, and he explained that the primary tumor, the large one, had grown surprisingly little since Jack's last MRI, but that there were several new smaller lesions. He stuck the film up in a lighted box on his wall and pointed them out. There were several of them, scattered around like tiny starfish clinging to rocks.

The bottom line, he told them kindly but firmly, was that Jack had done well to make it thus far, but that nothing had really changed. They should be optimistic, but not necessarily hopeful. He seemed to say that mostly to Emma.

Then he asked if he could have a few words alone with Jack and Emma offered to go get some coffee, but the doctor waved her back into her seat and said they'd walk and talk for a bit instead.

After they left, Emma walked over to the black and bright blue film on the wall. It was surreal to her, looking at the face of her enemy. She hesitantly reached out one finger and touched the largest of the tumors and felt a hatred she'd never felt before, coursing out through her fingertip to land on this evil, thieving thing that was in her husband's head.

Then she ran her eyes over every inch of the film, trying so hard to remember the parts of the brain, trying to recall what she had learned in anatomy, so that she could pinpoint where things were. Where on this film was the place where he remembered the first time they made love? Where was his dry sense of humor? Where was the part of his brain that told him he had fallen in love with her and which part stored the memories of every time they'd laughed?

She didn't find the answers to those questions before Jack walked back in with the doctor and she wasn't going to ask the doctor, either.

After giving Jack a prescription for several more refills of his medication, the doctor handed him an appointment card for October and told them to call if they had any questions or concerns. Five minutes later, they were back in the truck.

Emma got back onto I-85 and waited until she'd turned onto 82 before she spoke.

"What did he say to you?" she asked him.

Jack looked out the windshield for a minute before he answered without looking at her.

"He said there's a clinical trial going on at Duke," he said. "Some new immunotherapy they're working on."

Emma waited a minute and felt her hands shaking just a little on the steering wheel.

"What did you say?" she said.

"I said 'thank you' and that I needed to pee," he said.

"Jack."

Jack looked at her.

"Emma, he told me alone because he didn't want to get your hopes up," he said.

"So?"

"So what, baby?" he asked, though he knew.

"Will you go?"

"Let's not talk about it while we're driving, okay?" he asked. "Are you hungry, do you want to stop somewhere?"

"Not really," she said.

"Good. I just want to get back home and I'm of a mind to have some of your tuna fish and tomato soup."

When they pulled into the driveway and Emma shut off the truck, Jack reached for the door handle but Emma hit the locks again.

He looked over at her and saw the set of her jaw, the gleam of hope in her eye.

"Will you go?" she asked him again.

"I'll give it some thought and get back to you, okay, baby?"

Emma just sat and looked at him.

"I promise, okay?"

Emma swallowed and pushed the "unlock"

button.

"Okay," she said and they got out of the truck.

Emma left him alone about it for the next several days, finding things to do that didn't really need doing. Jack busied himself with helping Emma pick the apples that were in and running several baskets of unrealized peaches to Brother Fillmore. When he wasn't working with Emma in the orchard, he was doing something with Becca.

Jack was quiet on the topic of the clinical trial, but seemed to feel Emma needed a little extra affection in the absence of an answer he wasn't ready to give.

Every now and then he came by and hugged her from behind or grabbed her hand and kissed it. Each time, she made herself not ask.

Then one Friday night after dinner, Emma started the dishes while Jack tucked Becca into bed. He came back down and finished the dishes with her and they could smell rain in the air through the window over the sink.

"I'm going to go take a little walk, Emma Lee," Jack said as he hung up the dish towel. "I'll be back in just a little bit."

"Okay," she said and Jack gave her a hug and a quick kiss before heading out the back door.

Emma rinsed out the sponge and could just make Jack out in the twilight, as he walked off toward the orchard. A few minutes later, she realized that she was still squeezing the sponge and that it was as dry as it was going to get.

Jack sat down on a stump underneath the apple trees and tried to let his mind wander for a few minutes. Immunotherapy, chemotherapy, radiation, all of it a part of two of the worst years of his life. He hadn't done well with most of it, had lost his hair, lost his appetite, lost his energy and damn near lost his will to live after all.

The doctor had been honest and upfront about the fact that the clinical trial was promising, but his chances of benefiting from it were slim at best. He'd been kind in leaving Emma out of it, kind enough to let Jack decide whether she needed to know.

He'd also been kind to be straight up with him once they were alone. He didn't discourage Jack from going and he didn't say it was pointless, not by any means, but he didn't get effusive about it, either.

Jack sat there for a good while, even after a soft rain started in fits and spurts. But he couldn't arrive at an answer.

Finally, he bent his head and prayed, but he had an answer before he could even try to figure out how to phrase the question. He sat there for several minutes, just staring out at the dark.

It was certainly the fastest response he'd ever gotten from God and he thought maybe it was also the kindest and most loving one as well. He had many times thought that he had out-run, out-sinned and out-disappointed God's tolerance.

But with that one answer to a half-said prayer, he felt like God had disavowed forever the idea that he might have outlived God's love.

The rain was coming steady by the time Jack got back to the house, but it was a gentle mist more than a shower. Emma was sitting on the porch with a glass of wine when he got to the porch steps and stopped.

"Come here, Emma Lee," he said with a smile.

Emma put her wine down and went to stand at the top of the steps.

"Come here," he said again and held out his hand.

"It's raining," she said.

"I know. I've always thought it would be awfully romantic to slow dance in the rain," he said. "Come on, Emma, come dance with me."

Emma looked at him there below the steps with his hand out asking her to dance and it was almost exactly like the time he'd asked her at their wedding barbecue. Even with the rain starting to plaster his hair to his head and little drops of water hanging from his nose, he was the most beautiful thing she had ever seen.

She took his hand and let him lead her a little way into the yard and then pull her to him. He started swaying to his own inner music and she smiled before she laid her head in her spot.

"Now, isn't this romantic?" he sked her after a minute.

"Yes," she said and couldn't help smiling.

"You can call the doctor about the clinical trial, Emma," he said.

Emma stopped swaying and looked at him.

"Really, Jack?" she asked him.

"Yes," he said.

Emma grabbed his neck and pulled his head down to her to kiss him.

"I'll call them Monday," she said.

Jack smiled down at her and wiped the rain from her eyes.

"Okay, baby," he said and started dancing again.

After church on Sunday, Jack and Becca talked Emma into going fishing with them and Dew, and Emma packed a picnic and a book.

It was a good day for fishing and Jack and Dew were in rare form, discussing the football season with as much animation as a couple of lawyers battling it out in the courtroom.

They laughed a lot, argued a lot and got too much late September sun, but they caught a lot of fish and went home happy.

They ate far too much catfish at dinner and after Emma had done the dishes and Jack had tucked Becca in, Jack refused Emma's invitation to the porch and took her upstairs instead.

Jack tried to be romantic and suave and Emma tried to be sultry and seductive, but they ended up cracking each other up too much in the shower and gave up all hope of some kind of tryst like they saw in the movies.

Instead, they fell still wet onto the bed and made love the usual way, then fell asleep on the cool, damp sheets and let the breeze dry their uncovered bodies while they slept.

Emma woke in the middle of the night and went to the bathroom, then crawled back into bed, pulled the sheet up over them and laid her head on her favorite spot. *Thank you*, she thought, just before she fell back to sleep.

Jack got up with his usual headache and needed an extra cup of coffee before he could face walking Becca to the road to catch the bus. The sunlight was the worst thing about the morning headaches and he looked around the kitchen for his sunglasses, then thought *Screw it* and gave Emma a kiss on the neck before he and Becca headed out the front door.

The sun was like knives in his eyeballs and bleached all the color out of the trees and Jack closed his eyes as often as possible on his way out to the road. With these morning headaches, he skipped the pain pills as often as possible. They put him to sleep and made him lose half a day, so he either stayed inside until they passed, or just put on his sunglasses and took it like a man.

He listened to Becca talk about the birthday party she'd been invited to the next Saturday and tried to be cheerful and responsive, but he knew she didn't mind much. She was used to the headaches first thing in the day and she didn't ask much of him in the way of conversation.

When the bus ground to a stop at the end of the driveway, he kissed Becca on the cheek and said "See you, Little Bit" and she said "See you, Jack" back and he watched the bus pull away before he went inside to get another cup of coffee.

The sun was almost as bright in the kitchen as it was outside and Jack did a fairly good job of fixing his coffee with his eyes mostly closed. He looked out the window and saw Emma hanging sheets on the line. The light coming in was red and orange and white once it hit his eyeballs and he figured outside was as good as in, so he went outside to have his coffee.

He stopped and closed his eyes when he first got out the door, then blinked it off and sat down in his chair, set his coffee on the table and pinched the bridge of his nose before he subjected himself to the sun again.

The light was so bright that it had heat to it and he couldn't tell where the white-hot of the sun and the white-hot of the inside of his head began or ended. He squeezed his eyes shut again and felt it fade a bit, then cautiously opened his eyes and looked out into the yard.

The light was once again simply the sun's rays, bringing water to his eyes but not so much pain. He blinked and one droplet coursed down his right cheek as he looked over at Emma out at the clothesline.

The sunlight reflected on the gold streaks in her hair as she hung a billowing sheet from the line. She bent down to pull one of his tee shirts from the basket and as she straightened up, she saw him sitting there watching her. Before she turned to hang the shirt on the line, she threw him one of her big smiles.

She was the best last thing to see.

Epilogue

Six weeks later

EMMA HAD DECIDED that today would be the day she started working on Jack's edits.

She had tried to work up the motivation several times before, but the idea of reading his notes just left her sad and empty.

But today the October sun was bright and the air was crisp and cool. Fall had finally arrived, the time of year when she had the most sense of new beginnings. So, after taking Becca out to the bus, she grabbed a fresh cup of coffee and headed up to the bedroom.

She opened up the windows to let in the

fresh air, then went to get a sweater out of the closet. She opened the door and reached for her favorite pink cardigan, but her hand stopped in mid-air. Then she ran her hand along the shirts that were hanging there until she found the blue denim.

She slipped it off of the hanger and pulled it to her face. Cotton, maleness, peaches and just the barest whiff of Nautilus. She held it up by the collar and slid one arm in and as she did she heard something soft hit the floor.

She looked down and saw a piece of paper folded tightly into a little square. She got her other arm into the shirt, then bent down and picked up the paper.

It was a piece of her notebook paper. She opened it up and saw the handwriting, then she read the first few lines.

She stopped for a second, looked back up and caught her breath, then went to the desk to sit down.

> *Dear Emma Lee,*
> *One night out on the front porch, you said you wanted more than anything to just be able to sit down and plan the next five years of our lives. At the time, I really couldn't think of a way to answer you. But now I'll do you one better. I'll tell you how the whole rest of our*

life together goes.

Next year, you give birth to a little boy and we name him Matthew. I can see right away that we've been very fortunate. He got your looks, but my ability to interact with people. You also publish your first book and you swear it hurt more than going through labor.

In 2017, we celebrate my sixtieth birthday with a weekend in Gulf State Park. We discover that sex on the beach really isn't romantic at all, but we do get to watch the most amazing storm come in.

In 2019, I start to tell you something and you just let me do it. I damn near die of a heart attack.

In 2021, Matthew plays second base in his first Little League game. It's one of the proudest moments of my life. I spend every day teaching him how to swing a bat and Becca is now so beautiful that I decide I'd better teach her how to swing one, too.

In 2025, Becca goes to her senior prom without me and I cry like a girl out behind the barn. On our anniversary, you claim that you've managed to fall in love with me all over again. I declare you the smartest woman I know and let you get another cat.

In 2030, we have the best crop of peaches we've ever seen. I decide I'd plant twenty more trees just to watch you take that first bite of the summer. Your hair begins to turn to silver, just like Miss Margret's. You think about coloring it, but I tell you I'll stop sleeping with you. I win.

In 2032, Matthew is accepted to Ole Miss on an academic scholarship and that fat old cat Blackie finally passes away. He's 712. We're now all alone but we haven't run out of stuff to say. Every now and then I look at you across the table and I'm reminded yet again of all the ways that God saves us.

In 2035, Becca marries a man who isn't half the man her Daddy is. After all the wedding guests are gone, I have a slow dance with my woman. I might not be able to astonish and amaze you anymore, but you swear I can still slow dance better than most men make love.

In 2039, I go ahead and die after all. I pass away in my sleep, with your face on my back and your knees tucked in behind mine. I'm still not half done loving you but you'll be fine. You're the strongest woman I know and you have

Dawn Lee McKenna 399

all those idiot cats to keep you company.

You confused me and you slayed me and you made me laugh more than anyone I've ever known. You frustrated me and you fixed me, too. You made me want to choke you and you made me a whole person.

It was the best twenty-five years of my life.

See you,
Jack

The end.

For Margret Maxwell

I miss you, Grandma

and for my father, Jack McKenna, who inspired a love story

I miss you, too, Daddy

A Note from the Author

Dear Reader,

I would never be able to tell you how grateful I am to you without sounding like an awful dork, but I am.

Thank you for spending a few hours of your time to read Jack & Emma's story. I hope they stay with you a while, as they will stay with me.

If you enjoyed this book, please take a few more minutes of your time to leave a review on Amazon. Reviews are the lifeblood of indie authors and I will be in your debt yet again.

You can also sign up at www.dawnleemckenna.com to receive my newsletter, The Sweet Tea Chronicles, find out about my other books or drop me a line. I'd love to hear from you.

Please read on for a preview of The Cricket Jar, available on Amazon March 2015.

The Cricket Jar

chapter 1

I WAS EIGHT YEARS OLD the day I saw my Daddy get run over and killed by an ice cream truck. There's something bizarre about watching somebody die to the tune of Pop Goes the Weasel and, truth be told, I haven't had a Nutty Buddy since.

Getting run over by an ice cream truck is something of an accomplishment, since you could easily avoid it just by jogging along ahead of it. But the fact is that Daddy was out cold; he'd stumbled out into the street just previously, nearly unconscious already from a two-by-four administered by my Mama.

So I suppose that Mama was as much a contributing factor as the ice cream truck and Daddy really couldn't take much credit at all, but then he'd never been known for his achievements.

Shortly thereafter, Mama set her sights on losing her mind and even though it took her a few years, it was the one thing I know of that she actually finished on purpose. She started out slow, with a few pills and a lot of men, then finally worked herself up to a dead run.

I was thirteen when Mama took a handful of sleeping pills at the Sleepy Bear Motor Court. She was found the next day by Deputy Gordon Hayes, who was heard remarking a few years later that she'd still looked pretty good in that purple polyester jumpsuit. Mama would have appreciated that, as she had often told me that she and I were fortunate; it was okay to be poor as long as you were pretty.

Mama didn't even make the paper, but it was 1971 and Alabama had all kinds of other things on its mind.

That left me standing in the middle of the world with scabby knees, three hand-me-down dresses and four little children to see to. Brian was eight and Jessica was seven. Amy was five and had been the reason Daddy slapped Mama into a wall, which led to all of us ending up at the ice cream truck, me with Brian on my hip and a dripping Nutty Buddy in my hand, Daddy with tire marks on his head and Mama with a bloody board and somebody else's baby in her belly. She'd had another one later, too. Little Jeremy was three and also by Deputy Gordon Hayes, who really liked purple.

I was all set to pack us a suitcase and walk right out of our trailer, but the State of Alabama was suddenly apprised of our existence and concerned with our wellbeing. They packed us all up just a few hours after Mama was taken to the morgue. All we could take with us was a few paper bags from the Winn-Dixie, loaded with whatever clothes and toys I could grab.

We were driven to my Aunt Louise's by a pinch-faced woman in a navy blue suit and a baldheaded man with ketchup on his clip-on tie. Aunt Louise was my Daddy's older sister and was about the sorriest excuse for a grown-up that I had ever met, in that she acted like she was about nine. She simpered, she whined and she had a tendency to cry spontaneously, mostly when her husband Earl John yelled at her.

Earl John was a line supervisor at the textile mill and he pretended to be proud of it in front of his friends. But, at home, he took his altogether accurate feelings of inferiority out on Aunt Louise. The thing I liked least about her, aside from her lack of any feeling toward the kids, was that she just took it from Earl John. But I guess she and Daddy had learned from the same parents how women should expect to be treated.

Earl John and Aunt Louise would have turned us out in a minute if it wouldn't have made them look bad at church and among the neighbors. The fact that they got a whole bunch of food stamps for keeping us probably helped, too.

I got stuck with taking care of their ugly yellow house on DuPont Street and taking care of the kids besides, which made it an awful lot like being at home, except that the adults that should have been doing it were actually present.

I didn't mind taking care of the kids and I worried about little Jeremy when the rest of us were at school. I knew Jeremy would be shut up in our room all day while Aunt Louise smoked her Virginia Slims and watched *The Edge of Night* and *Search for Tomorrow*.

My real worry, though, was Earl John. Aside from being a wife-beater who looked like a redheaded gorilla and smelled of too much Aqua Velva, he had a way of looking at me when no one else was looking. It made me feel like his eyes left a slime trail down the side of my face, the way slugs do when they crawl across the porch. I despised him for it.

My only real relief during those years was the time I spent at school, although I loathed it with a real sincerity. I hated the way the girls treated me, all of them wearing brand new clothes and talking behind their hands. I hated the way the popular boys leered at me, like I was expected to be grateful that they'd noticed me at all. I think that, most of all, I hated the way the teachers either ignored me or resented me.

The teachers that disliked me seemed to be offended by the fact that I was intelligent but I couldn't be bothered with learning what they wanted to teach me. I didn't care about geometry or Home Ec or Spanish or typing. All I really wanted to do was read and if I wasn't working, sleeping or in the shower, I was reading a book.

I couldn't even do that like a normal girl, though. All the girls at school were reading idiotic love stories but I couldn't stand the things. I just didn't see the point of wasting a few hours reading something that I'd spend the rest of my life trying to unbelieve. I preferred reading Mark Twain, William Faulkner and F. Scott Fitzgerald.

I liked words. I liked long, beautiful, curvy words. I loved how they sounded like what they meant and I relished the way they felt in my mouth. A well-turned phrase had the same effect on me as David Cassidy had on those girls at school, with their permed and empty heads.

At home, after I'd washed and ironed the clothes, mopped the floors, scrubbed the bathroom and fed and bathed the kids, we all scurried out of harm's way and hid in our room. We had a double bed on one side for us girls and a twin bed on the other for the boys. I'd lock the bedroom door, we'd all gather on the girls' bed and I'd read out loud.

I'd read whatever I was reading at the time, since the little kids didn't own any books of their own and I didn't have the time or bus fare to take them to the library. The little ones might not have understood Light in August, but they sure liked the way it sounded.

Those evenings, the sounds of the crickets coming through the window and the sounds of words that came from someplace else soothed my heart. I read for them and I read for me and some days it was the only good thing we had besides each other.

I started working for real at the age of sixteen and worked after school and on weekend, cashing out ladies with big hair and blue hair at the Winn-Dixie. It didn't pay much but it paid more than cleaning Earl John and Louise's house and I saved every penny I could, like they were the last drops of water I might see in my life.

Even after I was eighteen and could have left that crowded, ugly little house and those broken, ugly people, I chose to stay. Earl John and Louise were only too happy to let me do it; they weren't of a mind to start raising children on their own.

I stayed as long as I could stand it, on account of I knew that it would be the cheapest place we'd ever live. I went full-time at Winn-Dix-

ie after I graduated high school, which I miracu-
lously managed to do with honors, in spite of my
thorough and impressive disinterest.

I also picked up another job nights and
weekends, cleaning up at Pearl's Couture Coif-
fures, which weren't the least bit couture at all. I
swept up piles of hair that would have been better
off left alone, dropped by women who didn't have
enough sense to know that this month's must-
have style was going to be next month's public
shame.

For two years, I did nothing but work, sleep
and try to keep the kids from raising themselves
while I was gone. We didn't have nearly as much
time for reading at bedtime and whenever the kids
were home I was usually sleeping or at work. Or
trying to make myself invisible to the man with
the slug eyes and the small-minded temper.

Two years was all I got, though. I came home
from work one afternoon and found Louise gone
and Earl John sitting at the kitchen table eating
chicken with his fingers like it wasn't the middle
of a Tuesday afternoon.

"Where's Aunt Louise?" I asked him and he
dragged his eyes across my chest and his greasy
fingers across his tongue and told me "Doctor."

I had to pass the kitchen table to get to our
little room down the hall and I had to change into
my other uniform before I could go to my other
job. I didn't think I could call Miss Pearl up and

tell her I wasn't able to come because a man with no table manners and a filthy mind was in my way.

So I headed for the hallway, walking around him as wide as I could, but his fat gorilla arm snaked out like a whip and he caught hold of the hem of my orange polyester tunic. He jerked me to a stop and I looked at him, tried to give him my death-dealing eye, but he just smiled and said, "Not this time."

That was when I slung my purse and got him up the side of his head, then grabbed his plate and hit him with that, too. It wasn't much in the way of violence, but I felt it made my thoughts clear and hoped that was enough.

It wasn't all that impressive I guess, because he came flying out of that chair like a man half his size and twice as smart and pinned me into the corner of the kitchen. He had just grabbed up the whole of my face in one hand and was going to kiss me with his mean, greasy lips when Louise walked in the back door and commenced with some screeching, followed up by an intolerable amount of whining and keening.

Ten minutes later, after I had run to my room to change, there was a banging on my door and I got told to get my snotty little siblings and my raggedy stuff and take my bony butt out the door.

I did just that, grabbing up what I could,

stuffing it into my consumptive little Vega and going straight to the kids' schools.

We spent two nights in that Vega, in the
parking lot of one workplace or the other, while I
tried to find a place we could afford to rent.

My salvation came in the form of the day
janitor at Winn-Dixie, an old black man named
Jeffrey whose aunt had just died, and left a house
behind.

Jeffrey told me that it was fearfully packed
with every variety of junk and needed a year of
cleaning, but I could have it if I did the work.

He told me, too, that it was all the way on
the other side of colored town, just outside the
county line on a dirt road that didn't have one
single other white family on it. But I could have
it if I wanted, and I could afford it so I wanted it,
and we made ourselves a deal.

Which is how I came to live in a forsaken
little white house outside of town. It's also how I
came to make my first best friend, dispose of my
first dead body and one day open my door to a
skinny-brown haired man with the prettiest eyes,
who had a bouquet of wildflowers in one hand
and a jar of crickets in the other.

Acknowledgements

I OWE A HUGE DEBT to several people who made this book a reality. Thank you, Katherine Scheideler, Linda Maxwell, Wendy Crawford, Theresa Crouse and Constance Whitley, for everything you have done and everything you have believed.

Bill Morrison, thank you for getting me on the right track and helping me speak in my own voice.

A very special and heartfelt thanks to book designer extraordinaire Colleen Sheehan of Write.Deam.Repeat. Without you, nobody would be reading this.

Note regarding Jack's illness:

Jacks' tumor, identified as malignant astrocytoma in this book, is a real illness in the family of brain tumors classified as gliomas. However, for the purposes of the story, Jack's symptoms, side effects and prognosis were taken from several different forms of glioma and shouldn't be misconstrued as an attempt to convey an accurate representation of malignant astrocytoma.

70300280R00248

Made in the USA
Columbia, SC
21 August 2019